THE FICTION OF DREAD

THE FICTION OF DREAD

Dystopia, Monstrosity, and Apocalypse

Robert T. Tally Jr.

BLOOMSBURY ACADEMIC
NEW YORK • LONDON • OXFORD • NEW DELHI • SYDNEY

BLOOMSBURY ACADEMIC
Bloomsbury Publishing Inc
1385 Broadway, New York, NY 10018, USA
50 Bedford Square, London, WC1B 3DP, UK

BLOOMSBURY, BLOOMSBURY ACADEMIC and the Diana logo
are trademarks of Bloomsbury Publishing Plc

First published in the United States of America 2024

Cover design by Eleanor Rose
Cover image: Abandoned hospital, Italy
© Martina Rigoli / iStock / Getty Images

Bloomsbury Publishing Inc does not have any control over, or responsibility
for, any third-party websites referred to or in this book. All internet addresses
given in this book were correct at the time of going to press. The author and
publisher regret any inconvenience caused if addresses have changed or sites
have ceased to exist, but can accept no responsibility for any such changes.

Library of Congress Cataloging-in-Publication Data
Names: Tally, Robert T., Jr., author.
Title: The fiction of dread : dystopia, monstrosity,
and apocalypse / Robert T. Tally Jr.
Description: New York : Bloomsbury Academic, 2024. |
Includes bibliographical references and index. |
Summary: "A history and examination of dystopia and angst in popular
culture that speaks to our current climate of dread"– Provided by publisher.
Identifiers: LCCN 2023025701 (print) | LCCN 2023025702 (ebook) |
ISBN 9781501375842 (paperback) | ISBN 9781501375859 (hardback) |
ISBN 9781501375866 (epub) | ISBN 9781501375873 (pdf) |
ISBN 9781501375880 (ebook other)
Subjects: LCSH: Dystopias in popular culture. | Monsters in
popular culture. | Apocalypse in popular culture.
Classification: LCC NX180.D97 T35 2023 (print) | LCC NX180.D97 (ebook) |
DDC 700/.474–dc23/eng/20230807
LC record available at https://lccn.loc.gov/2023025701
LC ebook record available at https://lccn.loc.gov/2023025702

ISBN: HB: 978-1-5013-7585-9
         PB: 978-1-5013-7584-2
         ePDF: 978-1-5013-7587-3
         eBook: 978-1-5013-7586-6

Typeset by Integra Software Services Pvt. Ltd.

To find out more about our authors and books visit www.bloomsbury.com
and sign up for our newsletters.

For Phillip E. Wegner,
who gives me hope

CONTENTS

ACKNOWLEDGMENTS

I began this project about ten years ago, and I think most would agree that the world we live in seems even more dystopian than it did at that time. Examples are too numerous to cite, but in the United States and elsewhere, increasingly repressive and authoritarian regimes have taken or maintained power, the return of fascism and rise of neo-fascist movements, ongoing environmental devastation along with negligent or cavalier attitudes toward the threat of climate change, ever more invasive technologies and media, police brutality and warfare, vicious forms of almost predatory capitalism empowered by further deregulation, attacks on health care, education, unemployment, welfare, and so on, not to mention a worldwide and ongoing pandemic that has caused millions of deaths, just to name a few, have made what was already a dreadful and precarious situation in the early twenty-first century all the worse as we approach the second quarter of that century. As if to employ the fantasy form to realistically reflect this world, popular culture has only multiplied its dystopian, monstrous, and apocalyptic offerings in recent years, and those themes show no signs of receding from view in literature, film, or television anytime soon. Undoubtedly, some good news makes its way through also, and as so many of these dystopian entertainments would assure us, one of the nice things about living amidst the apocalypse is the way it brings people together! (That's a bit of a joke, of course, but then all jokes have some sense of truth, after all.) Amid so much that is bad, one inevitably seeks, and sometimes finds, much that is good and even some promising signs. In any case, I am grateful to many people who make this place and time not only more bearable, but more enjoyable.

This book is dedicated to Phil Wegner, for his unflagging generosity, excellent teaching and mentoring, superior criticism and scholarship, and general bonhomie. Among his impressive and extensive list of publications, *Invoking Hope: Theory and Utopia in Dark Times* (2020) models a way of doing scholarly criticism in our dystopian era, and although we have our differences of opinion and viewpoint, I am grateful to Phil for always patiently showing the ways to find hope in a dismal situation, which often involves making visible those many entanglements with one another that can seem as vexing as they are illuminating. I am grateful to have had my life become entangled with Phil's, as with others along the way, and I have benefited greatly from it.

I want to thank the many people with whom I have discussed these matters, and whose generous feedback has helped me think more on the subjects. Even a very long list could not do justice to all who have helped, but I would like to name a few: Jonathan Arac, Ian Balfour, Paul A. Bové, Christopher Breu, Gerry Canavan, Andrew Cole, Jeffrey Di Leo, Caroline Edwards, Merve Emre, Ying Fang, David Greven, Katrina Goudey, Christian Haines, Caren Irr, Fredric Jameson, Youngmin Kim, Anna Kornbluh, Melody Yunzi Li, Sophia McClennen, Paul Allen Miller, Sianne Ngai, Mich Nyowalo, Daniel O'Hara, Ato Quayson, Robin A. Reid, Bruce Robbins, Amanda Rose, Ignacio Sánchez Prado, Russell Sbriglia, Benjamin Schreier, Nicole Simek, Kenneth Surin, Janelle Watson, Jeffrey Weinstock, Rob Sean Wilson, and Zahi Zalloua. Among the many others I should thank are my students and colleagues at Texas State University, including but not limited to Suparno Banerjee, Rebecca Bell-Metereau, Bianca Beronio, Sabah Carrim, Geneva Gano, Matt Hudson, Katie Kapurch, Simon Lee, Rui Ma, Whitney S. May, Kate McClancy, Susan S. Morrison, Sirsha Nandi, Benjamin Reed, Aimee Roundtree, Thais Rutledge, Leah Schwebel, Victoria Smith, and Graeme Wend-Walker.

I would also like to thank the people at Bloomsbury, including Hali Han and especially my editor Haaris Navqi, whose encouragement, support, and especially patience have gone above and well beyond the call of duty, as usual.

Over the past decade or so, I have had the opportunity to present some of these ideas at conferences and other events, and I am grateful to the organizations, organizers, participants, and audiences for the opportunity and for their valuable feedback. These include the *Conference on Science Fiction, Utopias and Dystopias: Relationships in Crisis*, sponsored by the Laboratory of Studies on the Novel (LERo) at the University of São Paulo, Brazil, in 2022; *Spatial Modernities: Mapping the Physical and Psychological World*, the annual conference of *Countervoices*, Centre for Modern Studies, Postgraduate Forum, York University, England, in 2021; and the annual meetings of the Society for Comparative Literature and the Arts in 2018, 2021, and 2022.

The overall idea from the book was summarized in my article "Monstrous Accumulation: Topographies of Fear in the Age of Globalization," which was published in *CLCWeb: Comparative Literature and Culture* 21.7 (December 2019), a special issue on "Monstrosity and Globalization," edited by Ju Young Jin and Jae H. Roe. Earlier versions of some of the material in *The Fiction of Dread* has been published previously: A slightly different version of Chapter 3 first appeared in *Blast, Corrupt, Dismantle, Erase: Contemporary North American Dystopian Literature*, edited by Brett Grubisic, Gisèle M. Baxter, and Tara Lee (Wilfrid Laurier University Press, 2014); a version of Chapter 4 was published in *Humanity in a Black Mirror: Essays on Posthuman Fantasies in a Technological Near Future*, edited by Jacob Blevins and Zahi Zalloua (McFarland Press, 2022); a different version of Chapter 6 appeared in *The New Americanist* 1.3 (Autumn 2019), a special issue on "American Fantasy Fiction in Theory," edited by James Gifford and Orion Kidder; Chapter 7 presents a revised version of an essay in *Other Globes: Past and Peripheral Imaginations of Globalization*, edited by Simon Ferdinand, Irene Villaescusa-Illán, and Esther Peeren (Palgrave, 2019); and part of Chapter 8 appeared in *The Map and the Territory: Exploring the Foundations of Science, Thought, and Reality*, edited by Shyam Wuppuluri and Francisco Antonio Doria (Springer, 2018). I thank the editors, publishers, and readers.

Above all, I want to thank Reiko Graham, who has always been there for me, as well as Dusty (in memoriam), Windy, Steve French, and Nigel for their part in the chaos that keeps things interesting in this place. Their contributions, like others named and unnamed in this section, help make life less dreadful.

INTRODUCTION:
MONSTROUS ACCUMULATION

At the beginning of the twentieth century, dystopian fiction was arguably a minor, recessive, or even nonexistent genre, while utopian visions seemed to predominate and proliferate. This is not to say that there were no dystopias being produced, and to the extent that cultural criticism employed dystopian ideas (sometimes in the form of satirical utopian novels, such as Samuel Butler's *Erewhon* [1872]), one could argue that dystopia served as an underlying force beneath a great deal of naturalist fiction, social commentary, and even utopian novels. But a vision of beneficent futurity associated with the progressive movement, among other things, gave a certain optative mood to the *fin-de-siècle* culture in the United States and Great Britain. Virginia Woolf suggested that the world changed in 1910, but most Europeans would probably characterize 1914 or 1917 as a more appropriate turning point.[1] The Great War did not put to rest the hopes of the Progressive Era; on the contrary, so-called progressives could take credit for many of the "achievements" of the post-war 1920s, but the scare-quotes here suggest the ambiguity of those achieved goals, which in the United States included many "positive" and "negative" changes (women's suffrage, e.g., but also eugenics, prohibition, nativism, and anti-immigration, and so on). Almost exactly 100 years ago, Woolf's Russian contemporary Yevgeny Zamyatin penned what many consider to be the foundational modern dystopian novel, *We*, written by 1921 but first published in English translation in 1924. In the aftermath of the first "world" war, among other cataclysmic events, the dystopian century might be said to have begun.

The zeal for utopian literature and thought at the end of the nineteenth century was rooted in part in a devastating social critique of the present, but it was also animated by a powerfully progressive vision of the future. Not surprisingly, many famous utopian narratives from this era involved time-travel, with a narrator waking up, Rip Van Winkle-style, to a world transformed. The emergence of twentieth-century dystopia challenges both the hopes for social reform and, more generally, the faith in a progressive arc of history. Time itself did not seem to work as it should, and the radical transformations of the world system in this period altered the spatiotemporal order, to which modernists in the arts as well as modern science attest with equal force. Starting with H. G. Wells's *The Time Machine* (1895), which along with Wells's subsequent body of work is arguably utopian and dystopian, we might say that that dystopia reflects and figures forth the image of a world system then emerging from the breakdown of traditional empire and the growth of multinational capitalism. Along those lines, we might propose that the utopian critique of industrial capitalism gives way to a dystopian perspective on multinational capitalism. If, as Karl Marx observed in the opening line of *Capital*, "the wealth of those societies in which the capitalist mode of production prevails, presents itself as 'a monstrous accumulation of commodities,'"[2] in the era of globalization, both the monstrosity and the accumulation expand exponentially, inaugurating a dystopian era of monsters, a teratocene in which the end of the world seems more imaginable, and perhaps even more desirable, than our present social condition.

The rise of dystopia remains crucial to understanding the system that has become so pervasive and powerful that even the thought of its destruction or evanescence seems nearly inconceivable today. In its original conception, in fact, *The Fiction of Dread: Dystopia, Monstrosity, and Apocalypse* was imagined as a sequel to my *Utopia in the Age of Globalization: Space, Representation, and the World System* (2013); indeed, in my working notes it was tentatively titled "Dystopia in the Age of Globalization." Elements of this conceptual framework remain, but I found that the investigation of dystopia involves very different work, for dystopia is not simply the flipside of utopia. Scholars of utopia and dystopia have long known this, of course, and the relationship between the literary forms on the one hand, and the social, political, economic, and cultural forces and networks on the other, are different in complex and interesting ways.[3] *Utopia in the Age of Globalization* focused on utopian theory in particular, drawing upon a Frankfurt School-inflected utopianism and looking especially at writings by Herbert Marcuse and Fredric Jameson in the context of a postmodern world system. *The Fiction of Dread* also draws upon these and related theoretical traditions, including Jameson's work, but it pays greater attention to the dystopian texts themselves: novels, films, and other media, as well as theory and criticism. In *Utopia in the Age of Globalization*, I argued that utopian theory represents less the effort to produce visions of ideal societies and more an attempt to map the present world system in its dynamic complexity. As a sort of sequel, *The Fiction of Dread* examines what appears to be an almost epochal shift from a dominant utopianism to a pervasive dystopianism in postmodernity. Looking at a variety of texts in different media, I explore these themes in relation to three broad, overlapping categories mentioned in the subtitle. In the twenty-first century, dystopian themes, proliferating monsters, and apocalyptic or post-apocalyptic visions appear dominant in popular culture and beyond.

The phrase "monstrous accumulation," borrowed from Marx, seems all too fitting a label for the immense and growing corpus of dystopian visions in our time. It is not just that there seems to be an unlimited reservoir of "monsters" with which to menace us in our present moment, but that the accumulation of dreadful things seems to proceed at an alarming rate. The perils of the postmodern condition, of late capitalism and globalization, that had been cause for such consternation and anxiety a generation or two ago appear almost quaint, in contrast to the far more pervasively gloomy worldviews that predominate the present. Dystopianism has arguably been a leading generic mode or sensibility in popular culture for the past century, but one feels that the acceleration and proliferation of bad places in the past forty years or so is especially disturbing. It sometimes feels that the present is fundamentally dystopian, beset on all sides with monstrous forebodings and terrors, amounting to a veritable teratocene or "age of monsters" in which various predictions of the end of the world, of some sort of apocalyptic or post-apocalyptic condition, becomes almost utopian in their own right.

The chapters of *The Fiction of Dread* examine this rise and spread of dystopianism in our time. Chapter 1, "Evoking Dread: The Reality of Possibility," begins with a discussion of China Miéville's defense of dread as a productive category for Marxist analyses and celebrations of the possible amid the real conditions of our time. As a foundational emotion in or concept underlying dystopian narratives, tales of monstrous horror, or end-of-the-world scenarios, dread seems to be the inversion of hope, the animating spirit of the utopian impulse. Whereas utopian narratives may invoke hope, dystopian ones evoke dread. Yet dread turns out to be a form of hope, a dialectical instance of the unity of opposites, perhaps, in empowering the imagination and positing of alternative futures.

Chapter 2, "Baleful Continuities; or, the Desire Called Dystopia," examines some of the formal differences between dystopia and utopia, and particularly how the former is usually connected to the romance, adventure, or fantasy genres, while also sharing with its putative rival a sort of spatial narrative structure. As Jameson and other critics have observed, utopias are fundamentally typified by a break, marked by islands and trenches in both space and time,[4] whereas I think dystopias tend to be characterized by a creeping, incremental horror, typical of the dreadful. The baleful continuities of dystopia are thus contrasted with the generative discontinuities associated with the utopian impulse. The "desire called dystopia," in this sense, represents a degree to which the modern condition and its effects permeate the scene, not allowing what Jameson calls "the desire called utopia" to disrupt the thematics of modernity in favor of radical alternatives.[5]

Chapter 3, "Lost in Grand Central: *American Gods*, Free Trade, and Globalization" focuses on Neil Gaiman's award-winning 2001 novel in the context of cross-border commerce and multinational capitalism at the turn of the twenty-first century. The regnant conceit animating *American Gods* is that immigrants bring their gods with them as they cross national boundaries. Moreover, the old gods native to those who have lived upon that soil remain, including ancient forgotten ones, while new gods, nourished by the power of their believers, come into being. In the novel, recent examples of such new deities include "gods of credit card and freeway, of Internet and telephone."[6] The story takes place within the United States, although Gaiman—an Englishman who at the time of writing *American Gods* had not yet spent much time in the country—admits that he had an image of the nation based mostly on its representations in popular culture. Indeed, it is "America," an idea, not the United States *per se*, that becomes the ground for this fantasy tale. America, which one character claims "has been Grand Central for ten thousand years or more,"[7] serves as a metaphysical free-trade zone in which fluid economies of belief alter the social landscape of the continent, and this North American "space" is depicted at the very moment of the North American Free Trade Agreement (NAFTA) and its effects in transforming the cultures of its regions. Thus, *American Gods* is a fable of metaphysical border-crossing, as well as a powerfully dystopian narrative, presenting a dialectical reversal of the utopian prospects of transgressive movements across porous national and social boundaries.

In Chapter 4, "The Utopia of the Mirror: The Postmodern *Mise en abyme*," I explore key themes sounded in the popular, largely dystopian British television series, *Black Mirror* (2011–19). Given the variety of themes and heterogeneity of styles visible across the many discrete episodes of the series, it is perhaps unwise to generalize about *Black*

Mirror as a whole, but certain topics are revisited frequently, as with the persistent question of technology in relation to personal identity, individual freedom, ethics, and memory. Taking a step farther back, one could look at the title itself for a clue to the unity to be found amid the narrative diversity. The mirror distorts, but also offers a sense of familiarity; it is radically unreal, since its image is an illusion, yet it becomes a crucial way for me to "know" myself. As Michel Foucault has put it, "[t]he mirror is, after all, a utopia, since it is a placeless place. In the mirror, I see myself there where I am not, in an unreal, virtual space."[8] For many characters in *Black Mirror*, the technologies enable a bizarre self-reflection as well, and in the overall eeriness of many of their experiences, the infamous Sartrean dictum "Hell is other people" is refracted into "Hell is myself (whatever that 'self' may be)." *Black Mirror* plays upon this existential anxiety or dread, but specifies a historical context, postmodernity, in which the uncanny becomes a figure for our subjective experience of globalization, a system of infinite mirroring, with its unmappably monstrous social and conceptual spaces.

The dominant dystopian visions in our time are complemented by, and subsumed within, a broader sense of the monstrous world system, which increasingly seems to involve the presence of actual monsters, suggestive that ours is an "age of monsters." Chapter 5, "Welcome to the Teratocene: Morbid Symptoms at the Present Conjuncture," examines this timely sense of the monstrous today. As the processes and effects of globalization become more starkly experienced, they are also often rendered invisible or unknowable, and individual and groups find themselves subject to an immense array of forces beyond their control. Starting with an oft-quoted, if misquoted, observation by Antonio Gramsci, "[t]he old world is dying, and the new world struggles to be born: now is the time of monsters," which has circulated in recent years as almost a truism regarding our own present, not necessarily Gramsci's earlier historical moment, I discuss the ways in which this misquote (the final part of the original sentence would be more literally translated as "in this interregnum a great variety of morbid symptoms appear") stands as a motto for our era nonetheless.[9] Revisiting Franco Moretti's elaboration of the dialectic of fear in connection with ideologies of the undead, I look at the ways that various monsters have become particularly significant in our time. Monsters and monstrosity have developed into critical embodiments of unnamed terrors in postmodernity, symbolizing aspects of globalization, thus making them into exemplary figures of late capitalist dread.

The popularity of monster narratives is itself a sign of the respect given by readers to authors who refuse to deny the existence of monsters. In Chapter 6, "Teratology as Ideology Critique; or, a Monster Under Every Bed," I look at a relatively simple narrative as an example of the means by which monstrosity can be employed in connection with a sort of cognitive mapping in an era of globalization. The presence of monsters, and of horror more generally, offers a figural representation of the world which reveals the unreality of the so-called "real world." In this sense, the monstrosity explored in horror literature is a form of ideology critique, as China Miéville has suggested in his discussion of radical fantasy.[10] That is, the world as seen through realism is itself unreal, inasmuch as it masks the underlying "truth" in its very surface-level realism. Similarly, with horror, these hidden realities may be rendered visible through fear or dread, combined with the imaginative process of projecting new models for understanding that allow one to overcome the fear. This chapter examines ways in which fantasy-horror functions as a means of demystifying and mapping the so-called "real world," in part by providing an exemplary reading of a children's picture-book, Mercer Mayer's *One Monster After Another* (1974), whose apparent simplicity is belied by the monstrous world system it discloses as being the absent presence for our most quotidian, commonplace, and even dull or boring practices, in which "nothing much" seems to ever happen.

Dystopian monster narratives, particularly those involving zombies or zombie-like creatures, frequently evoke the post-apocalyptic condition or other end-of-the-world-as-we-know-it scenarios. These notions permeate the postmodern scene with increasing urgency as greater attention is paid to climate change, natural disasters, and rampant capitalist expansion into and saturation of the remote corners of the planet and beyond. In many cases, apocalyptic and post-apocalyptic fictions feature dystopian regimes and monsters as well, and help to figure forth a new world that may be all the more desirable for existing *après le déluge*.

Chapter 7, "The End-of-the-World as World System," begins with what is by now a cliché, so well known that its frequent criers cannot seem to decide whether Žižek, Jameson, Mark Fisher, or someone else deserves attribution: to wit, that it is easier to imagine the end of the world than the end of capitalism. The quip has become a truism, as the once triumphalist or wary tone adopted by researchers into the phenomena of postmodernism or globalization has turned increasingly apocalyptic. In this, scholars join with popular culture, whose visions of a future tend to be almost exclusively dystopian. The apocalyptic sensibility or mode suggests that a "world system" under globalization can now only be imagined in terms of an end of the world. The global totality is, in a sense, more "representable" in its incipient end-of-the-world state than as an active, thriving system. This attitude represents both an impasse to thinking, barring in advance the conception of alternatives, and an opportunity for mapping the system itself. Analyzing this condition dialectically in relation to the cartographic imperative to map the emergent spaces of our world, we may find that, in a ruse of history, the apocalyptic end may reveal new beginnings for critically theorizing globalization in the twenty-first century.

Chapter 8, "In the Deserts of the Empire: The Map, the Territory, and the Heterotopian Enclave," takes its title from Jorge Luis Borges's infamous map in "Of Exactitude in Science." That parable about an ancient empire that created a map coextensive with the territory it purported to represent, ends on an elegiac note: "In the Deserts of the West, still today, there are Tattered Ruins of that Map, inhabited by Animals and Beggars; in all the Land there is no other Relic of the Disciplines of Geography."[11] In *Utopia in the Age of Globalization*, I had argued that utopia today is less a matter of trying to project an ideal future state than an attempt to map the world system itself. This is, in part, what Jameson had in mind in developing the notion of cognitive mapping as the appropriate strategy for addressing the postmodern condition. Dystopia, arguably, would have a similar vocation, except in this case it takes the catastrophic failure of such a representation at its point of departure. The deserts of cartography, those wastelands of representation, speak to the sense of the world system in the present moment, which is not only unable to represent it adequately, but which can only imagine it as something terrible, impersonal, and ultimately fatal. How does one construct a working map under these circumstances? How does one dwell in the remnants of the great maps? Can we find ways to map anew, to produce cartographies of the future worthy of living beings, as opposed to ghosts, the undead, and other monsters who inhabit these spaces but, perhaps, cannot truly live in them?

Finally, in a brief Conclusion, I draw upon Walter Benjamin's "angel of history" and Ernst Bloch's evocative image of "gold-bearing rubble" to imagine potentially utopian elements within the pervasively dreadful, dystopian, and monstrous postmodern condition. In the aftermath of the dystopian century, we find ourselves living with monsters in a figuratively post-apocalyptic space typified by its pervasive sense of dread, with little hope for relief in the future. And yet, arguably, the dominance of dystopian thought is itself a feature of some indescribable, perhaps unconscious, utopianism. By positing the destruction of existing society, for instance, dystopian narratives make possible alternative visions for constructing new forms. Amid the "gold-bearing rubble" left behind by postmodern dystopianism, we might detect the "the lastingly subversive and utopian contents" of such ideas, and imagine other ways of seeing and mapping the world. Faced with little alternative but to do the impossible, we can use that apparent impasse to revisit "the scandal of qualitative difference," as Herbert Marcuse had called it,[12] and to imagine totally different ways of being in the world.

After all, with our pervasive sense of dread, inhabiting bad places and living in dark times, amid monsters, and at what seems like the end of the world, what have we got to lose?

Notes

1   See Virginia Woolf, *Mr. Bennett and Mrs. Brown* (London: Hogarth Press, 1924), 4.

2   Karl Marx, *Capital, Volume 1*, trans. Ben Fowkes (New York: Penguin, 1990), 125, translation modified.

3   See, e.g., Tom Moylan, *Scraps of the Untainted Sky: Science Fiction, Utopia, Dystopia* (London: Routledge, 2000).

4   See Fredric Jameson, "Of Islands and Trenches," in *Ideologies of Theory* (London: Verso, 2008), 386–414.

5   See Jameson, *Archaeologies of the Future: The Desire Called Utopia and Other Science Fictions* (London: Verso, 2005).

6   Neil Gaiman, *American Gods* (New York: Harper Perennial, 2001), 137.

7   Ibid., 196.

8   Michel Foucault, "Of Other Spaces," trans. Jay Miskowiec, *Diacritics* 16 (Spring 1986): 24.

9   See Antonio Gramsci, *Selections from the Prison Notebooks*, ed. and trans. Quintin Hoare and Geoffrey Nowell Smith (New York: International Books, 1971), 276; for the "misquotation" of the line, see Slavoj Žižek, "A Permanent Economic Emergency," *New Left Review* 64 (July–August 2010): 95.

10   China Miéville, "Editorial Introduction: Marxism and Fantasy," *Historical Materialism* 10.4 (2002): 39–49.

11   Jorge Luis Borges, "On Exactitude in Science," in *Collected Fictions*, trans. Andrew Hurley (New York: Penguin, 1999), 325.

12   Herbert Marcuse, "The End of Utopia," in *Five Lectures: Psychoanalysis, Politics, and Utopia*, trans. Jeremy J. Shapiro and Shierry M. Weber (Boston: Beacon Press, 1970), 69.

Chapter 1

EVOKING DREAD:
THE REALITY OF POSSIBILITY

In "Marxism and Halloween," a talk presented at the *Socialism 2013* conference in Chicago that year, China Miéville guided listeners on a rousing and ranging tour of the uses of enchantment for those on the radical left. In the process, Miéville endeavored to wrest the holiday, along with other forms of fantasy and horror, from the bourgeois apologists of capitalist rapacity and the advocates of the conservative political ideologies more generally. As he put it, "I support a campaign to deny the right-wing any fun or pleasure in any arena possible, and therefore I want to take Halloween from them."[1] Miéville conceded that there has been an influential line of thinking within the socialist tradition to condemn or eschew various "unrealistic" cultural forms such as those found in fairy tales, fantasy, and horror, but Miéville took this attitude to be mistaken and wrongheaded. He argued for a surrealistic or "Gothic" Marxism that should and must embrace aspects of the supernatural in championing a radical, leftist political theory and practice.[2] In his defense of monsters and the supernatural, Miéville also made an elegant case for both the intrinsic and the political value of *dread*.

Miéville's trajectory from defending celebrations of Halloween to proclaiming a slogan of "Socialists for dread!" in the concluding lines is deliciously tortuous and covers a great deal of historical, cultural, political, and even biological ground, which is thus in keeping with the writer's marvelous eclecticism. (I heartily recommend listening to the entire speech, for no summary can do it justice.) At one point, to the obvious surprise of his audience, Miéville works into his discussion references to a then-recent scientific study of the use of half-coconut shells by octopuses, an admittedly strange juxtaposition, by any standard.[3] These cephalopods were apparently taking some pains to keep hold of coconut shells in order to deploy them as shields against would-be predators. Some may think of this as simple tool-use, cautions Miéville, but this is actually quite different. Unlike the use of a tool for the sake of achieving a desired outcome—as with "ant-fishing," whereby a chimpanzee might use a stick or reed to obtain food from an otherwise inaccessible place—here the octopus employs the putative "tool" in the hopes that *it not be used* at all.[4] That is, unlike a linear and causal model of instrumental "sentience," the octopus grasping the coconut half-shell is not doing so in furtherance of a clearly perceived and achievable goal, but with respect to a *possibility* that is not itself an end. This is the "dreaded outcome," something that quite unlike ants to be eaten *does not exist* but that *might* make its unwanted appearance. As Miéville marvels, "uniquely, in the entire animal kingdom, other than humans, this is the only case of any animal deploying a tool in the aspiration that it need never be used." It is as if the octopus dreads being attacked, even without the presence of a predator that would establish an existing threat. In Miéville's reckoning, this conception of dread goes beyond merely the anticipation of the future, even of a "bad" future event, but rather involves "a sense of alternative futures." Potentiality, in other words, becomes the most pressing concern.

Drawing lessons from this example, Miéville observes that what is at stake here is more specific than *fear*, which refers to something like a recognizable threat or perhaps to the more diffuse "fear of the unknown." It is *dread*, which involves "something that might be bad but is not concrete." As Miéville puts it, dread is "ultimately ineffable, it cannot be quite contained." There is undoubtedly much to fear in our time, but one could argue that the truly dystopian emotion is dread, or perhaps a feeling better exemplified by the existentialist keyword *angst*. The German word *Angst*, which also crosses over into English without need of translation, combines the meanings of anguish, anxiety, and dread, while also linking a persistent sense of uncertainty to our existential condition. Dystopias derive from this sense, and they offer a spatiotemporal figure (bad places, dark times) that serves to evoke, contain, and represent the condition or worldview.

The explosion of works featuring dystopian, monstrous, and apocalyptic themes in recent and contemporary literature, film, and other media, not to mention their broad popularity and avid consumption, is undoubtedly connected to a pervasive sense of dread in the postmodern condition. Although it may be compared with such other anticipatory sensibilities as *hope*, which many would view as its opposite (as I discuss below), dread tends to be less distinctive in its aims. One frequently imagines dread, like its close associate anxiety, as more diffuse, circumstantial or almost auratic, than either hope or fear, which in turn tend to have discernible objects and ends. I hope for this, and I fear that. To be sure, one might dread this or that, but often there is also a sense of dread without concrete object, dread of "something bad" with no clear idea of what that "thing" will look like. Dread is intimately connected to the imagination, such that it is not just about how one can imagine dreadful outcomes or objects, but it also means dread is integral to the imagination as a faculty, for the imagination is able to posit possibilities as realities. That is to say, arguably, all imagining involves some aspect of dread.

As the imagination is crucial to our understanding of ourselves and the world, dread typifies a certain comportment to the world, a way of experiencing and representing the world that helps to make sense of it. At a certain level, this is characteristic of a certain existential condition, and it is not surprising that *angst* would be a crucial concept in existentialism. Søren Kierkegaard's 1844 work, *Begrebet Angest* (translated as *The Concept of Dread* or *The Concept of Anxiety*), remains a foundational text within that inchoate tradition, and his analysis of anxiety or dread is closely connected to Jean-Paul Sartre's in the following century. For example, Kierkegaard's assertion that "anxiety is the dizziness of freedom" vividly anticipates Sartre's nausea.[5] However, my understanding of dread in the context of dystopia goes beyond this basic existentialist sense, even if it acknowledges that it too is present. This sense of dread is a core element of human rationality, but one that has become heightened in the twentieth and twenty-first centuries. Existential angst is undoubtedly part of the situation, but there is much more to it.

Specifically, there is a widespread sense of what might be called sociopolitical dread that animates so much of the cultural productions of the late-twentieth and twenty-first centuries. I am thinking especially of a dystopian imagination that has engendered so many books, films, television series, and other forms in the past century. Although the concept it names is clearly much older, the term *dystopia* in the sense we know it now was apparently coined only in 1952, in Glenn Negley and J. Max Patrick's *The Quest for Utopia*. As they put it, speaking of Joseph Hall's 1605 satirical novel, "The *Mundus Alter et Idem* is *utopia* in the sense of *nowhere*; but it is the opposite of *eutopia*, the ideal society: it is a *dystopia*, if it is permissible to coin a word."[6] Thus the term is conceived almost as the opposite of utopia, but scholars working in the areas have also noted that anti-utopia is clearly not the exact same thing as dystopia, even if there are overlapping territories to be explored.[7] Dystopia is not in itself a critique of utopia, but its satirical edge can be used against would-be reformers who are sometimes dismissed as "utopian," in the sense of being overly idealistic or unrealistic. Dystopia is thus defined in relation to utopia, even if that relation cannot be consistently characterized as antagonistic.[8] As with utopia but with significant differences as well, the dystopian imagination operates as a means by which to map a social or cultural system that is functionally unrepresentable in itself, but that is characterized by a pervasive sense of dread. In endeavoring to map this world system, dystopian texts evoke dread and give shape to it, thus rendering it provisionally cognizable and offering some hope of navigating its complex, shifting spaces.

As noted in the Introduction, *The Fiction of Dread* takes up three variations on the broader themes of dread and dystopian theory. Simply put, as labels, these could be named *dystopia*, *monstrosity*, and *apocalypse*. Or, to elaborate slightly more, they deal with the traditionally dystopian concerns of individual and collective freedom in connection to social, political, economic, and technological structures that threaten such freedom; the emergence and spread of "monsters" as both a menace to and a condition of our social being in the present time; and an impending sense of doom that characterizes the end-of-the-world as real, which in turn causes us to imagine a post-apocalyptic condition as our own. The book is divided into three parts accordingly, but it probably goes without saying—or maybe, as Michel Foucault liked to joke,[9] it goes better *with* saying—that these categories overlap and blend together, forming a more interrelated set of ideas than can be simplistically set forth as in a Venn diagram. Similarly needless to say, perhaps, these categories are just three among many potential ones, and they are not intended to be exhaustive in any way. Rather, they represent identifiable coordinates or nodes within the networks of cultural production in recent decades. There are others, of course, but I am most interested in these three interrelated themes.

Dystopia, monstrosity, and apocalypse may represent distinctive concepts or categories within a more generalized idea of the fiction of dread, but the three intertwine mightily in recent mass culture. There is, after all, much that is monstrous in a given dystopia, and many dystopias arise in conjunction with or in the aftermath of cataclysmic events such that many dystopias are themselves imagined as part of a post-apocalyptic condition, which itself is also often characterized by a proliferation of monsters. The "zombie apocalypse" is perhaps the most well known and timely such cultural form or genre in this regard. There are predecessors, of course, but George Romero's *Night of the Living Dead* (1968), with its mysteriously reanimated ghouls—not to mention the vague but timely suggestion that satellites or space probes may be to blame, allowing anxieties about the "space race" to creep into this horror from another direction—undoubtedly paved the way for the explosion of zombies to come, but who in the late 1960s would have foreseen the popularity of the *Resident Evil* film franchise (with seven films and counting since the first in 2002), *The Walking Dead* television series (2010–22), along its spin-offs *Fear the Walking Dead* (2015–present) and *The Walking Dead: World Beyond* (2020–present), among the many dozens of similar such offerings across a range of popular media? The popularity of this genre is notable in its own right. The intersections among various forms of dystopia, monstrosity, and apocalypse may be seen as key sites for the excavation and exploration of contemporary society and culture. In what persists as the postmodern condition, these dreadful forms have become increasingly prominent and perhaps also dominant.

Dystopian fiction, broadly conceived, could be said to evoke dread. In other words, it is not just that dystopianism represents fearful figures or dreaded outcomes, but it summons forth the underlying mood, giving it shape and form. To "evoke" is not simply to call for, as with the concept of invocation, but itself is more ambiguous and diffuse: it is to summon, to bring forth, as with a memory or some other dimly descried thing no longer present or "real," yet readily taken into consciousness, if often at first only unconsciously, passively, or even against one's desires. This is part of why dread (or *angst*) is so frequently associated with "the return of the repressed," since it is the very thing that we may have wished to forget or to keep at a distance that is brought home to us through evocation. In this way, it is similar to haunting or to being haunted.

Evoking dread thus might be seen as the flipside to invoking hope, in the sense used by Phillip E. Wegner. In *Invoking Hope: Theory and Utopia in Dark Times* (2020), Wegner argues for a practice of creative reading that combines both theory and utopia in response to our present, seemingly dystopian situation, the *finsteren Zeiten* ("dark times") in which we live. The subtitle's phrase comes from a line in Bertolt Brecht's 1939 poem "An die Nachgeborenen" ("To Those Born After"), which seems all too worth revisiting in the dark times we face in the twenty-first century. Wegner asserts that "utopia and theory are akin in that both aim to reeducate collective desire for other ways of being and doing in the world."[10] For Wegner, it is the much maligned idea of hope, *das Prinzip Hoffnung* (as Ernst Bloch named it), that lies at the core of our understanding of the world. The practical activity by which we come to this understanding Wegner names "creating reading." This involves a hermeneutic practices, as well as a comportment to the world as a whole, that is capable of discerning the utopian impulse or content in the most apparently ideological texts or hopeless situations. Wegner follows Jameson's lifelong understanding of what, in *The Political Unconscious*, he referred to as "the dialectic of utopia and ideology," and Wegner quotes from an even earlier work in which Jameson affirms that, "[t]o maintain that everything is a figure of Hope is to offer an analytical tool for detecting the presence of some utopian content even within the most degraded and degrading type of commercial product."[11] This analytical tool, which for Jameson as for Wegner could well be named *Marxism* itself, provides a means by which hope may be invoked, even, or especially, in the darkest of times.[12]

Not surprisingly, perhaps, my project in *The Fiction of Dread* will turn out to be sympathetically allied to Wegner's, but the differences may be related to this subtle distinction between evoking and invoking, as well as that between dread and hope or between dystopia and utopia. If utopia be conceived better as a means for figuratively mapping the existing world system than as a blueprint for an ideal system, as I argued in *Utopia in the Age of Globalization*, then the hermeneutic or "analytical tool" used to read its maps likely would need to invoke hope, to bring its force into the consideration of the texts and contexts being scrutinized. I imagine *dread* as slightly more elusive, diffuse, and subterranean. It is not so much directly called forth as ambiguously and unconsciously summoned, such that its arrival is initially imperceptible, and its appearance can be surprising. It just hits you, as it were, and by the time you recognize it, you realize it has been with you for some time already. In that sense, dystopian fictions do not so much call to the fore dread as allow it to become knowable. It is like that shapeless gloom being molded into gloomy shapes, as a Nathaniel Hawthorne character put it,[13] and once realized, its gloom pervades the scene. And yet, in making it visible and recognizable for the reader, such dystopian, monstrous, or apocalyptic evocations of dread make possible new imaginings, alternative vistas, and different ways of seeing the world. This is, in part, why Miéville was so insistent that dread be valued by socialists and others who wish not merely to interpret but also to change the world.

Dystopian, monstrous, and apocalyptic narratives can be interpreted as figural representations of the vast economic, political, social, and cultural system we understand as globalization. That is, in imagining and giving form to some sort of global catastrophe, we can thereby find ways to think the system too vast to analyze using more conventional generic or narrative models. Paradoxically, there is also a utopian element to these various dystopian doomsday scenarios, which sometimes arrives in the realization that the world system too complicated and too large to change through political means can, at the very least, be destroyed. The means of the global destruction is not terribly important, and if the end of the world as we know it is caused by asteroids, natural disasters, nuclear warfare, cosmic cataclysm, alien invasions, zombie apocalypses, or whatever, at least the totality of the world system can finally be realized, or at least manageably estimated, in theory and in practice.

What is more, the absolute leveling of what *had been* creates the possibility of some *new order* of things, as if the only way to get beyond the apparent impasse of historical development would be to wipe the slate clean and start over. Antonio Gramsci famously wrote in 1930, "the old is dying and the new cannot be born; in this interregnum a great variety of morbid symptoms appear."[14] Faced with a seemingly never-ending onslaught of morbid symptoms, of which the current omnipresence of monsters itself may be a sign—indeed, as I discuss in Chapter 5, Slavoj Žižek's well-known "misquote" of this line from Gramsci delivers the last clause as "now is the time of monsters"—we might be forgiven if, in our aesthetic productions and entertainments, we imagine single-shot cures to this global, social disease.[15] Where once such imaginative solutions to real social contradictions might have produced straightforwardly utopian narratives, such as Thomas More's foundational *Utopia* (1516), Edward Bellamy's *Looking Backward, 2000–1887* (1888), or even Ernest Callenbach's *Ecotopia* (1975), our own epoch of globalization seems better suited to dystopian visions of societal and even planetary destruction.

In this matter, could it be said that we have something like a desire called dystopia? The social organizations depicted in the classic dystopian narratives of the last century, such as Yevgeny Zamyatin's *We* (1924), Aldous Huxley's *Brave New World* (1932), or George Orwell's *Nineteen-Eighty-Four* (1949), in retrospect appear almost preferable to the societies in which we live. If nothing else, the conventional dystopian narrative offered a more simplified social system and a more easily imagined if not circumscribed social space, such as a single city or coherent national space, populated with recognizable if also ambiguous heroes and villains. Contemporary dystopian narratives, in order to reflect the realities facing twenty-first-century readers, would need to register the anxieties and dread associated with an unrepresentably vast, incomprehensibly dynamic world system in part by crafting allegories in which the invisible processes of globalization become discernible in a familiar, even homey image of the dystopian state or post-apocalyptic landscape. Ironically, perhaps, visions of dystopian futures provide comfort for many in what is arguably a dystopian present. Dystopian dread makes possible the imagination of alternative realities, which is itself indicative of a utopian impulse at a time when, as the cliché goes, it seems easier to imagine the end of the world than the end of our present forms of global capitalism.[16]

In his discussion of the coconut-carrying cephalopods, Miéville quotes another line from *The Prison Notebooks*—"octopuses clearly read Gramsci," Miéville jokes—in which the Italian Marxist theorist observes that "[p]ossibility is not reality: but it is in itself a reality."[17] Dread is all about possibility, about what may come into being or what may remain nonexistent. The dystopian society, the epoch of monsters, and the post-apocalyptic landscape give form to dreadful possibilities, to their reality in our own *hic et nunc*, and to the lineaments of alternative organizations and networks. In this manner, the fiction of dread allows us to experience this anxious condition in new ways via fantastic narrative, and thus it enables us to descry, if only in the abstract, both the worlds in which we live and those in which we aspire to live.

Notes

1   China Miéville, "Marxism and Halloween—Socialism 2013," *YouTube*, uploaded by We Are Many Media, October 30, 2013: https://www. youtube.com/watch?v=paCqiY1jwqc. All quotations are from this video; to my knowledge, no published transcript is currently available.

2   On the phrase "Gothic Marxism," see Margaret Cohen's superb study, *Profane Illumination: Walter Benjamin and the Paris of Surrealist Revolution* (Berkeley: University of California Press, 1993), which Miéville explicitly cites as well.

3   See Finn, Julian K., Tom Tregenza, and Mark D. Norman, "Defensive Tool Use in a Coconut-Carrying Octopus," *Current Biology* 19.23 (December 15, 2009): R1069–R1070.

4   In fact, as the researchers had pointed out, the octopus is very much encumbered but this coconut-carrying, which forces the creature to resort to "stilt-walking" (i.e., a rather awkward deviation from their normal modes of locomotion); the octopus thus takes on a burden that serves no purpose at all unless the octopus is later attacked, a prospect not directly foreseeable but certainly possible.

5   See Soren Kierkegaard, *The Concept of Anxiety*, ed. and trans. Alastair Hannay (New York: Liveright Publishing, 2014), 75; and Jean-Paul Sartre, *Nausea*, trans. Lloyd Alexander (New York: New Directions, 2013).

6   Glenn Negley and J. Max Patrick, *The Quest for Utopia: An Anthology of Imaginary Societies* (New York: Henry Schuman, 1952), 298. Variants of the word *dystopia* did appear earlier, as far back as 1747, as Lyman Tower Sargent has discussed: "*Dystopia* or *negative utopia*—a nonexistent society described in considerable detail and normally located in time and space that the author intended a contemporaneous reader to view as considerably worse than the society in which that reader lived. The first use of this word is usually ascribed to Negley and Patrick's 'Introduction' to their anthology, but there were much earlier uses. Deirdre Ni Chuanacháin has recently noted a 1747 use by Henry Lewis Younge in his *Utopia or Apollo's Golden Days* (Dublin: Ptd. by George Faulkner) spelled as 'dustopia' used as a clear negative contrast to utopia. Before this discovery, the earliest usage appeared to be in 1782. See Patricia Köster, '*Dystopia*: An Eighteenth Century Appearance', *Notes & Queries* 228 (n. s. 30, no. 1) (February 1983): 65–6, where she says that the first use was in 1782 by Noel Turner (1739–1826) as dys-topia [first three letters in Greek] in 'Letter VIII' of his *Candid Suggestions in Eight Letters to Soame Jenkins, Esq.* (London, 1782), 169–72. John Stuart Mill used 'dys-topian' in the House of Commons. *Hansard* (March 12, 1868, page 1517, column 1) reports him saying 'I may be permitted, as one who, in common with many of my betters, have been subjected to the charge of being Utopian, to congratulate the Government on having joined that goodly company. It is, perhaps, too complimentary to call them Utopians, they ought rather to be called dys-topians, or cacotopians. What is commonly called Utopian is something too good to be practicable, but what they appear to favour is too bad to be practicable.' According to the *OED*, Cacotopia was first used by Jeremy Bentham in his *Plan of Parliamentary Reform, in the Form of a Catechism* (1818, Bowring edition of his *Works*, 3: 493)." See Sargent, "In Defense of Utopia," *Diogenes* 53.1 (2006): 11–17.

7   See, for example, Fredric Jameson, *Archaeologies of the Future: The Desire Called Utopia and Other Science Fictions* (London: Verso, 2005), 198–9.

8   On the idea of "critical dystopia," see especially Tom Moylan, *Scraps of the Untainted Sky: Science Fiction, Utopia, Dystopia* (London: Routledge, 2000).

9   D. A. Miller quotes this "joke" of Foucault's in *The Novel and the Police* (Berkeley: University of California Press, 1988), viii.

10   Phillip E. Wegner, *Invoking Hope: Theory and Utopia in Dark Times* (Minneapolis: University of Minnesota Press, 2020), 24.

11   Fredric Jameson, "Introduction/Prospectus: To Reconsider the Relationship of Marxism to Utopian Thought," *Minnesota Review* 6 (1976): 58; quoted in Wegner, *Invoking Hope*, 16. See also my "On Always Historizing: The Dialectic of Utopia and Ideology Today," *PMLA* 137.3 (May 2022): 542–7.

12   See also Christian P. Haines, *The Desire Called America: Biopolitics, Utopia, and the Literary Commons* (New York: Fordham University

Press, 2019); and Sean Austin Grattan, *Hope Isn't Stupid: Utopian Affects in Contemporary American Literature* (Iowa City: University of Iowa Press, 2017).

13   See Nathaniel Hawthorne, *The House of the Seven Gables* (Oxford: Oxford University Press, 1991), 306.

14   Antonio Gramsci, *Selections from the Prison Notebooks*, ed. and trans. Quintin Hoare and Geoffrey Nowell Smith (New York: International Books, 1971), 276.

15   Slavoj Žižek, "A Permanent Economic Emergency," *New Left Review* 64 (July—August 2010): 95.

16   As I discuss in Chapter 7, the now overused phrase first expressed (somewhat differently) by Jameson in *The Seeds of Time* (1994), quoted by Žižek in *Mapping Ideology* (1994), and used as the basis for main argument of Mark Fisher's *Capitalist Realism* (2009), in which Fisher quotes both Jameson and Žižek, somehow circulates today with various attributions. See, for example, my *For a Ruthless Critique of All That Exists: Literature in an Age of Capitalist Realism* (Winchester: Zero Books, 2022), 17–39.

17   Gramsci, *Selections from the Prison Notebooks*, 360.

Chapter 2

BALEFUL CONTINUITIES;
OR, THE DESIRE CALLED DYSTOPIA

At the dawn of the twentieth century, a spirit of utopianism dominated cultural discourse in the United States and England. Notwithstanding the manifold social problems besetting those countries at the time— or, rather, perhaps, because of them—an enormous number of utopian narratives, plans, or ideas found their way into the public and were widely embraced. As Jean Pfaelzer has observed in her study, *The Utopian Novel in America*, over 100 utopian narratives appeared in the United States alone between the years 1886 and 1896, and a similar outpouring of utopian publications can be found in British and other literatures of this era.[1] Shortly thereafter, however, something changed. The spirit of utopia in the Western world seemed to dissipate, while increasingly dismal visions of the social order and its future possibilities came to predominate. This did not occur "all at once," but rather crept into the social imagination and its literary counterparts steadily during the first half of the twentieth century, when the new form of both literary genre and imagined social order did not yet even have a name. Although the word had its antecedents, it is generally accepted that the word *dystopia* came into widespread use only around the mid-twentieth century.[2] By the beginning of the next century, dystopia would be arguably one of the most popular literary genres and dystopianism would be a dominant theme in popular culture at large, as well as in political theory and the social imagination.

The transition from *fin-de-siècle* utopianism to a dominant mid-to-late-century dystopianism is not marked by a single event, even ones so notable as the First World War or the Russian Revolution. Although historical critics may point to various dates at which point "everything changed," the movements of social change are far too dynamic to pin down. Indeed, it seems that dystopianism in particular might be marked by its dreadful yet largely unnoticed arrival. That is, unlike utopias which are traditionally encountered at a newfound place or a distinct moment in time, as with the sudden discovery of the island nation in Thomas More's *Utopia* or the awakening into a fully formed utopian society in Edward Bellamy's *Looking Backward, 2000–1887*, dystopias seem to emerge more gradually, leaving those within them to ponder the origins of their now dismal condition.

Part of it, too, has to do with readerly tastes and expectations. As Fredric Jameson has suggested, what had disappeared from the earlier period was "a certain type of reader, whom we must imagine just as addicted to the bloodless forecasts of a Cabet or a Bellamy as we ourselves may be to Tolkien, *The Godfather*, *Ragtime*, or detective stories."[3] But Jameson also notes that the "level of tolerance for fantasy" (by which he here means the utopian imagination, not the marketing genre) had "in the windless closure of late capitalism" come to seem "increasingly futile and childish for people with a strong and particularly repressive reality-and-performance-principle to imagine tinkering with what exists, let alone its thoroughgoing restructuration."[4] This "windless closure" suggests the total system of late capitalism, which increasingly appears to extend to the furthest reaches of the planet and beyond as the era of globalization unfolds. If utopia is preeminently a modern or even modernist form, as Phillip E. Wegner has argued persuasively, perhaps it is not surprising to find dystopianism to be an aspect of the cultural dominant that is postmodernism.[5]

When the World Changed

Speaking of modernists … Virginia Woolf famously claimed that "the world changed" in 1910. She was not exactly thinking of utopia or dystopia, but arguably, in her assessment of the shifting social and cultural relations she identifies, her periodization might be instructive for thinking of the emergence of various dystopian visions in the years to come. "The change was not sudden and definite," writes Woolf,

> But a change there was, nevertheless; and since one must be arbitrary, let us date it about the year 1910. […] In life one can see the change, if I may use a homely illustration, in the character of one's cook. The Victorian cook lived like a leviathan in the lower depths, formidable, silent, obscure, inscrutable; the Georgian cook is a creature of sunshine and fresh air; in and out of the drawing-room, now to borrow *The Daily Herald*, now to ask advice about a hat.

This is a terribly classist example, of course, with Woolf suggesting that the very visibility and temerity of servants is a sign of epochal change in

Western Civilization. But she is also moved by a more feminist impulse, as she continues:

> Do you ask for more solemn instances of the power of the human race to change? Read the *Agamemnon*, and see whether, in process of time, your sympathies are not almost entirely with Clytemnestra. Or consider the married life of the Carlyles, and bewail the waste, the futility, for him and for her, of the horrible domestic tradition which made it seemly for a woman of genius to spend her time chasing beetles, scouring saucepans, instead of writing books?

As Woolf concludes, "All human relations have shifted—those between masters and servants, husbands and wives, parents and children. And when human relations change there is at the same time a change in religion, conduct, politics, and literature. Let us agree to place one of these changes about the year 1910."[6]

Woolf's periodization is connected to a polemic, for she is responding to a critic who, in her view, is behind the times in his reading of her work. However, Woolf's recognition of a world having changed and her instinct to try to identify a turning point or date upon which everything changed reflect a more widespread social anxiety. It is undoubtedly the shock of recognition that comes with that subtle, slippery, and seductive idea of modernism, famously likened by Marshall Berman to "a maelstrom of perpetual disintegration and renewal, of struggle and contradiction, of ambiguity and anguish."[7] Such a phenomenon may engender reactionary visions, nostalgia, or worse, just as easily as it may inspire revolutionary speculations or utopian visions. The key is the recognition, however evident or vague, that the present is quite distinct from the past. Modernism, like utopia, involves some idea of a break, in space or time or both. Ezra Pound's dictum, "Make it new," operates as a call for a break with the past, even as it expresses a sense that that rupture has already somehow occurred, and the duty to register this new incommensurability falls upon poets and artists of the newly *modern* world.

Might this too mark a turn from the more optative utopianisms of the late Victorian period to the generalized dystopianism that emerges afterwards? Whereas Oscar Wilde could declare in "The Soul of Man Under Socialism" (1891) that "[a] map of the world that does not include Utopia is not even worth glancing at," Woolf by the 1920s likely could not foresee "human progress" in the same way. Wilde's defense of the apparent utopianism of socialism is rooted in this belief in progress; as he explains, the reason a map without Utopia on it is useless is because "it leaves out the one country at which Humanity is always landing. And when Humanity lands there, it looks out, and, seeing a better country, sets sail. Progress is the realisation of Utopias."[8] This vision of a progressively improving future has not entirely disappeared, and the legacy of a variation of "Whiggish thought" still permeates a great deal of political and scientific discourse even in the twenty-first century, but the faith in its vision would seem to be shaken. Woolf's literary productions of the 1920s depicted a changed world, perhaps, but they do not seem to indicate any utopian condition to come from these social transformations. Yevgeny Zamyatin's *We*, which many consider to be the first modern "dystopian novel," was published in 1924, the very year in which Woolf wrote about the date when everything changed, as if to punctuate the moment further.[9]

The desire to mark a date upon which "everything changed" may itself be motivated by a somewhat modernist impulse. The imperative "Make it new," after all, insists upon a break with that which is not new, the past or a prior period, and if modernity is to be understood as a temporal form or category at all, then it must be established in connection to some sort of "break." As Wegner has put it, speaking of Jameson's notion of periodization and, more particularly his assertion that in our time "one cannot not periodize," "no 'theory' of a period makes sense unless it comes to terms with the hypothesis of a break."[10] Arguably, what we think of as a modernist aesthetic could be considered itself a means of meditating upon such a break, and Jameson notes that "'Modernity' always means setting a date and positing a beginning," although he later insists that "[n]o theory of modernity makes sense today unless it comes to terms with the hypothesis of a *postmodern* break with the modern."[11] That is, if we are to imagine this as a temporal period, its parameters must be identified, at least in theory, and in the case of modernity, only a sense of the postmodern makes it representable as such. In this manner, the period itself, like the island of Utopia, is set apart from the mainland or from the mainstream flow of history.

Woolf's sense of a discernible "break" with the past is, in its own way, part of a modernist and utopian *Weltanschauung*. To the extent that a certain postmodernist dystopianism has become a pervasive aspect of our own worldviews today, one might wonder about when that earlier period ended. If, as Jameson has suggested, we cannot really begin to theorize modernity (or modernism?) without some sense of a postmodern break from the modern, where do we locate such a break? Jameson's own efforts to periodize and to historicize postmodernism in connection with late capitalism or globalization have proved to be among the most evocative, imaginative, and for me convincing of all such impossible attempts. But perhaps even more so than with the "moment when everything changed" to become "modern," the postmodern resists dates and events. The postwar period offers some guidance, so perhaps 1945 still counts. Enthusiasts of the "space race" might name Sputnik and 1957, while many cultural critics in the United States still gesture toward that fuzzy and ill-defined historical being known as "the Sixties," which does not always stay put within the decade's ten-year span of 1960–9, of course. Leo Marx referred to the label, "the Sixties," as "the misnamed political upheaval" that happened from 1965 to 1975, for example.[12] For scholars of globalization and the permutations of finance capital, 1973 offers a good candidate, with the collapse of Bretton Woods, the oil crisis, and the subsequent explosion in financial derivatives markets, among other things.[13] Certainly Thatcherism and Reaganism, which may as well now function as code words for the attacks on and dismantling of the modern (modernist?) welfare state, play their parts in postmodern culture.

Perhaps this says something about dystopia in an age of globalization, another term that does not readily admit decisive inaugural "breaks"; despite efforts to name them, globalization, like the Anthropocene, can be somehow traced to the earliest days of mankind's movements across putative boundaries. Some far-seeing critics might speak of the old Silk Road or the Mediterranean in time of Caesar as early instances of globalization, just as some environmentalists have found the Anthropocene to have begun with man's discovery of fire. Even by the standards of an Annales School-styled *longue durée*, these sorts of periods do not seem particularly helpful, particularly when identifying key characteristics of our own "age," as it were. I tend to agree with Jameson that there is a periodizing imperative, much like a temporal variant on the cartographic imperative, and that we tend to establish periods—marking boundaries between a before-time and an after—whether we really intend to do so or not. This occurs at even the most basic levels of imagining beginnings and endings, as Frank Kermode put it in his famous *tick-tock* example, which functions as an extraordinarily simple "plot" by which humans yet make "fictive concords with origins and ends."[14] Although the periodizing imperative and the making of plots remain, it may be that part of the dread associated with contemporary dystopianism lies in the fact that it is so difficult to pin down a clearly identifiable moment of rupture, when everything changed.[15]

Discrepant Temporalities

Thus, perhaps one of the inherently dystopian features of modern or postmodern dystopias is the nagging sense that the utopian break, that *coupure épistémologique* or "the moment when everything changed," did not occur. Or, perhaps, if it did, we did not take sufficient notice of it, and now it is too late to do much about it. Unable to make the break that characterizes the utopian enclave in space or time, dystopia winds up being thematized in relation to its baleful continuities with the past.

Lest I risk overstating this, let me hastily add that, for the reader or viewer, the alterity of the dystopian society or cultural landscape is a key feature of the dystopian text. Part of the fun, after all, is seeing a world that is unlike the "real world" in which we live, hence the generic forms of and similarities with science fiction, fantasy, and supernatural horror. But another part of the fun is the way in which current social problems are exaggerated or extrapolated in such a way that the dystopian alternate or future society is reminiscent of the present. Instead of seeing imagined solutions to contemporary problems, as Raphael Hythlodaeus witnesses in the social organization of Utopia or as Julien West finds in the year-2000's socialist United States in *Looking Backward*, readers or viewers of many dystopian texts explore contemporary social problems taken to a further limit, as when *Soylent Green* extrapolates upon the theme of overpopulation or *The Hunger Games* tacitly comments on the intersections of entertainment, violence, and political repression. In many respects, dystopianism registers the social, political, or cultural failure to make a break with the past and its troubles, which may also be why some famous dystopian works partake of a profoundly anti-utopian sentiment, as with *Brave New World*, in which the putative advances and solutions found within the future society's utopian achievements turn out to be the very aspects that readers are supposed to find dystopian and dreadful.

This sense of historical continuity can also be seen in the formal character of dystopian narratives. In their attention to plot and character, as opposed to mere description of spaces or elaborate explanations of policies, dystopian texts often resemble the romance or adventure tale more than the more properly utopian ones, where a "spatial" or descriptive form predominates. For Jameson, among others, dystopia is much more like fantasy—a generic mode that he sharply distinguishes from science fiction in a chapter of *Archaeologies of the Future* tellingly titled "The Great Schism"—in its kinship with romance and with adventure stories in general.[16] Dystopian narratives, in contrast to the largely static utopian form, tend to be very plot heavy, with compelling characters with clear motives and a major quest of some sort or another, which itself may be undergirded by a moralizing motive (e.g., defeating "evil"). Jameson also notes that "the pleasures of the nightmare—evil monks, gulags, police states—have little enough to do with the butterfly temperament of great Utopians like Fourier, who are probably not intent on pleasures at all but rather or some other form of gratification."[17]

Jameson wishes to go beyond merely distinguishing dystopian from utopian modes, but in fact to disjoin their connections to one another entirely. As he and others have noted, the "opposite" of utopia is not dystopia, but rather anti-utopia, and thus dystopia is of an entirely different order, not directly associated with either utopia or anti-utopia, although a dystopian text may very well have its affinities with either or both. Citing Gilles Deleuze's careful disentangling of sadism from masochism, effectively rendering the more familiar *sadomasochism* an inherently flawed concept or false start for discussions of these phenomena, in his study of Leopold von Sacher-Masoch, *Masochism: Coldness and Cruelty*,[18] Jameson writes that he "should like to disjoin the pair Utopia/dystopia in much the same definitive way."[19]

Jameson begins by noting the fundamental formal difference, narrative versus nonnarrative, to which I have already alluded. Unlike the dystopian tale, which often "tells the story of some imminent disaster," according to Jameson, "the Utopian text does not tell a story at all; it describes a mechanism or even a kind of machine, it furnishes a blueprint rather than lingering upon the kinds of human relations that might be found in the Utopian condition or imagining the kinds of living we wish were available in some stable, well-nigh permanent availability."[20] In many respects, this is a requirement of the truly utopian text, for if it is to imagine a society that has not yet existed and as yet cannot come into existence—that is, if it is not a "reactionary" or degraded vision of some Edenic past, as Marx and Engels in the *Manifesto* so vehemently criticized "utopian socialists" for desiring—then it cannot really depict how we would experience such a place. As Jameson puts it, "if you already know what your longed-for exercise in a not-yet-existent freedom looks like, then the suspicion arises that it may not really express freedom after all but only repetition."[21]

This "repetition" is perhaps the sort of thing that dystopian narratives may, in their own way, highlight. To the extent that many famously dystopian narratives appear to be critiques of what might be considered utopian schemes—*Brave New World* is a classic, in this regard—the idea that the purported improvements made in the quality of human life in the future wind up being merely different ways of imposing the same sorts of unfreedom upon the populace amounts to the moral of the story. Even in such "failed utopias," if one wishes to call them such, the "break" turns out to have merely been another, perhaps differently configured "bridge" connecting the lamentable problems of the past to similar, if newly instantiated, versions of those same problems in the future. Indeed, the societies or cultures in such near-future dystopian fantasies are often depicted as *more* horrid, precisely because of the ways in which the people, their leaders, or the social organizations as a whole had tried to implement supposedly utopian policies. The road to Hell being paved with good intentions, after all, many critics and readers may find the intentions themselves to have been, in retrospect, deplorable. Moreover, as Jameson puts it, "the more surely a given Utopia asserts its radical difference from what currently is, to that very degree it becomes, not merely unrealizable but, what is worse, unimaginable."[22] Or, again, potentially deplorable, as some critics might see in the utterly alien world of the utopia something that is both fantastic, in the bad sense of being impossible and therefore unworthy of our consideration, and bad, insofar as its very impossibility and unreality may lead to consequences far worse than our current reality entails. Wegner has stated that, in Jameson, the "desire for Utopia" is effectively a "passion for totality," but that this passion also "accounts for the tremendous fear of Utopia in the anti-Utopia."[23] A *totally* different system is too alarming for some to want to imagine, it seems.

Hence the baleful continuities of dystopia, which may also help to explain the paradoxical sense that there is a widespread "desire called dystopia," to play upon Jameson's evocative phrase. Dystopias look oddly familiar, notwithstanding their setting in a more-or-less-distant future or some otherworld, and this connection to our own times and places provides a path by which the allure of alterity and the comforts of the quotidian can be equanimously trodden. Along those lines, dystopias also replace the potentially jarring break with the here and now, that spatiotemporal rupture at the heart of the utopian project, with the temporal coordinates of past, present, and future that serve as a kind of mapping in their own right, displaying the points along a timeline or within a matrix that register our relative position in time (and space, too) in ways that help to reconcile the discrepant temporalities in which we exist as finite beings in a broadly historical and natural world. The desire called dystopia, perversely perhaps, reflects a sense of nostalgia, as I discuss later (in Chapter 7), in terms of the way the dystopian fiction, especially of the apocalyptic or postapocalyptic variety, often offers reassuringly simpler and more manageable worlds that, even amid their existential terrors, are almost comforting when contrasted with the vast complexities of the present and, of course, with the precarity and uncertainty of the future. Indeed, the frequently appearing dystopian theme of historically retrogressive social forms—such as a Hobbesian *bellum omnium contra omnes*, primitive tribalism, or small, organic communities—registers a nostalgia for the future, a historical sleight of mind in which past and future blend together to make the present's own dreadfulness appear potentially manageable.

For enthusiasts of dystopia, it is possible that the end of history suggested by utopia, which in its spatiotemporal "totality" would amount to an escape from history itself, might appear frightening. As Jameson writes,

> at some point discussions of temporality always bifurcate into the two paths of existential experience (in which questions of memory seem to predominate) and of historical time, with its urgent interrogations of the future. I will argue that it is precisely in Utopia that these two dimensions are seamlessly reunited and that existential time is taken up into historical time which is paradoxically also the end of time, the end of history.[24]

Jameson understandably sees utopia, in its own way a sort of alternate name for communism and thus for the overall emancipation from the nightmare of history and vale of tears that is capitalist modernity, as a figure for this canceling, preserving, and abolishing of the contradiction between our earthly lived experience and those vaster systems with their own inhuman rhythms and processes to which we are subject, often unconsciously and sometimes unwillingly. In a sense, then, the "desire for narrative" that Jameson had discussed in an earlier examination of disparate temporalities might find some purchase in the space of the dystopian narrative: "The 'desire for Marx' can therefore also be called the desire for *narrative*, if by this we understand, not some vacuous notion of 'linearity' or even *telos*, but rather the impossible attempt to give representation to the multiple and incommensurable temporalities in which each of us exists."[25]

Of course, there is also the simpler explanation of why dystopian fiction might elicit pleasure and even comfort when compared with utopian variants. Those who are critical of dystopia and of what they imagine as fantasy more broadly cite the fundamentally reactionary or quietist politics associated with the genre,[26] and to some extent the fanciful presentation of near-future social horror does arguably help to make one more complacent with respect to the *status quo*, particularly when the problems identified in the texts can be made distant through the spatiotemporal matrix employed by the text itself. Bioengineering and Big Brother are already very much features of our experience with the world, yet the fiction of *Brave New World* or *Nineteen-Eighty-Four* keeps these menaces in an imagined future or at least in a fictional world. Science fiction and fantasy novels or films of all sorts do this, of course, as do works of so-called "serious" literature, realism and modernism, and so on. But the idea that our world is not so bad in comparison with a world in which our problems, fears, and worries are exacerbated and extended may offer some comfort, much in the way that consumers of horror are able to process their phobias through the medium, while finding pleasure in the experience. Similarly, the continuities between our familiar sense of the world and the dystopian worlds in which we both live and experience through different media may appear more comforting than the radical disjunctions we might have hoped would liberate our modern present or future from the past.

Divergent Mechanisms, or Soma and Surveillance

Does this desire for dystopia then undermine the monitory power of the genre, for which it has been so thoroughly praised by journalists, historians, and social critics? If the great pleasure associated with reading or watching these dystopian tales, novels, films, and series somehow mitigates the political efficacy of the message, such that warning us about the dangers of this or that social evil no longer has its intended effect, then why imagine dystopian fiction as potentially progressive or liberatory at all? In fact, might we begin to imagine a world in which the mania for dystopia is itself a sign of dystopia, as readers and audiences eagerly consume the very things they were to have been warned against?

These questions get at a "classic" bifurcation in the genre's exploration of modern dystopian experience. Specifically, how would the societies and cultures in which we live limit our freedoms and the possibilities of living a life without anxiety (*leben ohne Angst*, as Adorno put it), thwart our desires, and undermine our plans for the future? Various dystopian visions proliferate—from Kafka-esque bureaucratic absurdity, technological dependence (i.e., the "rise of the machine"), repressive governments or police forces, and so on—but the basic question of how these systems would affect people was mooted, in turn, by two of the most famous "dystopian" novels of the past century. Thus, famously, Aldous Huxley's *Brave New World* (1932) and George Orwell's *Nineteen-Eighty-Four* (1949), almost certainly the best known and most canonical of modern dystopian novels, present rather different visions of a dystopian society, but each of which effectively closes off the possibility for overcoming the social orders depicted in them, in part by presenting failed quests to do so. For Orwell, a painstaking process of repression and manipulation led Winston Smith to love Big Brother, as the last line of the novel would have it, but Huxley was far more concerned by the ways that modern societies could be organized so as to encourage the populace to embrace the chains that bind them.

In Huxley's depiction, genetic engineering and careful psychological conditioning in *Brave New World* produces a happy, productive, and docile populace, whose delights in social status, entertainment, and sex preclude them from revolting or questioning authority. Thanks to advances in social engineering, even at the level of fetal development, the rank and file of the population are already ordered in such a way that citizens "know their place" in the social hierarchies. A caste system is thus established that is internalized at the level of biology and neurochemistry, not just at the level of ideology. Moreover, should anyone experience any feelings of insecurity or anxiety, there is *soma*, a drug eagerly taken by members of the society. "A gramme is always better than a damn," as one character earnestly puts it.[27] The drug relieves them from feelings of angst or dread, but even it is merely supplementary to other pleasures and entertainments available, as games, movies, or other forms of popular pastimes—sex, above all, for Huxley's world is replete with casual, unlimited, and carefree sexual activity—also function as types of *soma*, relieving any personal stress and effectively barring any political criticism. To be outside this system almost literally requires remote enclaves in the desert, as well as a conscious hostility to the soma and other diversions available. But as the figures in *Brave New World* make clear, why should one actively resist pleasure, comfort, and serenity?

In Orwell's Oceania, by contrast, constant surveillance and brutal police repression keep the citizenry in line, and "Big Brother Is Watching" becomes the figure for the social life writ large. Moreover, in what may be chalked up to Orwell's own concerns about the politics of the English language and the manipulations of historical knowledge by the media, *Nineteen-Eighty-Four*'s dystopia features Newspeak, a perversion of the common tongue, and relentless revisions of history; in both cases, with the elimination of individual words or phrases and the erasure of people and events, the past and its traditions are destroyed as much as the so-called "freedoms" of the present. Indeed, as Orwell tries to make clear, these strategies work in tandem, for panoptic surveillance and the constant regulation of language and "truth" engender similar effects among the populace, which is unable to articulate or to remember the ideas needed to counteract the forces of a police state. In such a society, the protagonist Winston Smith feels rebellious just thinking his thoughts, which culminates in his "bold" assertion that "[f]reedom is the freedom to say two plus two equals four" (which, as it happens, is not entirely true, as he learns while being interrogated by O'Brien later). Winston's sexual relationship with Julia also functions as an act of supreme resistance to the totalitarian regime, which represses not only knowledge but also desire. The climax of the novel, arguably, is when Winston betrays Julia (who had apparently betrayed him earlier), thus allowing fear and capitulation to the state to overcome love and resistance.

Between Huxley and Orwell, these represent the two poles of the modern dystopia, the pleasurable distractions and the disciplining oversight, and in our own time, the technologies for each have developed almost infinitely beyond the rudimentary versions depicted in those novels. In many respects, it seems that Huxley's dystopian perspective has clearly won out in the twenty-first century, at least in the United States and Europe. After all, there is no need to airbrush photographs to remove embarrassing or unwelcome historical juxtapositions in a world where nobody cares about such things at all. (In a more strictly Orwellian world, the famous photographs of Donald Rumsfeld shaking hands with Saddam Hussein might have been more scandalous, but much as critics of the Iraq War hoped to use it to point out the Bush Administration's hypocrisy, there was never any sense that Rumsfeld, Bush, or anyone else would be in political peril over such images.) Along those lines, where politics is itself a form of entertainment, with self-proclaimed "news junkies" reveling in the latest gaffe by a perceived opponent or celebrating the way one's favorites scored points on their enemies, it is difficult to imagine real challenges to the structures of domination in the society, and that is not even to mention all the other entertaining distractions and opportunities for self-gratification available. However, Orwell's successors might rightly counter that omnipresent surveillance has only increased and spread throughout all levels of society, right down to people's GPS-located movements, social media monitoring, cell phones, and so forth. Also, police brutality and state-sponsored violence have hardly abated, such that physical repression and social discipline remain part of the modern world. Soma *and* surveillance continue to both operate effectively, and perhaps mutually, today.

Huxley admired Orwell's novel, even if he felt that Orwell's social critique was focused on the wrong side of this soma versus surveillance dichotomy. In an October 21, 1949, letter to Orwell, Huxley praised *Nineteen-Eighty-Four* before speaking of its main subject, "the ultimate revolution." As Huxley goes on,

> The first hints of a philosophy of the ultimate revolution—the revolution which lies beyond politics and economics, and which aims at total subversion of the individual's psychology and physiology—are to be found in the Marquis de Sade, who regarded himself as the continuator, the consummator, of Robespierre and Babeuf. The philosophy of the ruling minority in *Nineteen Eighty-Four* is a sadism which has been carried to its logical conclusion by going beyond sex and denying it. Whether in actual fact the policy of the boot-on-the-face can go on indefinitely seems doubtful. My own belief is that the ruling oligarchy will find less arduous and wasteful ways of governing and of satisfying its lust for power, and these ways will resemble those which I described in *Brave New World*.[28]

For Huxley, the terrible "revolution" to come is not to be confused merely with the growing hegemony of an American-styled capitalist cosmopolitanism or a Soviet-like totalitarian regime but with the "total subversion of the individual's psychology and physiology," which then leads him to discuss the significance of hypnosis and barbiturates in helping to make this revolution possible. Consequently, "infant conditioning and narco-hypnosis are more efficient, as instruments of government, than clubs and prisons" and "the lust for power can be just as completely satisfied by suggesting people into loving their servitude as by flogging and kicking them into obedience."[29]

Huxley concludes by saying "I feel that the nightmare of *Nineteen Eighty-Four* is destined to modulate into the nightmare of a world having more resemblance to that which I imagined in *Brave New World*," which is not surprising. Notably, he imagines the dystopia of *Brave New World* as inhabiting a later stage of or progression beyond the society of Orwell's novel, thus imagining the movement from panoptic surveillance and brutal repression toward the narco-hypnotic embrace of the chains that bind us as an almost natural progression of this long revolution that is modernity. But more noteworthy still is his explanation for this "progressive" movement: "The change will be brought about as a result of a felt need for increased efficiency."[30]

It is interesting that Huxley identified the "felt need for increased efficiency" as the motive force in modern society's dystopian development. Zamyatin's *We*, after all, was among other things a satirical critique of Taylorism, the "science" of management that preached efficiency above all.[31] In Huxley's view, a more efficient society would require less direct physical repression, particularly if the now psychologically conditioned laborers could embrace the chains that bind them by striving to be more efficient themselves. As it happens, a third British dystopian novel, published a decade after *Nineteen-Eighty-Four*, would identify and name the mechanism by which soma and surveillance could be united most effectively, and it would coin as a dystopian label a term that would within a short time become almost universally praised and championed by governmental and business leaders. In Michael Young's *The Rise of the Meritocracy* (1958), a society-wide system of locating, measuring, redistributing, and ultimately exploiting intelligence points to the apotheosis of the Huxley-like hedonists' Orwellian police state. Young's dystopia, perhaps even more than those of Huxley and Orwell, is most thoroughly realized in our own time, so much so that it is not even recognized as dystopian any longer. Hence, it is arguably dystopia perfected.

Merit as Dystopia

Somewhat like Edward Bellamy's *Looking Backward* in the previous century, *The Rise of the Meritocracy* was initially imagined as a nonfiction work of social commentary, but it became more of Bellamy-esque science fiction novel, as Young presents the narrative as an official report (written by a person named Michael Young) in 2034, which looks back upon the achievements and drawbacks of the meritocratic revolution in England over the past eighty years or so. Young, a socialist who later became a member of Parliament, saw meritocracy as a fundamental and pervasive ideology that would ultimately (perhaps inevitably) secure the upper class as the "ruling class"; indeed, it would do so far more effectively than the pre-industrial system of hereditary lordship could have done. As Young sums up the "argument" of the novel,

> if the soil creates castes the machine manufacturers classes—classes
> to which people can be assigned by their achievement rather than

ascribed by their birth. Insofar as this has happened, social inequality can be justified, and, to avoid too blatant a contradiction, such a justification is almost always needed in a democratic society which has bowed to equality at least as far as elections are concerned. Otherwise the people who exercise power are going to be undermined by self-doubt and people over whom the power is exercised become indignant and subversive because they deny that the others have the right to lord it.[32]

The brilliance of a concept like meritocracy, in practice, lies in the way that it at one and the same time seems to combat privilege while it actually establishes and reinforces privilege, making both those in power and those out of it feel all the more comfortable with their relative positions.

In a fantastic ruse of history, Young's term, *meritocracy*, which he had coined to describe a dismal, dystopian scenario, eventually became so almost universally admired that well-meaning pundits, university leaders, business executives, and heads of state came to use the word in praise of a system of ultimate fairness. That these are "people in power" is not coincidental, but even those most disadvantaged by this system seem to want to celebrate "merit," if only by condemning "unearned" privileges. For instance, both Tony Blair and Bill Clinton touted the virtues of meritocracy, vowing in the early 1990s to make sure that their nations maintained the ideals of such a system. Imagine a British Prime Minister or an American President bragging about their support for Big Brother! And yet, in some respects, that is what support for meritocracy amounts to, for the disciplinary surveillance used to maintain the Party's hegemony in *Nineteen-Eighty-Four* could be said to reach its apotheosis in the more acceptable forms of it that undergird meritocratic systems. To Young's great dismay, as he records in a 1993 Introduction to a new edition of his 1958 novel, the term is now embraced throughout the very societies in which he had hoped his book could serve as a warning. The devastating consequences of the meritocratic ideal are widely apparent today, even if the ideal itself has not suffered much ignominy among the rich and powerful.

Young's satirical exposé of meritocracy is, as he concedes in his 1993 retrospective on his novel, very *English*, which is also to say, it is part of a long tradition of English social satire, and "in those island clothes the book may not travel well."[33] In particular, the persistence of the peerage or aristocratic system in Britain long after the industrial revolution had supposedly sorted most of society into economic classes, as opposed to hereditary castes, makes the emergence of meritocracy all the more striking. When, for example, the posh, seven-year-old children featured in the first installment of Michael Apted's legendary *Up* documentary series (the first installment, *Seven Up!*, released in 1964), announce both matter-of-factly and condescendingly that they are already "down for" Cambridge or Oxford, they have underscored the degree to which birthright still appeared to reign in British culture. Of course, by noting that their privilege was acknowledged in part *through* the educational institutions for which they were bound, the children also perhaps unwittingly revealed the way that their system of social hierarchy was becoming based on much more meritocratic values, specifically those associated with educational attainment. Your Cambridge degree might well be more important than your father's name, as it turns out, even if you initially were able to enroll at Cambridge because of that name. In a sense, this would come across as a major change in the self-regard of the "upper classes" and of the society in general.

In the United States, by contrast, a core element of the national ideology going back to the eighteenth-century is the myth of the unencumbered individual who can succeed on his own merits, regardless of birth. The working-class born Benjamin Franklin became a living symbol of this in his time, and his example later was mythologized into something equally resonant with such politically diverse figures as Horatio Alger, Ayn Rand, Paul Goodman, and Martin Luther King Jr., all of whom—notwithstanding their very different political views and goals—plumped for the idea that "America" was a land of freedom in which all persons could, or should, be able to succeed equally, despite the very obvious history indicating the contrary. It is a myth, after all, but no less powerful for being one. Undoubtedly, a seven-year-old George W. Bush in 1953 (a year in which his Yale-educated father founded an oil company and his Yale-educated grandfather was a US Senator) likely could feel just as confident about his prospects of being accepted to their *alma mater*, Yale University, when the time came as those posh English boys did in *Seven Up!* That said, a young William Jefferson Clinton, just one month younger than Bush, was the son of a bigamous traveling salesman with no college education whatsoever and who died shortly before Bill was born; at age seven, perhaps Clinton would not have been as able to watch a future at Georgetown University, then Oxford, and later Yale Law School unfold before his mind's eye so smoothly. And yet, both the scion of a Bush clan whose wealth and power extended generations and the fatherless, Arkansan "Man from Hope" have been among the most fervent champions of "meritocracy" among visible national leaders in recent decades.

The distinctly American version of all this owes something to related concept, *individualism*. One of the twentieth century's most astute critics of this ideology, Kurt Vonnegut (another satirist known for maintaining a utopian's spirit while producing dystopian scenarios in his novels), wrote that this belief in individualism causes intense pain and guilt, since all people are told it is their own fault that they somehow fail to find themselves rich, powerful, and therefore happy. As Vonnegut has a character say it in *Slaughterhouse-Five*, referring to a saying that is at the heart of the American experience, "[i]f you're so smart, why ain't you rich?" In *Jailbird*, Vonnegut summarized a short story written by the fictional Kilgore Trout called "Asleep at the Switch," in which souls newly arrived in heaven are shown detailed retrospectives of their lives by auditors who point out opportunities missed—that is, times the person could have struck it rich, married the mate of one's dreams, garnered the respect and love of others, and so forth—punctuating each with, "[a]nd there you were, asleep at the switch." Needless to say, perhaps, it makes people miserable even in heaven to learn that they could have been happier on earth, had only they acted differently at the right times, but the audit shows them that they cannot complain (or blame God) about their lot in life. Each individual is utterly responsible for his or her choices in life, with the added sense that any failure to act, even through ignorance, is as damning as any "bad" act. But this in turn means that, while in life they might have felt unlucky or dissatisfied, in heaven they live in abject misery, knowing full well how they had many blown chances. By making individuals personally responsible for their relative success or failure, *structural conditions* for the possibility of their success or failure are left unquestioned and largely invisible.[34] As Young himself has put it, if "ordinary people […] think themselves inferior, if they think they deserve on merit to have less worldly goods and less worldly power than a select minority, they can be damaged in their own self-esteem, and generally demoralised."[35]

In Vonnegut's parable, the phrase "asleep at the switch" is the equivalent of "not being smart enough." Notably, the domain in which meritocracy operates and reproduces its power is *education*. This field has the advantage of conferring status upon individuals based on their intellect and industriousness. Indeed, in *The Rise of the Meritocracy*, Young provides the "formula" established by meritocracy: "IQ + Effort = Merit." Those who are successful in this system are thus encouraged to believe that they have earned their position through hard work, that they are smarter or at least better trained and often harder working than others beneath them, and that they are fully deserving of their status. In many cases, even today, when one hears of the qualifications that make a given leader worthy of leadership, it is often little more than a list of the schools attended; the irony is that "elite" schools are clearly themselves a feature of the older, aristocratic model, something most meritocrats winkingly fail to acknowledge. In the satirically dystopian Netflix movie, *Don't Look Up* (2021), the advisors to the President at the White House cast doubt on the scientists' credibility on the grounds that they teach at Michigan State University (which is, of course, a major research institution in its own right), rather than at a Harvard or a Princeton; this comedic take-down of official "elitism" is so effective precisely because we know how often attending "the Ivies" or other such elite institutions is so heavily valued by a credulous public, including most of those in power.

The topic requires further elaboration. It is not simply education itself, but the ways in which education is formed, measured, evaluated, and so on that matters most here. Michel Foucault's brilliant analysis of the *examination*, a form that might be called a "panopticon-on-paper," discloses the degree to which it simultaneously homogenizes and individualizes its subjects, establishing a standardized domain that is immediately hierarchized, and distributing the test-takers along a discontinuous continuum of apparently meritocratic outcomes, some of which are understood to minutely condition if not absolutely determine one's future successes or failures in a future too remote to accurately foresee. Virtually all students living in the late-twentieth and twenty-first century know all too well how their scores on standardized tests, possibly the most significant and visible way that meritocracy enforces its system in Young's dystopian novel, will affect them in different sectors of life outside of their current classrooms. In *Discipline and Punish*, Foucault offers an incisive reading of how these forms enact and maintain disciplinary power, perhaps far better than any surveillance-heavy prisons or factories could, in fact.[36] Given the ways that "good" test-takers are rewarded, one can even see the degree to which exams can be likened to soma as well as to surveillance in their widescale operation.

Critics of meritocracy often focus on how it becomes an ideology that masks the built-in privileges and advantages that abound in post-industrial societies, thus essentially showing how the discourse of our living in a meritocracy hides the fact that we do not live in a meritocracy. That is, although the privileges may no longer accrue directly according to bloodline or birthright, they nevertheless in reality tend to be found in those who do come from a certain class, and quite often they come from family members who had been in the ruling class of an earlier era. (Also, of course, inherited wealth and power never went away, regardless of the regimes of educational testing that were imposed on post-Second World War generations.) Fundamentally, these critics of meritocracy actually embrace the concept in theory, but lament that it does not truly exist in practice and that the illusion that it exists in reality does more harm than good.

However, there is good reason to criticize meritocracy on its own merits, as it were, by examining its most elementary claim: that those who are in the social position they find themselves in *deserve* to be in that position because they have *earned* it. That is, they have proven that that is where they *belong*. In practice, this means that if you are dissatisfied with the position you find yourself in, you have no one to blame but yourself, for you are too stupid, unskilled, or indolent to *place yourself* in a more desirable position. In an ideal meritocracy, at least, there would be no other explanation. But even if we believed that our society truly were a meritocracy, even if no one received unfair advantages based on non-merit-based factors, *why* should we want people in such a society to gain advantage over others, and *why* should we want those disadvantaged persons to remain so? Should the hungry not be fed? Should the sick not be healed? (Samuel Butler's *Erewhon* [1872] does imagine a utopia in which ill-health is punished with prison sentences and hard labor, but that was intended as social satire.) Should even the ineducable be made to suffer for their poor scholastic performances? Ironically, perhaps, the defenders of meritocracy if only unconsciously are more likely to embrace the idea that the sick, hungry, uneducated, and poor be left to their just deserts than an earlier, ostensibly crueler generation might have. As Young writes, "granted that the best astronomer should be made Royal, [but] why should he get a larger emolument than the bricklayer who built his observatory?"[37]

The Rise of the Meritocracy astutely identified key social problems in the then-present that were only to become more acute and widespread, just as Huxley and Orwell had. "Merit" in our society has functioned very much like soma, in that it deadens resistance and makes acceptance—nay, embrace—of the *status quo* almost inevitable. It also involves panoptic surveillance as the unending regimens of exams, measurement, evaluation, and training all see to it that a version of Big Brother, here understood as merit itself, maintains a constant vigil.

The meritocratic system has resulted in starker class divisions and greater dynastic transmission of wealth and privileges than those found in previously aristocratic or even feudal societies in the United States and UK. The alternatives are also much more difficult to imagine and enact, since meritocracy virtually ensures the consent of those most damaged by its practices, even as the underlying resentments fuel different forms of resistance. Neo-fascism, for instance, seems to be a direct consequence of this model, as the critique of liberalism takes on ever more right-wing, racist, and nationalist freight. Populist movements in the United States and elsewhere have also aimed at criticizing the "elites" who purportedly look down upon the "ordinary" people. Yet these would-be resisters are nevertheless also supporters of meritocracy, for instance, blaming minorities or immigrants for "unearned" advantages or hand-outs, but not interested in seeing that everyone gets hand-outs. (In fact, the right-wing discourse in the United States has made "hand-outs" something that only one's enemies are unfairly given, while the corporate welfare, government-backed farm subsidies or small-business loans, and even food stamps are well-deserved when benefiting themselves or their "kind.") So well disciplined, in the Foucauldian sense, are the supporters of meritocracy than they can hardly imagine the real problem, is not the distribution of the prizes, but the prizes themselves.

Kwame Anthony Appiah, writing specifically about *The Rise of the Meritocracy* as well as about the ethical problems associated with meritocracy more generally, has explained that

> [f]urther democratising the opportunities for advancement is something we know how to do, even if the state of current politics in Britain and the US has made it increasingly unlikely that it will be done anytime soon. But such measures were envisaged in Young's meritocratic dystopia, where inheritance was to hold little sway. His deeper point was that we also need to apply ourselves to something we do not yet quite know how to do: to eradicate contempt for those who are disfavoured by the ethic of effortful competition.

Appiah notes that "we live in a plenitude of incommensurable hierarchies," even if we do not always agree on how they are formed or maintained (e.g., faster runners win footraces, actors with "better" performances win Academy Awards, and so on). "But class identities do not have to internalise those injuries of class. It remains an urgent collective endeavour to revise the ways we think about human worth in the service of moral equality."[38]

Appiah also cites the concept of "institutional desert," by which, for example, lottery winners "deserve" to win, not because they performed better than others, but merely because they played by the rules of the game (i.e., they purchased their tickets in hopes of winning and without cheating, just as other did). "Institutional desert, however, has nothing to do with the intrinsic worthiness of the people who get into college or who get the jobs, any more than lottery winners are people of special merit and losers are somehow less worthy."[39] This may itself be worth thinking about given the degree to which lives within these dystopian meritocracies often feel like they are determined by random chance or otherwise indeterminate forces, despite all the cant about education and training.

The answer, if there is one, would probably lie in what Herbert Marcuse called "the scandal of qualitative difference," which is to say (in the Marcusean idiom), utopia itself. "Marxism must risk defining freedom in such a way that people become conscious of and recognize it as something that is nowhere already in existence."[40] This requires a thoroughgoing critique of the current ways of seeing merit and "just deserts," thus, overcoming the complementary powers of soma and surveillance, and empowering the social imagination more generally.

Conclusion: "This Is Fine"

Arguably, Marcuse's sense that freedom as we ought to try to define it exists nowhere in our world is itself a potentially dystopian sentiment, particularly if we imagine dystopias, as Huxley and Orwell apparently did, as societies in which basic human freedoms had been attenuated or eliminated. If freedom as it should be viewed does not currently exist, then we may well be living in supremely dystopian times and places. Marcuse had elsewhere characterized utopian experience, "the ultimate form of freedom," in reference to his old friend Theodor W. Adorno's phrase, *ohne Angst leben* ("to live without anxiety").[41] Ours certainly remains a time in which *Angst* persists, perhaps even more than before, at virtually all levels of daily life we are forced to confront ever greater uncertainty and precarity, owing in part to the very system that so many today have come to take as utterly inalterable. Once upon a time it was easier to imagine the end of the world than the end of capitalism, as the cliché goes, but in many respects it today seems easier to imagine the end of the world than slightly better healthcare, increased wages, safer roads and bridges, educational access, affordable housing, or ways to reduce gun violence. The seeming impossibility of securing even such modest "freedoms" is undoubtedly a sign of the dystopian condition in which we live in the twenty-first century.

Looking back in search of a turning point or moment when everything changed, perhaps we can look to the early 1950s, which in the United States at least was in many ways a time of peace and plenty for some, a time of great conflict and trouble for others, and above all an instant of momentous change with largely unforeseeable consequences. Perhaps it is not surprising that this is when Young coined his term *meritocracy* while imagining the baleful transformation of his society, and perhaps it is fitting that the very word *dystopia* in its current meaning is apparently established around this time, as noted above. In such a case, the unexpected reemergence of utopianism in the 1960s may well be viewed as the misleadingly bright afterglow of a *residual* form, in Raymond Williams's sense, where the creeping dystopianism that would find fuller flourish during and after the Reagan-era could be seen as *emergent* in that earlier moment.[42]

As dystopias are hardly "intentional communities," in contrast to many utopias, it makes sense that such a vexed cultural and social form would emerge in often unseen or little noticed increments. Denizens of dystopias may thus be likened to the proverbial frog in the pot of water who, as the apologue would have it, is acclimatized to the increasing heat by its very graduality; we don't know we're cooked until it's too late. Perhaps a more apt and timely figure could be found in the popular social-media meme depicting a cartoon dog, calmly sipping coffee while sitting in a house engulfed by flames, who thinks to himself, "This is fine."[43] In many respects, the twenty-first-century consumers' complacency with respect to their pervasive sense of dread, their learning to live amid the disasters as a sort of "new normal," their embrace of postcritical "surface readings" and its tacit affirmation of the *status quo* ("it is what it is"), and their inability or unwillingness to imagine radical alternatives, these may prove to be the most dystopian aspects of the present time. Little wonder then that dystopia, monstrosity, and the end of the world feature so prominently in our popular culture.

Notes

1   Jean Pfaelzer, *The Utopian Novel in America, 1886–1896: The Politics of Form* (Pittsburgh: University of Pittsburgh Press, 1984), 3.
2   The modern coinage of the term is sometimes attributed to Glenn Negley and J. Max Patrick, *The Quest for Utopia: An Anthology of Imaginary*

Societies (New York: Henry Schuman, 1952), 298; but see also *infra* Chapter 1, note 5.

3   Fredric Jameson, "Of Islands and Trenches," in *Ideologies of Theory* (London: Verso, 2008), 386.

4   Ibid.

5   See Phillip E. Wegner, *Imaginary Communities: Utopia, the Nation, and the Spatial Histories of Modernity* (Berkeley: University of California Press, 2002); see also Phillip E. Wegner, "The Modernisms of Science Fiction: Toward a Periodizing History," in *Shockwaves of Possibility: Essays on Science Fiction, Globalization, and Utopia* (Bern: Peter Lang, 2014), 1–63.

6   Virginia Woolf, *Mr. Bennett and Mrs. Brown* (London: Hogarth Press, 1924), 4–5. Needless to say, perhaps, but in the U.K., 1910 also marks the beginning of the reign of King George V, and in a society that conveniently labels its historical periods after the rule of an individual sovereign, Woolf's choice to refer to Victorian *versus* Georgian-era servant behavior, without reference to the Edwardian interim (1901–10), might itself be noteworthy.

7   Marshall Berman, *All That Is Solid Melts Into Air: The Experience of Modernity* (New York: Penguin, 1988), 15.

8   Oscar Wilde, *The Soul of Man Under Socialism and Other Selected Critical Prose*, ed. Linda Dowling (New York: Penguin, 2001), 141.

9   Written in Russian by 1921, *We* was first published in English translation in 1924; the first Russian edition did not appear until 1952. This novel's obvious influence on Aldous Huxley and George Orwell, among many others, has helped to solidify its canonical status as the "first" dystopian novels, although there were obviously many predecessors throughout the nineteenth and early-twentieth centuries. *We's* continuing influence is undeniable. For example, while reflecting on his first novel, *Player Piano*, which drew heavily upon his own observations of working at the General Electric Company, Kurt Vonnegut said that he "cheerfully ripped off the plot of *Brave New World*, whose plot had been cheerfully ripped off from Eugene Zamiatin's [sic] *We*." See Vonnegut, *Wampeters, Foma, and Granfalloons (Opinions)* (New York: Dial Press, 1999), 263.

10   Wegner, *Periodizing Jameson: Dialectics, the University, and the Desire for Narrative* (Evanston: Northwestern University Press, 2014), 17. For Jameson's proposition that "one cannot not periodize," see Jameson, *A Singular Modernity: Essay on the Ontology of the Present* (London: Verso, 2002), 94.

11   Jameson, *A Singular Modernity*, 31, 94, emphasis supplied.

12   Leo Marx, "On Recovering the 'Ur' Theory of American Studies," *American Literary History* 17.1 (Spring 2005): 122.

13   See, for example, Edward LiPuma and Benjamin Lee, *Financial Derivatives and the Globalization of Risk* (Durham: Duke University Press, 2004), 67–71.

14   Frank Kermode, *The Sense of An Ending: Studies in the Theory of Fiction* (Oxford: Oxford University Press, 1967), 45, 7.

15 In one contemporary dystopian genre, at least, this seems not to be the case. I'm thinking of the apocalypse, the zombie apocalypse more particularly, in which the "outbreak" is often a crucial starting point, by which to distinguish the world and the plot that is centered upon an "aftermath." Moreover, many dystopian narratives posit, at least in theory, a "before-time," a "long, long ago," but part of the dystopian worldview, it seems, involves the increasing ignorance or forgottenness of such a "break" in social history, as in Orwell's *Nineteen-Eighty-Four*. Some narratives, like Cormac McCarthy's *The Road*, omit the apocalyptic "event" out of the picture entirely, leaving the reader to ponder what sorts of disasters must have happened in the past to render the world a hellscape in the now present.

16 See Jameson, *Archaeologies of the Future: The Desire Called Utopia and Other Science Fictions* (London: Verso, 2005), 57–71.

17 Jameson, *The Seeds of Time* (New York: Columbia University Press, 1994), 55.

18 Ibid. See also Gilles Deleuze, *Masochism: Coldness and Cruelty*, trans. Jean McNeil (New York: Zone Books, 1991), 7–141; this volume also includes the text of Sacher-Masoch's 1870 novella *Venus in Furs*.

19 Jameson, *The Seeds of Time*, 55.

20 Ibid., 56.

21 Ibid.

22 Jameson, *Archaeologies of the Future*, xv.

23 Wegner, *Periodizing Jameson*, 200.

24 Jameson, *Archaeologies of the Future*, 7.

25 Jameson, *The Ideologies of Theory, Volume 1: Situations of Theory* (Minneapolis: University of Minnesota Press, 1988), xxxviii.

26 Carl Freedman, in fact, refers to the very term *dystopia* as "a popular solecism," urging that it not be used at all since, that by positing a "bad place," the concept displaces the fundamental estrangement of utopia (*outopia* rather than *eutopia*) with a moral dimension, positive or negative, relative to the society in which it is produced. See Freedman, *Critical Theory and Science Fiction* (Middletown, CT: Wesleyan University Press, 2000), 74, note 38. But see also China Miéville, "Cognition as Ideology: A Dialectic of SF Theory," in *Red Planets: Marxism and Science Fiction*, ed. Mark Bould and China Miéville (Middletown, CT: Wesleyan University Press, 2009), 231–48.

27 Aldous Huxley, *Brace New World and Brave New World Revisited* (New York: Harper Perennial, 2004), 89.

28 Huxley, *Letters of Aldous Huxley*, ed. Grover Smith (New York: Harper & Row, 1970), 604.

29 Ibid., 605.

30 Ibid.

31 Named for Frederick Winslow Taylor, author of *The Principles of Scientific Management* (1911), Taylorism (or Taylorization) referred to the regimented discipline of labor as described in Taylor's theories. Efficiency, above all, was the goal.

32 Michael Young, *The Rise of the Meritocracy* (London: Routledge, 1994), xiii.

33 Ibid., xv.

34 See Kurt Vonnegut, *Slaughterhouse-Five* (New York: Dial Press, 2009), 165; Vonnegut, *Jailbird* (New York: Dial Press, 2011), 245–7.

35 Young, *The Rise of the Meritocracy*, xvi.

36 Michel Foucault, *Discipline and Punish: The Birth of the Prison*, trans. Alan Sheridan (New York: Vintage Books, 1977), 184–92.

37 Young, *The Rise of the Meritocracy*, 145.

38 Kwame Anthony Appiah, "The Myth of the Meritocracy: Who Really Gets What They Deserve?" *The Guardian* (October 19, 2018): https:// www.theguardian.com/news/2018/oct/19/the-myth-of-meritocracy-who-really-gets-what-they-deserve.

39 Ibid.

40 Herbert Marcuse, "The End of Utopia," in *Five Lectures: Psychoanalysis, Politics, and Utopia*, trans. Jeremy J. Shapiro and Shierry M. Weber (Boston: Beacon Press, 1970), 69.

41 Marcuse, *Eros and Civilization: A Philosophical Inquiry into Freud* (Boston: Beacon Press, 1966), 149–50.

42 For his famous discussion of emergent, dominant, and residual formations, see Raymond Williams, *Marxism and Literature* (Oxford: Oxford University Press, 1977), especially 121–7.

43 The drawing itself was created by Web comic artist KC Green in 2013. See Emma Bowman, "A Decade On, the 'This Is Fine' Creator Wants to Put the Famous Dog to Rest," *NPR's All Things Considered* (January 16, 2023): https://www.npr.org/2023/01/16/1149232763/this-is-fine-meme-anniversary-gunshow-web-comic.

Chapter 3

LOST IN GRAND CENTRAL:
AMERICAN GODS, FREE TRADE,
AND GLOBALIZATION

Dystopia never appears all at once. One does not stumble upon the "bad place" out of the blue, like an island in the middle of the sea or an enclave just over the range. Rather, one slowly apprehends that she or he has been living there all along. Famously, some dystopias emerge from the attempts to form some sort of utopian society (as in the notorious visions of Yevgeny Zamyatin's *We* [1924], Aldous Huxley's *Brave New World* [1932], or perhaps even George Orwell's *Nineteen-Eighty-Four* [1949]),[1] but more often the dystopian aura envelops a reality that has simply proceeded along in its quotidian ways. One goes about one's everyday life and work, while as time passes noting this or that odd occurrence that might be a sign; a creeping suspicion evolves toward certainty, a gloomy presentiment congeals into visible shape, and dystopia appears, right here and right now, where it has been for a while. As Herman Melville put it, in a way that only barely discloses the sense of dread aroused by the words, "[s]hadows present, foreshadowing deeper shadows to come."[2] Like a shadow, suggestive of simultaneous absence and presence, the gathering darkness of dystopia colors our perception of the world, even when we cannot be sure it is really there at all.

If "dystopia became the dominant literary form" of the twentieth century, it is at least partly because of a pervasive dystopian mood or anxiety that increased its momentum throughout that century.[3] By the beginning of the 1990s, in the United States as elsewhere, ever more menacing storm clouds congregated on the horizon, and the final decade of the twentieth century brought with it a deep sense of foreboding and unease. In the United States, the triumphal rhetoric that accompanied the "end of the Cold War," spectacularly represented by the fall of the Berlin Wall in December 1989, was inflated by the optative mood of early criers for a "borderless world" of free trade, globalization, and multiculturalism.[4] At the same time, however, these very victories appeared to augur greater calamity, as the aftermath of crumbling Soviet Bloc brought not only new freedoms but intense sectarian violence, war, even genocide; the economic *glasnost* and burgeoning world market provided hitherto unimagined productivity and wealth, but also bred greater economic instability, transforming communities and restructuring worldviews. If the industrial age had already created the conditions under which "all that is solid melts into air, all that is holy is profaned, and man is at last compelled to face with sober senses his real conditions of life and his relations with his kind," then the postmodern moment of multinational capitalism and global finance in the final years of the twentieth century compounded this situation immeasurably.[5] This generalized unease and social malaise characterized the public mood during the debates over the formation of the North American Free Trade Agreement (NAFTA) in the early 1990s, as the promise of fluid, cross-border movements of goods and services was necessarily tempered by a nameless fear of the radical, likely unforeseeable transformations such "free trade" would engender or entail.

Neil Gaiman's 2001 fantasy novel, *American Gods*,[6] explores the sorts of anxieties that typify the NAFTA era. *American Gods* offers a portrait of "U.S. Culture in the Long Nineties."[7] *American Gods* dramatizes the era's dystopian atmosphere by highlighting the role of transgression or transgressivity: movement, border-crossing, liminality, illicitness, and indeterminate danger. Although most readers would place *American Gods* in the genre of fantasy, rather than utopian or dystopian literature, Gaiman's use of the fantastic mode—more specifically, his blending of fantasy and realism—helps to vivify the dystopian narrative in the novel.[8] Gaiman's fantasy thus provides a more visceral, though less overt critique of the contemporary scene, while also maintaining a pervading spirit of ambiguity and vague menace. The ominous suspicion of a potential conspiracy amplifies the unease, and the inability to map the shifting landscape and one's place in it becomes the most persistent form of existential anxiety for North Americans at the end of the millennium. In *American Gods*, the dystopian moment of the post-NAFTA United States is illustrated in the transgressive movement of its tenebrous hero in his attempt to make sense of the "bad place" he inhabits. In the conclusion of the narrative, the dystopian condition and the method by which to counteract it coalesce into a single conception, that of transgression itself.

"A Contemporary American Phantasmagoria"

As Hank Wagner, Christopher Golden, and Stephen R. Bissette argue in their *Prince of Stories: The Many Worlds of Neil Gaiman*, "*American Gods* is a novel that only Gaiman could have written [...] The novel reflects his deep fascination with and love for his adopted country, but also subtly reflects its harshness, and strangeness, and flaws."⁹ In an unpaginated interview appended to the text of *American Gods*, Gaiman describes the tortuous paths he took in first conceiving, then writing the novel, which he labels "a contemporary American phantasmagoria." At that point, he is speaking strictly as a writer of imaginative fiction, and the twists-and-turns involve his many abortive attempts to create a protagonist, one who would become Shadow, to latch onto a novelistic concept, to orchestrate multiple movements, to flesh out the other characters, and so on. But pointedly, Gaiman's own peripatetic biography asserts itself in subtle ways in how he imagined this book.

A descendant of Polish Jewry, whose ancestor emigrated to England from the Netherlands, Gaiman grew up in England, began his career in London, and moved to Minnesota in 1992. Gaiman's early career reflects the breadth of his interests, as well as the roller-coastering fortunes of a would-be professional writer. His first books include a pop "biography" of the band Duran Duran (1984), a biography of Douglas Adams that also served as a critical study of Adams's *Hitchhiker's Guide to the Galaxy* series (*Don't Panic* [1985]), and a work of comedic fantasy co-authored with Terry Pratchett, *Good Omens* (1990); also, beginning in 1989, his immensely well-respected comic book series, *The Sandman*, began its run of seventy-five issues. In response to the question in the interview appended to *American Gods* of how his life and work changed now that he lives in the United States, Gaiman refers to *The Sandman*, pointing out that

> I wrote about America a lot in *Sandman*, but it was a slightly delirious America—one built up from movies and TV and other books. When I came out here I found it very different from the country I'd encountered in fiction, and wanted to write about that. *American Gods* was, in many ways, my attempt to make sense of the country I was living in.

Even at this personal level, then, *American Gods* represents the perspective of the transgressor, the border-crosser, who moves into a foreign domain while retaining a hybrid identity: old world and new, native and foreign, fantastic and realistic, and so forth. America appears as both a real and an imaginary place, or perhaps in Edward Soja's appropriately hydridized notion, a *real-and-imagined* space, in which the author represents both the mental and material spaces of the place simultaneously.¹⁰ *American Gods* is in some respects a form of literary cartography or cognitive mapping. That is, the novel could be said to represent, in part, Gaiman's own attempt to map the spaces of his newly adopted but still foreign territory: a stranger strangely *at home* in a strange land.[11]

Along those lines, Gaiman includes, by way of preface, a "Caveat, and Warning for Travelers," in which he writes: "[w]hile the geography of the United States of America in this tale is not entirely imaginary—many of the landmarks in this book can be visited, paths can be followed, ways can be mapped—I have taken liberties. Fewer liberties than you might imagine, but liberties nonetheless" (n.p.). Thus Gaiman invites the reader to explore the fantastic, imaginary geography of the country with his fictional characters, while conceding that the maps are not to be trusted, and "[o]nly the gods are real."

Transgressivity animates the whole of *American Gods*, which is if nothing else a story of wanderers, immigrants, border-crossers, and travelers from afar. The foundational concept of the novel is that those people who immigrated to the United States (or elsewhere) brought their gods with them as they traversed oceans and national boundaries. Moreover, the old gods native to that North American soil remain, and Gaiman duly records aspects of Native American or First Nations myths and religions, such as when Shadow encounters such deities as Whiskey Jack (Wisakedjak), the Buffalo Man, or the Thunderbird. What is more, the gods carried over by the transients and settlers are not necessarily the same as those left behind in their old worlds. In the novel's postscript, for instance, Shadow meets an Odin character rather different from the Wednesday he had worked for in the United States; these two (and many others, of course) are the "same" god, but they are also imbued with a different character specific to their current time and place. Such characteristics, like their powers *as* gods, derive from the force of belief on the part of those who worship them. A god is only as powerful as the belief in him or her that the faithful maintain, and "gods die once they are forgotten" (514).[12] Retaining many aspects of their immortal identities, these gods also take on new forms in the changing society. Cairo (pronounced "KAY-ro"), Illinois, home to several Nile Delta deities, is not Cairo, Egypt, after all. America, which one character claims "has been Grand Central for ten thousand years or more" (196), is a metaphysical free-trade zone in which fluid economies of belief alter the social landscape of the continent. Displaced from their native soil, put into circulation in a spiritual marketplace, subject to metaphysical competition from new and more powerful objects of faith, the gods experience a kind of perpetual crisis. Beliefs, like goods and services, are also subject to the vicissitudes of international trade.

It follows that, if the old gods are given life through the faith of their believers, circumstances will produce new believers able to engender new gods who will in turn be nourished by the power of their adherents. In *American Gods*, we find a haughty cadre of young, powerful deities, some displaying open disdain for the ancient gods. The new American gods include "gods of credit card and freeway, of Internet and telephone, of radio and hospital and television, gods of plastic and of beeper and of neon. Proud gods, fat and foolish creatures, puffed up with their own newness and importance" (137–8). A large part of the drama in *American Gods* comes down to a putative war between the old and the new gods, between gods on the brink of extinction, eking out some meager existence at the furthest margins of their former glory (like poor Bilquis, Queen of Sheba, whose legendary, erotic powers are put into service as a sex worker in the quest for worshippers), and those thrilling to the ecstatic rush of their novel and seemingly limitless power (like the gods of television and computers). Upon this unstable ground, the apparent plot of *American Gods* unfolds.

And, yet, this is not really the main narrative in the novel. Rather, as is hinted at by the many coin-tricks and confidence games in the text, the metaphysical war is a diversion, a sleight-of-hand ploy intended to distract attention from the much more powerfully dystopian theme in the novel. *American Gods* is a fable of transgression, and transgressivity is eventually disclosed to be not only the state of things in the dystopian, end-of-the-millennium United States, but also the means by which to navigate the spaces of dystopia. America, which in so much of its nationalist ideology, going all the way back to the earliest settlements, had been conceived as a utopia,[13] is fundamentally dystopian. In *American Gods*, the state of transgressivity within the United States is a dialectical reversal of the utopian prospects of transgressive movements across porous national and social boundaries. With its tenebrous hero Shadow winding his way around the continental United States on his odyssey to find himself, the novel's mood is anxious and foreboding, consistent with Peter Fitting's view that the dystopian mood is "a sense of a threatened near future," but without the science-fiction projection of a future tense at all.[14] *American Gods* is set very much in the present, and the otherworldly aspects of that present are not technological but, in the language of Darko Suvin, "metaphysical."[15] But the dystopian mood is quite fitting as the action seems to be leading up to a veritable Ragnarök, the *Götterdämmerung*, and the final doom of all creation. Amid the gloom, the utopian impulse to carve out new spaces of liberty unfolds as a dystopian confrontation between the new and old, which reveals the country to be "a bad place for gods," as one character in the novel puts it (586). "Bad place" is, after all, what the very word *dystopia* means, but the dystopia in *American Gods* will have more to do with the movements of the shadows than with the twilight of the gods.

Fables of Transgression

American Gods is ultimately about transgression. The original meaning of the word, from its Latin root, is a "step across" and had a specifically spatial sense. As Bertrand Westphal notes in *Geocriticism*, "[a]mong the Romans, one transgressed when passing to the other side of a boundary or a river [...] The *transgressio* could also be an infraction: one does not cross a boundary without departing from the norm. But the Romans did not give priority to that sense of the word."[16] The foundational conceit of *American Gods*—that is, that gods and legends accompany their believers who cross into new territories—requires this image of transgression, and the primary narrative trajectory, Shadow's circuitous travels ultimately lead him to the revelation of his own identity, but along the way he repeatedly enacts different instances of boundary-crossing. However, the more modern meaning, with its moral valences, is also pertinent. Not only is the protagonist Shadow a shady figure (ahem), with a criminal past and presently engaged in continuous, illicit activities while abetting Wednesday's swindles, but the generalized sense of lawlessness throughout the narrative, including the idea that nearly all the novel's characters are somehow operating outside or only on the margins of the national *nomos*, along with the almost constant allusions to trickery, illusion, and deception, mark *American Gods* as a transgressive text in even the less than literal sense. Indeed, most transgressive of all is the novel's clever insinuation that transgressivity is itself an essential constitutive feature of America, the grounds upon which dystopia discloses itself as dystopian. Shadow's transcontinental itinerary merely traces some of the contours of the transgressive space that is the dystopian United States at the end of the twentieth century.

The novel announces its theme of transgression from the start. In the opening pages, the protagonist is completing his prison sentence, time served for a crime he most certainly did commit, so the commonplace contemporary understanding of the word *transgression* is established as a theme even before Shadow's peripatetic movements begin. He is released from prison early because his wife, Laura, has died. He later discovers the circumstances, how she died in a car crash while performing a sex act upon Shadow's best friend and business partner, as the "transgressions" begin to pile up in the novel. Infidelity and betrayal thus color the reader's initial ideas about Shadow's relationship with his spouse, but Laura proves more faithful in the liminal, living-death existence she maintains after her funeral, as she (or her ghost-like, revenant persona) frequently comes to his aid throughout the narrative. With no one to return home to, Shadow agrees to work for a mysterious stranger he meets on an airplane, a Mr. Wednesday who we soon discover is Odin, the All-Father, of Norse mythology. True to the multiple meanings of *transgression*, Shadow follows Wednesday as he engages in a series of illegal or morally questionable activities, all while traveling to different places to meet with odd persons, who themselves turn out to be avatars of various deities from different theological or folkloric traditions and of diverse, multiple geographic origins.

These movements are punctuated by a few layovers in which Shadow is able to pause, and the reader is able to gain greater insight into the overall scheme of things. First, in his time with the Egyptian deities who are working as undertakers in Cairo, Illinois, Shadow discovers the breadth and depth of the metaphysical free-trade zone that is North America. Then, in the town of Lakeside, Wisconsin, Shadow experiences a sort of utopian space outside of the flows of commerce and history; in the end, he discovers the dark secret behind the town's timelessness and resistance to change. Finally, in his suspension—literally, as he is hanging by ropes from the World Tree—between life and death, Shadow discovers the truths about his own origins and identity, preparing himself (and the reader) for the final conflict between the new and old gods, a battle that turns out to be little more than an elaborately orchestrated confidence game. At the conclusion of this apocalyptic ruse, Shadow returns to Lakeside, where he helps to return that anomalous site to the spatiotemporal flux of American dystopia, before eventually moving on further, "transgressing" beyond those national borders, to Iceland, and thence … beyond.

An additional, fascinating feature of *American Gods* is its use of brief interludes or excurses labeled "Coming to America" (or "Somewhere in America"), which depict scenes of immigrants and their gods finding, and in some respects, *creating* themselves in the New World's spaces. We learn that Mr. Ibis, the Egyptian deity and Illinois undertaker, is the author of these vignettes. In addition to breaking up the narrative trajectory of Shadow's journey, these scenes—most of which do not bear directly or at all on that plotline—help to populate the American world with gods, legends, and folkloric figures, as well as showing the ways in which strangers in this strange land long for the connections to their ancient gods, even as they experience the wonders of a brave new world. Yet the punctual interventions that these episodes provide help to color the entire world of *American Gods*, demonstrating both the ongoing desire for an evanescing tradition and the transformative force of movement and displacement. The dystopia of America is thus tied to its utopian aspects. In "coming to America," the horrors of transgression, of crossing over the borders, are mitigated by the old spirits, but a new god tortures the past and shapes it into something barely recognizable. First and foremost, one powerful "new god" is the mythical entity that is "America" itself. In these "Coming to America" passages, the admixture of transgression and dystopia is dramatized, and the reader's pause in these moments makes the headlong rush of the Shadow-centered narrative more meaningful.

A Metaphysical Free Trade Zone

"This country has been Grand Central for ten thousand years or more" (196). Early in the book Mr. Ibis, who provides so much background information for Shadow and for the reader, asserts the astonishing proposition that voyagers over many millennia have traveled to and around North America, leaving their remains and establishing their gods upon this new soil. According to Ibis, the city of Cairo, Illinois, was once a trading post, visited by people of the Nile Delta over 3,500 years ago. Indeed, a kind of free trade is the basis for all of these improbable—Ibis calls them "impossible"—voyages to America, which include those of the aboriginal race of Japan, the Ainu, 9,000 years ago, of Polynesians to California two millennia later, of the Irish during the dark ages, of the Welsh and the Vikings, of West African traders in South America, of Chinese adventurers exploring the Oregon coastline, of Basque fishermen tending their nets off the coast of Newfoundland in the eighth century, and so on. Indeed, the primitive conditions of transoceanic travel were no impediment. As Ibis continues in his lecture, "[m]y people, the Nile folk, we discovered that a reed boat will take you around the world, if you have the patience and enough jars of sweet water" (198). What mattered was not technology or transportation, but goods and services to trade. "You see, the biggest problem with coming to America in the old days was that there wasn't a lot here that anyone wanted to trade" (198). But after Columbus, so the story goes, the traffic within this Grand Central becomes heavier, as the North American trade zone expands. With all this movement and circulation, the long-hidden dystopian character of place creeps into view as well.

As another incarnation of Odin observes late in the novel, America "is a good place for men, but a bad place for gods" (586). There are several reasons why this may be, and one lies in the formulation itself. If it is a "good place" (or *eutopia*) for humans, then it may be because America favors the present, the material, the novel, the living, and the mortal. As "foreign" visitors such as Alexis de Tocqueville or Jean Baudrillard have long recognized and commented upon, Americans appear to have little regard for the traditions of the past, the intellectual sphere, or even matters of the spirit, notwithstanding or, perhaps, *owing* to the profoundly potent forms of religious observance and zeal on display throughout the country and its history. These metaphysical notions play small roles in the public spaces of the national culture in the United States, although, as American literature frequently reveals, such ideas become quite powerful in the dream world of Americans. *American Gods* also makes great use of dreams, as omens, portents, or merely vistas into times and places not always available to the waking mind. The shadowy and liminal sphere of that space between conscious thought and unconscious flows provides yet another figure of transgression in *American Gods*.

One reason why America may be understood as a "bad place" (or *dystopia*) for gods is that "America" is itself a kind of religious artifact, a totem or mythic device, an imaginary construct to which natives and immigrants alike must imbue with divine substance and bow down before. Whether in the old Puritan rhetoric of the "city on a hill" or a New Jerusalem, in the providential decree of a Manifest Destiny, in the rhetorical of "the American Dream," or even more strongly perhaps in profoundly effective fiction a twentieth-century America as a utopian space of freedom in a world beset by totalitarianism or terror, the entity known as "America" becomes something to be "believed in."[17] As far back as 1693, Cotton Mather had suggested that the early pilgrims had hoped to find Thomas More's Utopia, but ended up creating one instead, and this vision continues to color the national and nationalist rhetoric well into the twenty-first century. Indeed, in some cases, even the harshest critics of United States and its policies often launch their criticism from this quasi-religious and utopian view of America as a place of freedom, bemoaning the "fact" that America is not living up to its purported mission.[18] What gods could be more powerful than this mythic, national deity who can (ideologically if not always practically) unite all parties arrayed along its political spectrum under this divine banner? In this, the utopianism of America is also its most dystopian feature, as the dissatisfaction with a failure to be utopia is felt more strongly than anything else.

Thus, in its own somewhat apolitical way, *American Gods* launches its own critique of the state of the United States' national identity as a technological and political pseudo-utopia, one that ideologically welds together individual freedom, economic opportunity, and collective harmony. Shadow's apparent disgust with several of the new gods (such as the god of television, who appears as Lucille Ball in *I Love Lucy* and offers to show him "Lucy's tits" [176]) registers his relative indifference to these modern achievements that are supposed to make the New World superior to the Old.[19] *American Gods* is not utopian, then, but it is not really anti-utopian either, and the distinction between dystopia and anti-utopia ought to be emphasized. As many critics have argued, dystopia (rather like utopia, in fact) is fundamentally critical. Even in offering what seems an ambiguous or bleak image of the threatened near future, dystopian narratives are not really critiques of utopian schemes so much as critiques of the *status quo* itself. Often, in dystopian narratives, the future disaster is extrapolated from a present condition, and the critical edge of the text lies in its ability to identify and challenge the state of things. Fitting notes that the "critique of contemporary society expressed in the dystopia implies (or asserts) the need for change; the anti-utopia is, on the other hand, explicitly or implicitly a defense of the status quo."[20] Similarly, Tom Moylan has introduced the concept of "critical dystopia" to emphasize how, "[f]aced by the delegitimation of Utopia and the hegemonic cynicism of Anti-Utopia," certain recent dystopian texts "do not go easily toward that better world [of utopia]. Rather, they linger in the terrors of the present even as they exemplify what is needed to transform it."[21] In *American Gods*, the dystopian mood of the millennial moment is suffused with a sense of movement and change, transgressions that simultaneously render the present both a "bad place" and a site of possibility for alternative formations.

Some readers might legitimately object that *American Gods* is not exactly a dystopian novel, and since it is not likely to be confused with utopian fiction either, the traditional association or binary opposition between utopia and dystopia is not entirely apt. However, Jameson's description of a key, categorical difference between the two genres indicates the degree to which *American Gods* might be called a dystopian text. Tacitly drawing upon Georg Lukács's distinction between narration and description,[22] Jameson observes that "dystopia is generally a narrative, which happens to a specific subject or character, whereas the Utopian text is mostly nonnarrative." Jameson goes on to posit that, in general, whereas the utopian text "does not tell a story at all" but "describes a mechanism," "the dystopia is always and essentially what in the language of science fiction is called a 'near-future' novel: it tells the story of an imminent disaster—ecology, overpopulation, plague, drought, the stray comet or nuclear accident—waiting to come to pass in our own near future, which is fast-forwarded in the time of the novel."[23] Assiduously narrative even in its few descriptive scenes, *American Gods* certain fits the bill here, with Shadow's own personal story dominating the plot even as the broader depiction of a dystopian United States at spiritual war provides the necessary context.

More fantasy than any other clearly discernible marketing genre, Gaiman's novel enables the reader to detect a dystopian aura inherent in the otherworldly, yet real, America presented through Shadow's tale.[24] Peter Paik, in his exploration of the apocalyptic science fiction of certain recent comic books or graphic novels, argues in part that the combination of realism and fantasy in such works makes possible a clearer rendering of the dystopian conditions of the present moment and offers the possibility of imagining other conditions. As Paik says, "[i]It is perhaps only such a fantastic realism that is at present capable of opening up a critical space for reflection between the alternatives of an enlightened obedience to a devouring and deteriorating beast and a headlong embrace of fate that masquerades as a godlike freedom."[25] Gaiman's fantastic realism in *American Gods*, while not as openly political as that employed in many other dystopian texts, nevertheless clears room for this "critical space for reflection" of the shifting social relations of the late-1990s' United States.

"There's Going to Be a Lot More Trouble"

The events taking place in Lakeside, Wisconsin, offer one allegorical example within *American Gods*. After the apparently climactic scene at Rock City, Shadow returns to Lakeside to uncover the town's terrible secret. From time immemorial, each year a child had gone missing, presumably runaways or possibly victims of kidnapping, and Shadow discovered the grisly connection between such a regular misfortune and the annual "klunker" raffle, where everyone in town participates in guessing the date and time at which an old, derelict, donated car will break through the melting ice and fall to the bottom of the lake. Shadow has discovered that, in each klunker's trunk, a dead child sinks beneath the water, in what amounts to a macabre, annual ritual. Hinzelmann, the old man in charge of the raffle, turns out to be an Old World kobold, a totemic spirit who re-enacts the yearly child-sacrifice in order to protect the town. Hinzelmann had hinted that the "good town" survived the insidious advances of economic turbulence through "hard work" (277), but in the end Shadow sees how this tiny utopian space was artificially created by a magic that, with Hinzelmann's death, no longer has power. As he tells Lakeside's police chief,

> this town is going to change now. It's not going to be the only good town in a depressed region anymore. It's going to be a lot more like the rest of this part of the world. There's going to be a lot more trouble. People out of work. People out of their heads. More people getting hurt. More bad shit going down. (573)

In other words, Lakeside will return to history itself, re-entering the late-twentieth-century's post-NAFTA world of economic uncertainty and dystopia.

A one-man (or one-kobold) scheme is not exactly a conspiracy, but the idea that some well-organized and often nefarious plot can be revealed in order to explain how all of these odd and threatening circumstances came to be is itself of pervasive feature of the late twentieth century. In addition to the diffuse millenarian paranoia of the turn-of-the-century moment, the old-fashioned fears of one-world governments and Big Brother accompanied some of the louder, if marginal, debates over the passage of NAFTA in the US Congress in 1994. The notion that the mysteriously swirling, seemingly unfathomable conditions affecting our everyday lives may be explicable in terms of some conspiracy is a paradoxically comforting thought. If nothing else, the vast conspiracy would explain the inexplicable, putting an evil face on and offering a distinctive enemy in lieu of the vague insecurities permeating the society at the time. In the smaller-scale explanation of Lakeside's mysterious good fortune, being the rare "good town" amid a decaying Rust Belt, the idea of magical forces, even those employing "dark magic" and murder, may be oddly satisfying, and the chaos of sheer luck or the perplexities of global finance and commerce are far too horrible and vast to think about.

American Gods is also suffused with various notions of false consciousness, if not in the strictly ideological sense, then in the more inchoate and elusive meaning attached to discovering that one is being "fooled." Illusions permeate the text, whether in the form of Shadow's good-natured sleight of hand magic and coin tricks, Wednesday's petty cons or his larger "two-man con" executed with the aid of Low Key (or Loki), or the menacing "men in black" agents of those vicious new gods. Of these latter mysterious figures, with names like Wood, Stone, Town, and World, the goddess Easter (or Eostre) explains: "They exist because everyone knows they must exist" (309). Referring to the genre of "conspiracy films," Jameson has suggested that narratives depicting such a grand scheme may offer one of the few ways in which individuals can imagine the global totality that is now the horizon of their existence; conspiracy then functions as a kind of allegorical or cognitive map by which individuals can imagine collective action at all.[26] In *American Gods*, the elaborate confidence game pulled off by Wednesday and Loki is revealed in the end as a means of explaining Shadow's entire life, but this is also the moment at which he both fulfills his destiny and moves on. Again, the dystopia is transgressive, in both positive and negative senses.

Conclusion: Shadows in Motion

Shadow himself, as well as the image of the shadow more generally, becomes the indistinct but defining feature of the transgressive dystopia in *American Gods*. Shadow is a liminal figure, assiduously occupying a space *in-between*, straddling presence and absence, here and there, life and death, and so forth. As in Melville's deliberately ambiguous deconstruction of the black-and-white narrative in "Benito Cereno," the shadows (which are, after all, a mixture of black and white) only foreshadow deeper shadows to come. These ambiguities point to what Siegfried Kracauer called the "Utopia of the in-between," but in *American Gods*, one might also recognize it as a sort of dystopia of the in-between as well.[27] The conclusion of *American Gods* does not offer a clean victory for one side over the other, since the entire battle turns out to have been a complicated con. Shadow in the final pages continues his wanderings, now in Reykjavik, where he does not really intend to stay, but nor does he intend to return to America or to go to some other particular place. The novel's final line—"He walked away and he kept on walking" (588)—suggests further transgression, perpetual motion, but no fixed state.

Movement, displacement, relocation, translation, and above all transgression provide the conceptual underpinnings of the dystopian phantasmagoria that is *American Gods*. The transgressive dystopia of *American Gods* is also positive, positing a given state that is also a sort of flux, insofar as transgressivity itself becomes the *status quo*. The postmodern condition is thus reconstellated in relation to networks of divine beings, gods and monsters. This is certainly not the *eutopian* state of happiness, but nor is it an *outopian* or nonexistent no-place; rather, it is the "bad place" in which we inexorably move, struggle, and live. The state of transgressivity, which is also the state of dystopia, is the condition of our historical being itself, and no otherworldly Ragnarök can impose celestial meaning upon things. The shadowy, inconclusive, or open-ended ending allows for mere continuation or radical changes with no discernible clues, beyond Shadow's own personal revelations, as to the nature of that "new" America about to emerge in the next millennium. The metaphysical free trade zone of "Grand Central" continues its operations unabated, presumably, and the cosmopolitan Shadow continues his uncertain wandering. *American Gods* leaves us in the dystopia we were already in, but in the novel's attention to the transgressivity, which is both a distinctive feature of the American dystopia in an era of globalization and a means of making sense of it, thereby perhaps also preparing ourselves to aid in transforming it, we see that other spaces are not only still possible, but that we are already shaping them by our perpetual, border-crossing movements.

Notes

1   Some scholars have even questioned whether *dystopia* ought to be a separate category of science fiction or fantasy at all. For example, Gerry Canavan has written that dystopia "is only ever utopia in negative." See Canavan, "The Suvin Event," in Darko Suvin, *Metamorphoses of Science Fiction: On the Poetics and History of a Literary Genre*, ed. Gerry Canavan (Bern: Peter Lang, 2016), xxv.

2   Herman Melville, "Benito Cereno," in *The Piazza Tales and Other Prose Pieces, 1839–1860*, ed. Harrison Hayford, Alma A. MacDougall, G. Thomas Tanselle, et al. (Evanston and Chicago: Northwestern University Press and the Newberry Library, 1987), 46.

3   Lyman Tower Sargent, *Utopianism: A Very Brief Introduction* (Oxford: Oxford University Press, 2010), 29.

4   See, for example, Kenichi Ohmae, *The Borderless World: Power and Strategy in the Interlinked Economy*, rev. ed. (New York: HarperCollins, 1999).

5   Karl Marx and Friedrich Engels, *The Communist Manifesto* (London: Penguin, 1998), 54.

6   Neil Gaiman, *American Gods* (New York: Harper Perennial, 2001).
    All references to *American Gods*, hereinafter cited parenthetically in the
    text, are to this edition.
7   See Phillip E. Wegner, *Life Between Two Deaths, 1989–2001: U.S. Culture
    in the Long Nineties* (Durham: Duke University Press, 2009).
8   All of Gaimain's books could probably be characterized as *fantasy* in
    a broad sense, but his writings have ranged across media and genres,
    including comic books and television screenplays in addition to his more
    traditionally novelistic or short form narratives. But then his novels also
    range widely over various literary and marketing genres, partaking of
    both gritty realism and fanciful romance, and frequently operating within
    the subgenres of children's literature, horror, mystery, and so on. For
    instance, *Good Omens* (1990), co-authored with Terry Pratchett, was a
    comic end-of-the-world mystery, as a demon and an angel rush to avert
    Armageddon. *Neverwhere* (1996), which began life as a BBC mini-series
    before Gaiman transformed his script into a novel, blends fairy-tale
    characters, such as Puss in Boots, with somewhat realistic cityscape of
    then present-day London. *Stardust* (1998) is an enchanting fairy tale in
    its own right. *American Gods* (2001) was followed by *Anansi Boys* (2005),
    a sort of sequel in that it is set in the same world, but which does not
    necessarily follow from the events of *American Gods*. His many children's
    books—although Gaiman does not always agree that they are meant for
    children exclusively—include *Coraline* (2002) and *The Graveyard Book*
    (2008), the latter a sort of re-imagining of Rudyard Kipling's *The Jungle
    Book*, in which an orphaned child is raised by ghosts, rather than wild
    animals, featuring a profoundly philosophical coming-of-age narrative
    (see, e.g., my "Nobody's Home: The Spectral Existentialism of *The
    Graveyard Book*," in *Neil Gaiman and Philosophy*, ed. Tracy Bealer et al.
    [Chicago: Open Court, 2012], 169–82.) More recently, he has published
    Norse Mythology (2017), in which he introduces and retells a number
    of mythic tales for both children and adult readers. Thus, although the
    fantastic *mode* pervades Gaiman's entire corpus, Gaiman's work tends to
    resist generic pigeon-holing.
9   Hank Wagner, Christopher Golden, and Stephen R. Bissette, *Prince of
    Stories: The Many Worlds of Neil Gaiman* (New York: St. Martin's Press,
    2008), 331
10 See Edward W. Soja, *Thirdspace: Journeys to Los Angeles and Other
    Real-and-Imagined Places* (Oxford: Blackwell, 1996).
11 On "cognitive mapping," see Fredric Jameson, *Postmodernism, or, the
    Cultural Logic of Late Capitalism* (Durham: Duke University Press, 1991),
    especially 51–4, 409–18.
12 The same principle is evident in a number of key intertexts. For example,
    in Terry Pratchett's *Small Gods*, we learn that the more powerful the
    belief, the more powerful the god. In that novel, a formerly mighty deity is

shocked to discover himself almost utterly powerless, since—even though the society of his purported believers is essentially a theocracy—he has only one faithful follower. But we meet other "gods," such as the Sea, who are immensely powerful, for she has many believers. See Pratchett, *Small Gods* (New York: Harper, 1992).

13   No less a person than Cotton Mather made the direct comparison between the early British settlers of New England and More *Utopia*: "Such great Persons [...] who mistook Sir Thomas Moor's UTOPIA, for a Country really existent, and stirr'd up some Divines charitably to undertake a Voyage thither, might now have certainly found a Truth in their Mistake; *New England* was a true *Utopia*." See Cotton Mather, *The Wonders of the Invisible World* [1693] (London: John Russell Smith, 1862), 12.

14   Peter Fitting, "Utopia, Dystopia, and Science Fiction," in *The Cambridge Companion to Utopian Literature*, ed. Gregory Claeys (Cambridge: Cambridge University Press, 2010), 140.

15   Darko Suvin, *The Metamorphoses of Science Fiction: On the Poetics and History of a Literary Genre* (New Haven: Yale University Press, 1979), 61.

16   Bertrand Westphal, *Geocriticism: Real and Fictional Spaces*, trans. Robert T. Tally Jr. (New York: Palgrave Macmillan, 2011), 41–2.

17   See my "'Believing in America': The Ideology of American Studies," in *The Critical Situation: Vexed Perspectives in Postmodern Literary Studies* (London: Anthem Press, 2023), 89–104.

18   As Sacvan Bercovitch, discussing the way that protesters in the 1960s regularly invoked the mythical idea of "America" in their critiques of racism, war, poverty, and so on, memorably put it: "I felt like Sancho Panza in a land of Don Quixotes. It was not just that the dream was a patent fiction. It was that the fiction involved an entire hermeneutic system. [...] You were supposed to discover it as a believer unveils scripture. America's meaning was implicit in its destiny, and its destiny was manifest to all who had the grace to discover its meaning. To a Canadian skeptic, a gentile in God's Country, it made for a breathtaking scene: a poly-ethnic, multi-racial, openly materialistic, self-consciously individualistic people knit together in the bonds of myth, voluntarily, with a force of belief unsurpassed by any other modern society." See Bercovitch, *The Rites of Assent: Transformations in the Symbolic Construction of America* (London: Routledge, 1993), 29.

19   These terms, *New World* and *Old World*, simultaneous register both history and geography, time and space, in distinguishing the "new" American world from the "old" worlds—Europe, especially, but also any region where immigrants to the Americas have come from before. That novelty, particularly in the United States, carries a "positive" semantic charge, makes the "new world" seem superior to the "old" almost inherently, and when the valuation is reversed, that often seems merely nostalgic or elegiac. This is also a pervasive theme in *American Gods*.

20 Fitting, "Utopia, Dystopia, and Science Fiction," 141.

21 Tom Moylan, *Scraps of the Untainted Sky: Science Fiction, Utopia, Dystopia* (Boulder: Westview Press, 2000), 198–9.

22 See Georg Lukács, "Narrate or Describe?" in *Writer and Critic and Other Essays*, ed. and trans. Arthur D. Kahn (New York: Grosset and Dunlap, 1970), 110–48.

23 Jameson, *The Seeds of Time* (New York: Columbia University Press, 1994), 56.

24 In *Archaeologies of the Future*, Jameson makes the case for a clear distinction between fantasy and science fiction (or utopia), but I argue that the radical alterity of both enables similar critical programs, even where the methods are demonstrably different. See Jameson, *Archaeologies of the Future: The Desire Called Utopia and Other Science Fictions* (London: Verso, 2005), especially 57–71; see also my *Utopia in the Age of Globalization: Space, Narrative, and the World-System* (New York: Palgrave Macmillan, 2013), 94–101.

25 Peter Y. Paik, *From Utopia to Apocalypse: Science Fiction and the Politics of Catastrophe* (Minneapolis: University of Minnesota Press, 2010), 22.

26 See Jameson, "Totality as Conspiracy," in *The Geopolitical Aesthetic: Cinema and Space in the World System* (Indianapolis and London: Indiana University Press and the British Film Institute, 1992), 9–84.

27 See Siegfried Kracauer, *History: The Last Things Before the Last*, ed. Paul Oskar Kristeller (Oxford: Oxford University Press, 1969), 217; see also my "Utopia of the In-Between, or, Limning the Liminal," in *Landscapes of Liminality: Between Space and Place*, ed. Dara Downey, Ian Kinane, and Elizabeth Parker (Lanham, MD: Rowman & Littlefield International, 2016), ix–xv.

Chapter 4

THE UTOPIA OF THE MIRROR:
THE POSTMODERN *MISE EN ABYME*

In Vladimir Nabokov's 1935 novel, *Invitation to a Beheading*, there is a scene in which the condemned man's mother recalls some of the "marvelous gimmicks" she had seen in her youth, the most striking of which was a kind of mirror. As she recounts,

> when I was a child, there were objects called '*nonnons*' that were popular, and not only among children, but among adults too, and, you see, a special mirror came with them, not just crooked, but completely distorted. You couldn't make out anything of it, it was all gaps and jumble and made no sense to the eye—yet the crookedness was no ordinary one, but calculated in just such a way as to … Or rather, to match its crookedness they had made … No, wait a minute, I am explaining badly.[1]

The fact that she must pause to collect her thoughts and to try to explain more clearly is itself significant. The sheer strangeness of both the mirror and the experience of it requires her to concentrate, to remember more vividly, and to articulate the memory as best as she can. She continues,

> [w]ell, you would have a crazy mirror like that and a whole collection of different "*nonnons*," absolutely absurd objects, shapeless, mottled, pockmarked, knobby things, like some kind of fossils—but the mirror, which completely distorted ordinary objects, now, you see, got real food, that is, when you placed one of these incomprehensible, monstrous objects so that is was reflected in the incomprehensible, monstrous mirror, a marvellous thing happened; minus by minus equalled plus, everything was restored, everything was fine, and the shapeless speckledness became in the mirror a wonderful, sensible image; flowers, a ship, a person, a landscape. You could have your own portrait custom made, that is, you received some nightmarish jumble, and this thing was you, only the key to you was held by the mirror. Oh, I remember what fun it was, and how

it was a little frightening—what if suddenly nothing should come out?—to pick up a new, incomprehensible "*nonnon*" and bring it near the mirror, and see your hand get all scrambled, and at the same time see the meaningless "*nonnon*" turn into a charming picture, so very, very clear ...[2]

As she is speaking, her son notices the curious expression in his mother's eyes, "just for an instant, an instant—but it was as if something real, unquestionable (in this world, where everything was subject to question), had passed through, as if a corner of this horrible life had curled up, and there was a glimpse of the lining."[3] In recounting even the mere memory of this "incomprehensible, monstrous mirror," the storyteller discloses a vista into a disturbing "real" condition hidden behind the variously unreal and defamiliarizing reflections.

Reading it now, the experience with the trick mirror, the memory of it and the recounting of it, along with the effect it has on the storyteller and the audience in *Invitation to a Beheading*, all calls to mind the sorts of mixed feelings one has in watching the television series *Black Mirror*. The individual episodes could be likened to these *nonnons*, double-negative monstrosities that when reflected in the incomprehensible mirror of the television screen become something clear, real, and in many cases rather disturbing. The veil is lifted, if only slightly, to reveal a formerly unseen corner of the reality distorted or hidden in the mirror image itself. Although each episode stands alone as a complete story, much like in the older *Twilight Zone* series that inspired it, there is an underlying continuity of theme, mood, or tone. The episodes cross traditional generic boundaries, such that examples of comedy, horror, romance, detective stories, fantasy, and science fiction can be found in abundance, but in its eerie blend of entertainment and anxiety, *Black Mirror* could be said to occupy its own unique genre. Given the variety of themes and heterogeneity of styles visible across the many discrete episodes of the series, it is perhaps unwise to generalize about *Black Mirror* as a whole. However, it is also fair to notice how certain topics are revisited, as with the persistent question of technology in relation to personal identity, individual freedom, ethics, and memory.

Taking a step farther back, one could look at the title itself for a clue to the unity to be found amid the narrative diversity. In a 2011 article in *The Guardian*, series creator Charlie Brooker explained the show is set "between delight and discomfort," and that "[t]he 'black mirror' of the title is the one you'll find on every wall, on every desk, in the palm of every hand: the cold, shiny screen of a TV, a monitor, a smartphone."[4] The mirror distorts, but also offers a sense of familiarity; it is radically unreal, since its image is an illusion, yet it becomes a crucial way for me to "know" myself. For many characters in *Black Mirror*, the technologies enable a bizarre self-reflection as well, and in the overall eeriness of many of their experiences, the inescapable Sartrean dictum "Hell is other people" is refracted into "Hell is myself," which may in some respects turn out to be the same thing, as one's self is conditioned upon the multifaceted gaze of all those surrounding it.[5] The mirror is at once comforting and dangerous, a site of identity and difference, of familiarity and estrangement, and of presence and absence. There I am, but there is also no *there* there.

Black Mirror plays upon this existential angst, but also specifies a historical context, postmodernity, in which the uncanny becomes a figure for our subjective experience of globalization, a system of infinite mirroring, with its unmappably vast social and conceptual spaces. In what follows, I discuss these aspects of *Black Mirror* in the context of contemporary utopian and dystopian impulses.

A Placeless Place

At its most fundamental level, as a television series which speaks to its historical moment and to that moment's dominant social formations in postmodern culture, *Black Mirror* is about contemporary anxiety. *Angst* is its basic *métier*, and the sense of anxiety or dread establishes the basic mood of many of *Black Mirror*'s episodes. Frequently, the anxious feeling is located in the protagonist, who is experiencing some bewildering and terrible ordeal during the course of the narrative. In "Shut Up and Dance," for instance, the main character is caught in an embarrassing act by a mysterious organization using Malware to monitor his computer, and things only get more alarming as he tries to satisfy their increasingly dangerous demands. The fact that all of his efforts, right down to the life or death struggle in the final act, are for naught—the ransomware terrorists reveal his horrible, secret sin to everyone anyway—leaves the characters with a sense of helpless futility that is actually worse than the anxious dread that had preceded it, for at least then there had been the element of a fool's hope.

Nearly as often, it is the viewing audience whose levels of anxiety and dread are established early in the episode and ratcheted up throughout. The indefiniteness is part of this, as the vague sense of unease without a direct object can be all the more dreadful. "In anxiety one feels 'uncanny' [*unheimlich*]," writes Heidegger, and this anxiety comes from an "indefinite" place, "the nothing and the nowhere."[6] "Uncanny," with its characteristic mixture of the homely and the otherworldly (as Freud had noted in his essay on the subject), is perhaps the perfect word for describing the effects of so many episodes of *Black Mirror*, as the disorientation and estrangement of the worlds depicted are also eerily familiar, reflecting a condition and a society so much like our own in the UK or United States in the twenty-first century as to produce an almost electric shock of recognition. Like Nabokov's "*nonnons*," the grotesque and formless visions take on distinctive shapes, becoming all too real in the mirror's reflected illusions, whereas the apparently "real" world and selves are bounced back in bizarre, phantasmagoric forms that, like ghosts, are all the more frightening for *seeming* real.

This returns us to the figure of the literal mirror, which offers a vision that is simultaneously real, in the sense of being faithfully mimetic, and unreal, in the sense of being an optical illusion. In his famous discussion of the heterotopia, for instance, Michel Foucault has observed that the mirror occupies a privileged and strange location directly between the utopian and the heterotopian. "The mirror is, after all, a utopia, since it is a placeless place." As Foucault explains, "[i]n the mirror, I see myself there where I am not, in an unreal, virtual space that opens up behind the surface; I am over there, there where I am not, a sort of shadow that gives my own visibility to myself, that enables me to see myself there where I am absent: such is the utopia of the mirror."[7] However, Foucault continues,

> it is also a heterotopia in so far as the mirror does exist in reality, where it exerts a sort of counteraction on the position that I occupy. From the standpoint of the mirror I discover my absence from the place where I am since I see myself over there. Starting from this gaze that is, as it were, directed toward me, from the ground of this virtual space that is on the other side of the glass, I come back toward myself; I begin again to direct my eyes toward myself and to reconstitute myself there where I am. The mirror functions as a heterotopia in this respect: it makes this place that I occupy at the moment when I look at myself in the glass at once absolutely real, connected with all the space that surrounds it, and absolutely unreal, since in order to be perceived it has to pass through this virtual point which is over there.[8]

Foucault is, of course, speaking of literal mirrors and their actual effects, but taken in a more metaphorical or allegorical sense, the utopia and heterotopia of the mirror functions as a useful trope for imagining the ways that *Black Mirror* presents its worlds.

In *Dissemination*, as part of his elaborate reading of Phillipe Sollers's experimental novel *Numbers*, Jacques Derrida reflects upon a related, but rather different idea of the mirror, the flipside, one might say. His thoughts appear in a section curiously titled "wriTing, encAsIng, screeNing," and even those familiar with Derrida's frequently playful use of language and the conventions of writing might well wonder about his decision to capitalize those letters in the middle of otherwise ordinary words. Given how far from ordinary the word "tain" is—who knew that that is what the backside of the mirror is called?—looking at the capital letters themselves might not seem helpful, until Derrida continues his reading. He there examines a space, specifically the fourth side of a three-sided box, somewhat like the "fourth wall" in staged drama, television, and cinema; he refers to this space as "a closed opening, neither quite open nor quite closed," which he characterizes first as a "false exit," then as a "mirror." But he quickly adds that in this case the mirror is turned away from the audience, "offering us only the sight of its tain, in sum."[9] Derrida continues,

> [w]hich would (not) be *anything* if the tain were not also transparent, or rather transformative of what it lets show through. The tain in this mirror thus reflects—imperfectly—what comes to it—imperfectly— from the three walls and lets through—presently—the ghost of what it reflects, the shadow deformed and reformed according to the figure of what is called present.[10]

One might say, in this context, that the "tain of the mirror" is itself a kind of "black mirror." As with the distortions and wild reimaginations that come with such a tricky looking-glass, in so many episodes of *Black Mirror* there is that eldritch mélange of the seemingly real and familiar, on the one hand, and of the utterly bizarre and mystifying on the other. In Derrida's words, it is like "a tainless mirror, or at any rate a mirror whose tain lets 'images' and 'persons' through, endowing them with a certain index of transformation and permutation."[11]

Rodolphe Gasché borrows this image and makes it the title of his brilliant study of Derrida's work, *The Tain of the Mirror*. Gasché explains his title thusly:

> *Tain*, a word altered from the French *étain*, according to the OED, refers to the tinfoil, the silver lining, the lusterless back of the mirror. Derrida's philosophy, rather than being a philosophy of reflection, is engaged in that systematic exploration of that dull surface without

which no reflection and no specular and speculative activity would be possible, but which at the same time has no place and no part in reflection's scintillating play.[12]

In the same section of *Dissemination*, Derrida notes that the "tain" he has been discussing effectively becomes a *screen*. "It shelters and conceals. Holds in reserve and exposes to view. The screen: at once the visible projection surface for images, and that which prevents one from seeing the other side." As something that simultaneously shows us things while obstructing our vision, the "screen-mirror" (as Derrida calls it) invites itself to be broken, to be pierced or penetrated, in order to reveal that something else which is either distorted in or hidden by its surface. "The mirror takes place—try to think out the taking-place of a mirror—as something designed to be broken."[13]

In what some viewers, might consider the happier endings of various episodes of *Black Mirror*, the mirror is arguably broken.[14] For example, in "Hang the DJ," the lovers who had been tormented with one terrible relationship after another in their virtual reality dating world finally destroy the system by flouting its rules. Of course, that merely confirms the system's overall effectiveness, as in the final moments of the episode, we learn that the protagonists had been operating only virtually within an elaborate computer simulation, which now has proven to be as effective as advertised. (The two had been promised a 99.8 percent chance of meeting their perfect match, and it turns out that these two virtual "theys" had chosen to escape the system 998 out of 1,000 times in the now revealed to be concurrent simulations.) The startling appearance of 998 identical versions of themselves in an otherwise ethereal, "blank" space evokes the perplexities of the hall of mirrors, with its seemingly endless "false" images and the notorious difficulty of determining which, if any, is the "real" one. Discovering one's "self" to be merely an element in a computer simulation is cause for unease, but to see oneself reflected in an indefinite number of others' eyes is more disturbing still, even if, in this one case, the result is an apparent happy one.

A Panopticon of Mirrors

It is perhaps a telling sign of the *Zeitgeist* that so many *Black Mirror* episodes revolve around surveillance. Part of this is undoubtedly a way for the writers and producers to highlight the profoundly televisual nature of contemporary culture, such that those ubiquitous "black mirrors"—that is, television and computer screens, tablets, cell phones, and so on—can be shown to exert their outsized power over individual and collective subjects in late postmodernity. In using the term "late postmodernity," I draw upon Phillip E. Wegner's analysis in *Life Between Two Deaths, 1989–2001: U.S. Culture in the Long Nineties*, in which he distinguishes recent postmodern culture from the earlier period of what might in retrospect be considered "high" postmodernism.[15] As we are further removed in time from those monuments of postmodernism from the 1960s through the 1980s, for instance, the very terms "postmodernity" and "postmodernism" are possibly losing their lustrous significance, but Fredric Jameson's admonition that "we have to name the system" seems all the more relevant in the current moment,[16] when—as shows like *Black Mirror* demonstrate clearly—the potentially bewildering hyperspace and technological sublime of postmodernity are undoubtedly raising problems that seem more urgent than before, while our capacity to make sense of the system as a whole is likely hampered to a degree formerly unimaginable.

If in the worlds of *The Parallax View* or *Three Days of the Condor*, not to mention the earlier visions of *Brave New World*, *Nineteen-Eighty-Four*, or *Fahrenheit 451* (all canonical ancestors of *Black Mirror*, of course), one could fear being spied on or monitored by secretive corporations or "the government," today's levels of and capacity for panoptic surveillance by governmental agencies, corporations, and even friends or acquaintances are not only exponentially greater in our own time, but—perhaps more shockingly to those mid-twentieth-century generations who warned us never to give out personal information and who demanded ever more expansive "rights" to privacy—these methods of surveillance are actively embraced by individuals throughout the social body. True, there are still many who express concerns about governmental interference in personal lives or about corporate espionage and so forth, but the very existence of social media like Facebook, Twitter, Instagram, Snapchat, WeChat, and TikTok (to name but a few of the most famous brands), not to mention their overwhelming popularity worldwide, suggests the remarkable degree to which consumers voluntarily welcome corporate surveillance, marketing, and even the sale of their personal information, including such private matters as one's tastes and desires. Even outside of these social media, most people have no trouble signing up for programs (sometimes marketed as "discount" or "rewards" programs) that catalog each and every purchase made by the consumer, cross-referencing those with potential products and services, which then subject the individual to increasingly personalized, yet also thoroughly homogenized, "targeted" advertising. The very ubiquity of cell phones, which after all could not operate without also making sure to geolocate and keep track of each user at all times, indicates the largely joyful or at least resigned capitulation to the most Orwellian aspects of a society organized around total, panoptic surveillance and disciplinary power.

Needless to say, *Black Mirror* makes much of this. There are several episodes in which the more traditional forms of Big Brotherly, government surveillance appear. For instance, in "Hated in the Nation," which ostensibly unfolds as a police procedural narrative involving weaponized mechanical honeybees, it is discovered that the UK government was using the robot-bees along with facial recognition software to keep track of all citizens everywhere; hence, what supposedly began as an environmentally minded, Green program to save the farming and ecosystems after the collapse of bee colonies turned out to be a massive Orwellian program of nationwide police surveillance. Interestingly, however, this aspect of the episode is almost a footnote, as the outrage over the inappropriate governmental overreach is displaced by the exigencies of the murder investigation, and the crimes are revealed to have much more to do with social media users and their own abusive practices than with the police's or the military's malfeasance. In the end, the cops are the "good guys," the murdering-mastermind a villain, but almost everyone who ever "tweeted" a cruel comment on Twitter are the real "bad" people, if also victims of the criminal plot. In this episode, as in others, the problem of surveillance is less ones involving nefarious governmental or corporate powers and more rooted in our own personal or collective desires to see and be seen.

A good example may be found in the eerie and ultimately heart-wrenching "Arkangel," in which the insertion of a microchip and the downloading of an "app" allow a mother to monitor and to control what her child sees and does. The guiding conceit, that the loving parent wishes to make sure her child is safe and free from anxiety, fits well within the sort of justifications for panoptic surveillance in society at large. That is, this technology and the surveillance it enables are simply ways of making us safer, more healthy, and ultimately happier. In "Arkangel," the program comes with parental controls that actually modify the child's ability to experience things, especially visually, such that potentially disturbing images—the aggressive barking of a neighbor's dog, violent imagery in a video game, sexual content in movies, and so on—can be occluded and "blocked," as with parental controls on cable television channels. Additionally, the parent can monitor the location and the activities of the child, even literally allowing the parent to see as if through the child's eyes. Such an intrusion is justified, in part, along the same grounds as requiring seat belts or bicycle helmets; that is, just because your parents' generation did not use them does not mean that ours shouldn't take advantage of these advances in safety and security (as the mother explains to her own skeptical father). In the episode the child, so protected and monitored, is spared potential traumas, but predictably never learns to process the emotions associated with them, effectively retarding her own mental development. When as an adolescent she discovers this program, she demands that her mother leave her alone, respect her privacy, and allow her to experience the world in a normal way. But the mother cannot resist spying when she suspects her daughter of doing drugs and having sex, and she even secretly adds a contraceptive to her drink, causing the daughter become sick at school and eventually revealing what the mother had done. In a rage, the daughter beats her mother with the mother's own laptop (unaware of the damage she is doing, owing to the parental control software's having been activated), and runs away from home. This is a tragedy of surveillance writ small, in the case of an overprotective mother in a one-parent, single-child household, but the terrible condition and effects of panoptic, 24/7 visibility are made clear.

In other episodes, the surveillance is even more intimate, such that the guard in the Panopticon's tower and the prisoner in the cell are one and the same. In "The Entire History of You," a device allows one to record and later replay all of one's experiences; again, the visual register is dominant, so one watches the memories of lived experiences as if it were simply watching videos of it. This allows one to "remember" an experience by rewatching it on a screen, and others can watch as well. In this episode, a jealous man demands that his wife replay scenes of her infidelity, thereby ultimately destroying their marriage and his sanity.

More common are the ways in which the multitudes in postmodern society as a whole are depicted as voyeuristic and all too willing to discipline and punish each other. In the aforementioned "Hated in the Nation," the murderer's criminal plans depend upon, and are eventually shown to have been motivated by, the willingness of millions of self-righteous and "good" people to wish death upon those who they think deserve their opprobrium. In "White Bear," the terrified victim of bizarre circumstances and murderous hordes pleads in vain while dozens of onlookers gleefully watch and record her every move on their cellphones; later, it is discovered that they are enthusiastic consumers enjoying a penal spectacle, and that their presence as voyeurs is certainly part of the punishment. That is, we were witnessing what was in effect a public execution, dragged out into a longer and "entertaining" spectacle, in which the public is at once the witnesses to and the participants in the capital punishment. In "Fifteen Million Merits," the entire dystopian society of the spectacle is organized around the production and viewing of television shows, nearly all of which involve some levels of degradation, from abject pornography to fat-shaming game shows; the machine operates both thanks to and in order to entertain masses who gladly toil in order to feed their lust for televisual *Schadenfreude*. In the more overtly political episodes, such as "National Anthem" and "The Waldo Moment," the public's insatiable appetite for watching and also (or thus) contributing to the anguish and shame of others is highlighted, revealing again the ways that individual discipline and torment can be administered by anyone throughout the capillary juridico-political system of the social totality, and that mass media and computer technologies have facilitated this to an alarming degree.

As Foucault observes, regarding the Panopticon's basic principle when extended beyond the prison walls, "[t]he seeing machine was once a sort of dark room into which individuals spied; it has become a transparent building in which the exercise of power may be supervised by society as a whole."[17] In such a total system, what might rebellion or resistance look like?

Freedom Is the Freedom to Say "Fuck You!"

"Visibility is a trap," as Foucault famously put it.[18] As we have seen, *Black Mirror* features a number of episodes in which the panoptic surveillance and concomitant discipline (and punishment) of the postmodern condition in advanced, late capitalist societies are highlighted. An especially fascinating episode, inasmuch as it seamlessly combines elements of sheer farce and others of terrifying dystopianism, "Nosedive" establishes itself as a long, patiently delivered joke, whose punch line is all the more satisfying for its meticulous revelation of the horrors implied throughout.

Briefly, "Nosedive" depicts a seemingly futuristic world in which today's familiar consumer-rating models of social media, but also of Yelp, Uber, and other services, have become so pervasive as to influence if not determine all areas of human life. That is, for example, not only can one "rate" a restaurant on the quality of its food or service, and not only can one rate one's *maître d'*, waiter, cook, or busboy at the restaurant individually for their contributions to one's dining experience, but one can rate everyone—fellow customers at other tables, strangers waiting in line, that guy who is (or seems to be) staring at you from across the room as you rate him, and so on—and such ratings have profound real-world consequences. For example, the protagonist (Lacie) is desperate to increase her personal score, going so far as to hire a consultant to help her strategize different ways of doing so. She hopes to move to a more desirable apartment complex, but she needs a higher rating to be able to afford to do so. The idea that "high quality" people get discounted rent along with preferable consideration helps to underscore the ways in which such ratings pervade all aspects of daily life. (What apartment complex wouldn't want as many "5-star" residents as possible, after all?) The opportunity to impress "high quality" others at a wedding by being her highly rated childhood friend's maid of honor becomes Lacie's holy grail, but a tragicomedy of errors ensues once her ratings drop: Lacie is unable to board a plane, she is limited in her choice of rental car, and so on. At one point, she is able to get a ride from a very low-rated truck driver, who compassionately lectures her on the evils of this system, but Lacie persists in holding out hope that the wedding will turn her life around. In the meantime, her bride-friend has changed her mind and, mortified at the thought of someone with such a low rating serving as a member of her wedding party, orders Lacie not to come. Lacie persists, nonetheless.

Not long after this episode aired, coincidentally, news outlets began reporting on the government's "social credit" system in China, which seemed to indicate that the sort of things happening to Lacie's character and others in "Nosedive" were already befalling Chinese citizens. For instance, citizens whose social credit scores had fallen below a certain point might not be allowed to board airplanes or trains, effectively preventing them from traveling at all. According to data released by the PRC's National Development and Reform Commission, by June 2019, the government has "stopped 26.82 million people from buying air tickets and 5.96 million from travelling on the high-speed rail network."[19] Ostensibly aimed at targeting corruption and fostering a more "honest society" by identifying "untrustworthy" individuals, the system would functionally regulate and punish a wide range of behaviors. The sort of infractions that could cause one's social credit score to be reduced include such major crimes as bribery or embezzlement, but also such minor offenses as jaywalking or other traffic violations, and even basic examples of rudeness, such as playing music too loudly on public transit or canceling hotel reservations without sufficient notice. In fact, even intensely personal matters, such as having an extra-marital sexual affair, could be grounds for lowering one's social credit score. Then again, on the carrot side of the carrot-and-stick approach, socially "positive" activities, such as giving money to charities, volunteering for community service, and donating blood, would help to increase one's ratings, presumably allowing one to thus be able to continue enjoying the benefits accorded to the country's most trustworthy, and therefore also most acceptable, citizenry. All of these activities would be monitored and administered via panoptic surveillance of the most thorough yet quotidian kind, using among other things face-recognition software and satellite imagery to monitor the population. Undoubtedly, the vast legions of would-be policemen, not least of which would be actual police departments and officers, would help to keep track of and enforce these activities, such that hotel managers or blood donation drive leaders could weigh in. Ultimately, as in the Orwellian or *Black Mirror* vision, all other people, everywhere throughout society, along with impersonal cameras and other forms of technology, would contribute to the social credit system in all its complex yet crystalline totality.

It is probably worth noting that the methods and technologies involved in China's social credit system are not at all uniquely Chinese, and that much of the reporting on these phenomena by the Western media has been ideologically motivated as well. For example, aspects of the Chinese system are in place in the United States and Canada, Europe, and elsewhere already, and a certain racially motivated Sinophobia as well as a politically motivated anti-Communism has influenced the breathlessly urgent reporting of this "Orwellian" development in China. As Louise Matsakis recently wrote in *Wired*,

> [t]he exaggerated portrayals may also help to downplay surveillance efforts in other parts of the world. "Because China is often held up as the extreme of one end of a spectrum, I think that it moves the goalposts for the whole conversation," says [Jeremy] Daum [a senior research fellow at Yale Law School's Paul Tsai China Center in Beijing], "So that anything less invasive than our imagined version of social credit seems sort of acceptable, because *at least we're not as bad as China*."[20]

Indeed, if one displaces the fears from the older vision of a totalitarian government to the more current image of the neoliberal and globalized political economy, it becomes apparent that the corporate surveillance of the Google, Amazon, and Facebook variety, nominally in the service of advertising and sales rather than in governmentality and rule, is already outstripping the public sector's best efforts in these areas.

In "Nosedive," there is almost certainly a distant form of a Big Brotherly government lurking in the background, and the repressive state apparatus in the forms of the police and the jail cell is invoked directly. However, the real fear comes not from agents (secret or otherwise) of the state, but from our own friends and acquaintances. The co-worker whom you did not even know you had slighted in some workplace misunderstanding, the neighbor you had failed to waive to while checking your mail, the barista at the coffee shop who found your politeness insufficiently authentic, the stranger in the elevator who didn't like the look on your face, and even the dear friend who has just had *enough* of you for one day: any and all of these people become beat cops, psychiatrists, judges, juries, and perhaps executioners whose assessments of you at any given moment can profoundly affect the quality of your life and your ability to live it. *And*, more significantly, every last one of them is bound up in the same complicated system, whereby your own judgment of their behavior, attitude, looks, and overall mien might have devastating effects upon their lives. The visibility that is a trap becomes an endless array of trick mirrors—but then, as we have seen, all mirrors are trick mirrors—in which the potential images are reflected and refracted in a terrible *mise en abyme*. This is a hellish landscape, and here *l'Enfer* really is *les autres*.

"Nosedive" ends, as I have said, with a punch line, ultimately revealing the episode to have been a comedy all along, if perhaps a comedy of errors mingled with the theater of the absurd, plus a healthy dose of dystopian satire. After much travail and crashing the party, Lacie delivers her maid-of-honor speech at her friend's wedding, before being arrested for trespassing. Locked in her jail cell, still wearing her ripped and muddy bridesmaid's dress, mascara lines scarring her face from the tears of conjoined sadness, anguish, and frustration, our heroine looks out to see a man in an adjacent cell, presumably one who has been having his own terrible day of which we can know nothing. Utterly exasperated, she asks (rudely) "What are you looking at?" and his response is similarly impolite. She offers a blunt retort, he makes an incautious comment about her appearance, she insults him, he mocks her, and so on and on until the two are pressing their faces against the walls of their respective cells, shouting invectives at each other while smiling as they had never truly done before, now that they had nothing left to lose. The final scene makes it clear, in this moment of fantastically joyous, indeed ecstatic rudeness, these two are finally free.

Whereas in *Nineteen-Eighty-Four*, Winston Smith had averred that "Freedom is the freedom to say two plus two equals four" (before O'Brien disabuses him of this article of faith), "Nosedive" affirms that in a neoliberal society bent on reducing all social relations to the model of customer service, freedom is the freedom to say "Fuck you!" The jubilation that comes with this freedom is evident on the faces of the prisoners, but one cannot help noting the irony that such freedom has only become possible when the "free" subjects are locked up. They are almost exactly mirror images of each other, the "Fuck you"-shouting man and woman, locked in each person's respective jail cell, and for all the happiness on their faces, we know that they are not free at all.

Through a Glass, Darkly

In discussing the scene from Nabokov's *Invitation to a Beheading* referenced at the beginning of this chapter, Merve Emre concludes that "[b]ehind the mirror lurks something monstrous—an idea of art as device, an object whose representational powers can distort and devalue just as easily as they can estrange and enchant."[21] This, too, seems to be an apt way of considering the effects of *Black Mirror*, whose variegated episodes operate as similar artistic devices, transforming the realities depicted in them and delivering representations of our world that are eerie in their familiarity and, at the same time, shocking in their estrangement. *Black Mirror* plays on this notion of itself as a mirror for our lives in late postmodern societies in almost every episode. To the extent that the series operates as science fiction, it has been noted that, for all the seemingly "futuristic" aspects of so many episodes, the series is really far more a reflection of the present. That is, while some of the technologies featured do not (yet) exist, the ethical, political, and social problems raised in their use are all-too-real in our own world. To see "through a glass, darkly" is, as in the Biblical allusion,[22] to know imperfectly, but it is nevertheless a way of knowing, and in providing these distorted, enchanting, uncanny, and yet homely reflections, the art of *Black Mirror* provides fascinating insights into knowing the contemporary world and our place in it.

Notes

1   Vladimir Nabokov, *Invitation to a Beheading*, trans. Dimitri Nabokov (New York: Vintage, 1989), 135–6, ellipses in original. (I am grateful to Merve Emre for adverting my attention to this scene.)

2   Ibid., 135–6, ellipses in original.

3   Ibid., 136.

4   Charlie Brooker, "The Dark Side of Our Gadget Addiction," *The Guardian* (December 1, 2011): https://www.theguardian.com/technology/2011/dec/01/charlie-brooker-dark-side-gadget-addiction-black-mirror (accessed November 7, 2020).

5   Here one might also add a discussion of the famous "mirror stage" in Lacanian psychoanalytic theory, perhaps. See Jacques Lacan, "The Mirror Stage as Formative of the *I* Function as Revealed in Psychoanalytic Experience," in *Écrits: The First Complete Edition in English*, trans. Barney Fink (New York: W.W. Norton, 2006), 75–81.

6   Martin Heidegger, *Being and Time*, trans. John Macquarrie and Edward Robinson (New York: Harper and Row, 1962), 67.

7   Michel Foucault, "Of Other Spaces," trans. Jay Miskowiec, *Diacritics* 16 (Spring 1986): 24.

8   Ibid.

9   Jacques Derrida, *Dissemination*, trans. Barbara Johnson (Chicago: University of Chicago Press, 1981), 345.

10   Ibid.

11   Ibid.

12   Rodolphe Gasché, *The Tain of the Mirror: Derrida and the Philosophy of Reflection* (Cambridge: Harvard University Press, 1986), 6.

13   Derrida, *Dissemination*, 346.

14   Several episodes feature broken mirrors or otherwise breaking glass in a quite literal sense, as in "San Junipero," when the protagonist, ashamed of herself, smashes her pseudo-self-image in the mirror.

15   See Phillip E. Wegner, *Life Between Two Deaths, 1989–2001: U.S. Culture in the Long Nineties* (Durham: Duke University Press, 2009), 5–6.

16   See Fredric Jameson, *Postmodernism, or, the Cultural Logic of Late Capitalism* (Durham: Duke University Press, 1991), 418.

17   Foucault, *Discipline and Punish: The Birth of the Prison*, trans. Alan Sheridan (New York: Vintage Books, 1977), 207.

18   Foucault, *Discipline and Punish*, 200.

19   See Orange Wang, "China's Social Credit System Will Not Lead to Citizens Losing Access to Public Services, Beijing Says," *South China Morning Post* (June 19, 2019): https://www.scmp.com/economy/china-economy/article/3019333/chinas-social-credit-system-will-not-lead-citizens-losing (accessed November 24, 2020).

20 Louise Matsakis, "How the West Got China's Social Credit System Wrong," *Wired* (July 29, 2019): https://www.wired.com/story/china-social-credit-score-system/ (accessed November 24, 2020), ellipses in the original.

21 Merve Emre, "Our Love-Hate Relationship with Gimmicks," *The New Yorker* online edition (November 9, 2020): https://www.newyorker.com/magazine/2020/11/16/our-love-hate-relationship-with-gimmicks (accessed November 9, 2020).

22 See 1 Cor. 13: 12.

Chapter 5

WELCOME TO THE TERATOCENE: MORBID SYMPTOMS AT THE PRESENT CONJUNCTURE

"The old world is dying, and the new world struggles to be born: now is the time of monsters." This sentence, attributed to the Italian Marxist theorist and critic Antonio Gramsci, seems a fitting epigraph for our era, which may well appear to be a sort of *teratocene* or "age of monsters." In recent years, the evocative line has been quoted extensively, over and over again, across a range of venues from mainstream journalism and social media to academic research and cultural studies.[1] The popularity of the phrase and the idea it presents is quite telling, all the more so given that Gramsci did not actually say it. Arguably, it works far better as a misquotation involving "the time of monsters" than as a more accurate translation of Gramsci's words. That this is so, in itself, may represent a morbid symptom of the present era.

As for the quotation and its widespread popular usage, it seems that Slavoj Žižek may be to blame (or, depending on one's point of view, he may deserve the credit). In a 2010 *New Left Review* article, "A Permanent Economic Emergency," Žižek assessed the situation of the global financial crisis, the austerity measures imposed by various governments, and the resistance movements these events had summoned forth, and he argued that we were then on the brink of a new period in history, reminiscent of but quite different from the post-revolutionary moment of the 1920s. As he writes,

[o]urs is thus the very opposite of the classical early twentieth-century situation, in which the left knew what had to be done (establish the dictatorship of the proletariat), but had to wait patiently for the proper moment of execution. Today we do not know what we have to do, but we have to act now, because the consequence of non-action could be disastrous. We will be forced to live "as if we were free." We will have to risk taking steps into the abyss, in totally inappropriate situations; we will have to reinvent aspects of the new, just to keep the machinery going and maintain what was good in the old—education, healthcare, basic social services.

Then, for his concluding line, Žižek adds: "as Gramsci said, characterizing the epoch that began with the First World War, 'the old world is dying, and the new world struggles to be born: now is the time of monsters.'"[2]

Apt as the slogan may seem, the words seemed a bit off for those of us weaned on the well-known *Selections from the Prison Notebooks* volume first published in 1971, where Gramsci's sentence appears quite differently in English. In the original Italian, it reads *La crisi consiste appunto nel fatto che il vecchio muore e il nuovo non può nascere: in questo interregno si verificano i fenomeni morbosi più svariati*, which Quintin Hoare translates, somewhat literally, as follows: "The crisis consists precisely in the fact that the old is dying and the new cannot be born; in this interregnum a great variety of morbid symptoms appear."[3] However, Žižek's "misquotation" is not exactly invented *ex nihilo*, for it seems likely that he first encountered Gramsci through a French translation of the *Prison Notebooks*, in which that sentence was rendered, rather poetically, *Le vieux monde se meurt, le nouveau monde tarde à apparaître et dans ce clair-obscur surgissent les monstres*. Ross Wolfe, in a 2015 blog post on *The Charnel-House*, discusses this connection, and he cites Žižek's reading of the French translations as the origin of his use of "the time of monsters." Wolfe also notes that Italian versions of the phrase, effectively retranslating the French translation back into Italian, have even begun to appear: *Il vecchio mondo sta morendo. Quello nuovo tarda a comparire. E in questo chiaroscuro nascono i mostri.*[4] It is interesting that Gramsci's interregnum (*interregno*) became a more artsy or poetic "light-dark" (*clair-obscur* or *chiaroscuro*) in this version, which effectively transcodes some of the political and juridical character of the observation onto a more allegorical plane in which the play of light and shadow set the stage for the monsters to come. Thus, in a monstrous ruse of history, Gramsci's repressed monsters return to his corpus even among fluent readers of Italian.[5]

Apart from the delights of tracing misquotations, misattributions, and mistranslations, we might observe just how welcome this phrase, popularized by Žižek and always now attributed to Gramsci, has become in recent years. Gramsci himself lends authority and *gravitas* to the matter, and Žižek's always provocative and even "cool" theorizing undoubtedly helps. But there is also something that seems rather appropriate about imagining our own period as both a moment of transition (and what moment isn't, after all?) and a time of monsters. We seem to be living in a veritable teratocene.

An Age of Monsters

As David McNally announces in the opening line of *Monsters of the Market* (2011), "[w]e live in an age of monsters,"[6] and hence the *teratocene* seems as appropriate a term as any used to name the present era. Such a label in our time undoubtedly conjures the specter of the anthropocene and invites comparisons. I do not mean to invoke the full discourse on the anthropocene here, but it does seem that elements of the global, environmental crises at the heart of that epochal analysis are tied to aspects of monstrosity as well, as may be seen clearly in Mark Bould's magnificent study, *The Anthropocene Unconscious: Climate, Catastrophe, Culture* (2021).[7] Donna Haraway's use of the term "Chthulucene" as a name for our time, an epoch in her view distinct from both the anthropocene and the capitalocene, already indicates a sense of the monstrous, not only in the way that it evokes the tentacular terror of the monster Cthulhu from H. P. Lovecraft's weird fiction, but also more generally, with respect to the Greek root (*khthōn*) and idea behind that name. As Haraway puts it, "Chthonic ones are beings of the earth, both ancient and up-to-the-minute. [...] Chthonic ones are monsters in the best sense; they demonstrate and perform the material meaningfulness of earth processes and critters. They also demonstrate and perform consequences."[8] Beings of the earth, "critters" and chthonic ones, also partake of the monstrous, in Haraway's view, and she spells *Chthulucene* as she does in part to avoid any resemblance to a "singleton monster or deity."[9]

As with any periodization, especially so when attempting to name entire "ages" perhaps, the teratocene could be said to have begun at various times, with a given *durée* lasting longer or shorter, depending on the interests of the investigator. For example, the concept of the anthropocene, despite its massive success in gaining widespread usage, has been roundly criticized for its lack of precision on the one hand and its ideological assumptions and occlusions on the other. In the first case, it is clear that for as long as humans have existed they have had some effect on the "natural world," although the perpetuation of a simplistic model of "mankind-versus-nature" is itself problematic. When Paul J. Crutzen and Eugene F. Stoermer first popularized the term *anthropocene*, they suggested a beginning date of roughly 1784 (a date that "coincides with James Watt's invention of the steam engine"), but others have suggested much later or earlier dates, such as 1964 (fallout from nuclear weapons testing) or 1610 (precipitous drop in carbon dioxide levels worldwide), and some have posited even "ancient" anthropocene origins, as with the emergence of neolithic farming practices 5,000 to 7,000 years ago.[10] In the second case, a label like *anthropocene* arguably provides cover for the real malefactors behind environmental devastation and climate change, as Christopher Nealon has pointed out: "It doesn't take a genius to recognize that capitalism is the engine behind the environmental crises of the early twenty-first century. It doesn't even take a Marxist: as the French environmental journalist Hervé Kempf put it in a recent book, it's not so much *Homo sapiens* as the rich who are destroying the earth—rich people, rich nations."[11]

On roughly those political and historical grounds, Jason W. Moore has suggested that the term *capitalocene* makes better sense, both as a descriptor and for the sake of making arguments about environmental justice.[12] McKenzie Wark finds the term *misanthropocene* fairly compelling, but notes that, in any case, one will want to name the ecological and historical world system *something*.[13] Bould, referring the *le deluge terminologique* that followed Crutzen's popularization of the word *anthropocene*, lists no fewer than thirty-seven variants (not to mention the three "&c." with which the list concludes). As Bould states, "[t]his proliferation of terms […] is trace evidence of an already-rich history of thinking through what it means for humans to have become a geological force."[14] "The glory of the Anthropocene," as Fredric Jameson has suggested, always on the lookout for the utopian potential within the most ideological forms, "has been to show us that we really can change the world."[15] The *teratocene*, for its part, indicates a world both changed and changing.

I am not suggesting *teratocene* as an alternative term for the anthropocene or as a successor to it, like Haraway's chthulucene, with its networks of tentacular kinships replacing the human-centered visions of the anthropo- and capitalocenes. I use the label in this part and in this book in order to highlight the "monstrous" character of contemporary culture, which contributes mightily to the dystopian sensibilities of this era. Needless to say, anyone searching for pre-twentieth-century versions of this will have no difficulty in finding them, and some of the recent "monster theory" emerges from scholars and critics interested in nineteenth-century, early modern, medieval, or even earlier epochs.[16] For example, in his "natural history" of dystopia, Gregory Claeys finds the ancient origins of his putatively modern subject in the figure of the monster. "Monsters inhabit the primordial *terra incognita* of the earth," asserts Claeys, adding "they define the original dystopian space in which fear predominates. As such, they mark the beginning of the natural history of dystopia."[17] Yet whatever background monsters, dystopia, and monstrous dystopia might have that extends into the distant past and across many cultures worldwide, the prevalence of monsters in recent dystopian visions is noteworthy. The *teratocene* is a somewhat tongue-in-cheek label for this periodization, but it seems fitting as well.

"Ungeheures *Is a Very Strong Word*"

In this, as elsewhere, size matters. It is not entirely accidental that the term "monstrous" is frequently used as a synonym for "large," nor it is merely coincidental that our era should be characterized by a menacing sense of hugeness that seems to permeate culture and society. In *Minima Moralia* (1951), in a section labeled "Mammoth," Theodor W. Adorno imagines the sociopolitical effects of this sense of monstrosity in relation to the monsters of popular culture at the time. Referring to a recent news report of a new species of dinosaur, Adorno wrote that "[s]uch pieces of news, like the repulsive humoristic craze for the Loch Ness Monster and the King Kong film, are collective projections of the monstrous total State. People prepare themselves for its terrors by familiarizing themselves with gigantic images. In its absurd readiness to accept these, impotently prostrate humanity tries desperately to assimilate to experience what defies all experience."[18] Even in Adorno's pessimistic evaluation of the phenomenon, one finds a need to grasp this metaphorical vastness of a social system now too large to be experienced or even to be understood empirically at all. It is "monstrous," in fact. Monstrosity, in the sense both of mere enormity and of terrifying otherworldly creatures, typifies this condition, and thus a certain political unconscious of the monster mania Adorno ridicules would disclose a more basic desire to map the world system in which such monsters emerge and proliferate.

The phrase "monstrous accumulation" comes from the well-known opening lines of the first chapter of *Capital*, where Karl Marx asserts that "the wealth of those societies in which the capitalist mode of production prevails, presents itself as 'a monstrous accumulation of commodities.'"[19] Ben Fowkes translates the German adjective *ungeheure* as "immense," which is consistent with earlier translations, but China Miéville points out that *ungeheure* does mean "monstrous." Miéville cites this in connection with his defense of the fantasy from a Marxist perspective, along with his own general teratophilia, and he insists that Marxist critique be able to benefit from fantastic tales of monsters or horror. As Miéville explains,

[i]n a fantastic cultural work, the artist pretends that things known to be impossible are not only possible but real, which creates the mental space redefining—or pretending to redefine—the impossible. This is sleight of mind, altering the categories of the not-real. Bearing in mind Marx's point that the real and the not-real are constantly cross-referenced in the productive activity by which humans interact with the world, changing the not-real allows one to think differently about the real, its potentialities and actualities.

Let me emphatically stress that this is *not* to make the ridiculous suggestion that fantastic fiction gives a clear view of political possibilities or acts as a guide to political action. I am claiming that the fantastic, particularly because "reality" is a grotesque "fantastic form," is *good to think with*. Marx, whose theory is a haunted house of spectres and vampires, knew this. Why else does he open *Capital* not quite with an "immense," as the modern English translation has it, but with a "monstrous" [*ungeheure*] collection of commodities?[20]

In a sense, of course, Marx is indicating size or magnitude anyway, so whether the phrase reads the "immense collection" or "monstrous accumulation," each version works to define the enormous heaps of commodities in question. However, given the veritable phantasmagoria of otherworldly metaphors in *Capital*, with its frequent references to monsters, including vampires, ghosts, dragons, and evil spirits, the term *monstrous* seems especially apt.

McNally goes so far as to suggest that Marx required this discourse in order to find "the means for depicting the actual horrors of capitalism," such as child labor, slavery, and environmental devastations. "Pillaging popular and literary imagination, from vampire-tales to Goethe's *Faust*, he cast capitalism as both a modern horror-story and a mystery tale, each inexplicable outside the language of monstrosity."[21] Along similar lines, William Clare Roberts has argued that Marx's *Capital* effectively relaunched the project of Dante's *Inferno* in a secular, materialist way, in order to depict the hellscape that is modern industrial capitalism.[22] For Marx, as these and other critics have argued convincingly, the epoch in which the capitalist mode of production predominates is, almost by definition, an age of monsters.

In the twentieth and twenty-first centuries, as simpler forms of industrial capitalism have made way for, incorporated, been succeed by, and ultimately been transformed by other regimes of monopoly, postindustrial, multinational, global, or "late" capitalism, the monsters of Marx's folkloric and literary traditions have only multiplied and grown more monstrous. A comprehensive sense of this postmodern monstrosity is likely impossible and certainly elusive, for even a somewhat tentative, uncertain, but searching explanation for these dynamic phenomena would involve due consideration of the world system today and of our situation with respect to and within it. As the processes and effects of the globalization of capitalism become more starkly experienced, they are also often rendered increasingly invisible or unknowable, for both individuals and groups find themselves subject to an immense array of forces beyond not only their control but their ken. As such, they appear "monstrous" in so many ways.

In *Adultery and the Novel*, Tony Tanner provides a close reading of a key passage from Goethe's *Elective Affinities* in which the narrator refers uncomfortably to the "monstrous rights" [*ungeheures Recht*] of the present era. Tanner notes that *ungeheures* is "a very strong word: *das Ungeheuer* is 'the monster', *nicht geheuer* is 'uncanny' or 'haunted', and oddly enough, there is no positive *geheuer*—it is a thing, quality, an aspect of experience, a sensation, a feeling that is only defined by the negative—or, as we say, by an absence, something not—*nicht, un*."[23] The term is in a weird way fundamentally negative, negative without a positive with which to contrast it. Such a pure negation seems eerie, and it is suggestive of alternative dimensions. Tanner goes on to observe that the monster "warns us that our world is not the world, and that there are margins or fissures or gaps, or black holes, or other levels of being— whatever—through which or from which may issue things not dreamt of in our orthodoxies."[24] In this sense, the monstrous accumulation in our time may be linked to the anxieties surrounding an unmappable system.

That said, it may be that monsters, by introducing us to alternate realities, even frightening ones, can also open up the possibilities for better ways of seeing ourselves and our situations. If the world as seen through realism is itself unreal, inasmuch as it masks the underlying "truth" in its very surface-level realism, then the otherworldliness of fantasy may allow us to find the truth in different guises. In Miéville's rehearsal of Marx's theory, for example, the truth of labor power is hidden from view by appearing as commodities, and the general process of reification has concealed the human and historical reality that may be disclosed precisely through the mechanisms of fantasy. "'Real' life under capitalism *is a fantasy*: 'realism', narrowly defined is therefore a 'realistic' depiction of 'an absurdity which is true', but no less absurd for that."[25] In other words, in a world where reality is itself unreal, the non-realism of fantasy may offer the means to get at these hidden truths. Any inquiry into the topographies of dread that characterize the real-and-imagined spaces of our world today must reckon with this world of monsters. Between and among these various sites, a properly critical theory would need to draw connections, ultimately forming a constellation that might serve, provisionally, as a frame of reference for further research into a largely unrepresentable but powerfully effective social totality. The monstrous accumulation is ongoing, not surprisingly, and its effects are only partially comprehended.

"Monsters Are Meaning Machines"

In *The Anthropocene Unconscious*, Bould connects a vast array of recent popular media to this broader sense of dread, in making the bold argument that all narrative today is in some way or another *about* climate change and its simultaneously vague and all-too-real threats. This includes stories about monsters, of course, and the rise in popularity of certain subgenres of the monster-movie tellingly reveals the more diffuse sense of dread that permeates societies in the twenty-first century. As Bould writes,

> [t]he fantastic expresses our fears and anxieties, our desires and sometimes even our hopes. Frankenstein's monster embodies the terrors of reproduction, foreshadows proletarian and anti-colonial revolution. King Kong rampaging through Manhattan enacts white fears of black masculinity and colonial comeuppance. Bodysnatching aliens are avatars of consumerist conformism. Robots are our dehumanised selves. Godzilla is the bomb.

From this, Bould asserts: "So the first thing you should always ask of a monster is: what does it represent?"[26]

Various monsters represent many different things, and a system of monsters in this teratocene can produce varied and elaborate *structures of feeling*, to use Raymond Williams's elegant term,[27] in an era of globalization. But the key point Bould makes is that monsters are never just "given"; there is never mere monstrosity, without some aspect of allegorical or figural power associated with them. While it is not always so simple as "Godzilla is the bomb," as Bould himself points out, it is always the case that monsters are meaningful. Indeed, as Jack Halberstam put it some years ago, "[m]onsters are meaning machines."[28]

Recent trends in mass media monstrosity have included the return of the great nineteenth-century terrors, vampires, and zombies, the latter broadly conceived, so as to incorporate such forms as Frankenstein's creature, mummies, and such more novel variations as the "infected" humans of *28 Days Later* (2002), *Train to Busan* (2016), or *The Last of Us* (2023). Hostile aliens, monstrous "natural" critters (e.g., sharks, with or without their tornadoes), ghosts or other spectral forms, demons, even angels as dangerously otherworldly beings (e.g., in *The Prophecy* movie franchise or, more humorously, in Kevin Smith's irreverent *Dogma*), and many others all remain part of the grand menagerie of monsters inflicted upon audiences in recent decades. Circumstances also create unexpected monsters, in some cases leading to a sort of inversion of hope and dread, of the familiar and the strange.

Take, for example, clowns. Although many of us today—including a majority of children, apparently—might find clowns to be inherently frightening, such a view would almost certainly come as a surprise to those (US-based) children in the 1950s and 1960s who tuned in to see "Freddie the Freeloader" on *The Red Skelton Show*, Clarabell the Clown on *The Howdy Doody Show*, and Bozo the Clown, a character franchised so that different television markets each had their own version of the clown and his show, or similar such fare.[29] Once upon a time, not long ago, the clown was about as wholesome and beloved a figure as there was in popular culture, and clowns were associated not only with the carnivalesque pleasures of the circus, but also with children's birthday parties, television programming, and corporate sponsorship. Even amid the proliferating "phobias" and the pathologization of everyday life in the mid-twentieth-century, there was no term for "fear of clowns." To the extent that one exists now, it was not until at least the 1980s or early 1990s, when *coulrophobia* was apparently coined—its origins are unknown—and the now somewhat widely used label only became recognized by the *OED Online* in 2010.[30]

As Whitney S. May has shown, the unexpected rise of the clown as a figure of horror occurs during the Reagan era, timing that she finds not entirely accidental. To be sure, there are potential predecessors (e.g., DC Comics' *Batman* antagonist "The Joker," for one), but the true emergence of the "evil clown" in popular culture in the United States seems to have occurred in the 1980s. It arguably started with Stephen King's terrifying Pennywise character in his 1986 novel *IT*, with perhaps a due reference to the "evil" clown doll in *Poltergeist* (1982) before, along with the campier aliens in the 1988 film *Killer Klowns from Outer Space* a bit later. The phenomenon has expanded exponentially in the decades since, with numerous evil clown characters featuring in horror films or television series. Evil clownery has even been found bleeding out into the "real world" from time to time, as reports of mysterious "clown sightings" periodically provoke local panics here or there. In 2014 in the UK and in 2016 in the United States, for example, a spate of such sightings led McDonald's, the largest restaurant chain in the world, to temporarily de-emphasize the use of their iconic Ronald McDonald spokesclown, who in fact now appears to be semi-retired.[31]

The rapid transformation of the clown from a delightful entertainer of children to the creepy, menacing fiend might itself be a symptom of the postmodern society of the spectacle in which delights and horrors are so utterly comingled as to have become indistinguishable. To say that the United States in the Reagan-era had become something of a carnival of nightmares may have been seen as hyperbolic when cultural critics suggested it at the time, but in the twenty-first century that insight almost seems to be among those "basic banalities" with which we live.[32]

In King's novel *IT*, the narrative is divided into two acts, one set in a somewhat stereotypical 1950s (evoking a sort of "nostalgia for the present," as Jameson famously dubbed it),[33] the other in the then-present early 1980s, as we learn that the monstrous villain reappears in the fictional town of Derry every twenty-seven years. In the two-part film version released in 2017 and 2019, this timeline is advanced by three decades, such that the earlier phase is set in the 1980s and the second in an American *hic et nunc* typified by, among so many other things, the absurd figure of Donald Trump in the White House. Or, as May puts it with delicious understatement, the shift in timing of the film adaptation registers "the clown-laden political imagery surrounding the 2016 U.S. presidential election and its subsequent administration." May astutely points out that "[b]etween these two eras—between Reagan and now, between the period of Morning in America and the Mourning Period in America—lies a landscape of fear appropriately peopled (or monstered) by clowns."[34] Where King in 1986 likely saw a tantalizing opportunity to take an archetype beloved by children in the 1950s and turn it into a terrifying monster for us in the Reagan era, Pennywise the Dancing Clown in the film adaptions thirty years later takes on an even more sinister role, as the menace of popular entertainment across various spheres (including politics) was no longer hidden or latent, but all too terrifyingly real.

Thus, one could argue, the absurd combination of neoconservativism and neoliberalism that found its ideological mooring in Reaganism or

Thatcherism could generate stranger than usual "monsters," ones that managed to overturn a century's worth of goodwill and warm feelings. After all, Reagan himself seemed a mostly harmless, likable entertainer in that earlier period, and his generally affability and personal charms were thought to make way for his pernicious electoral appeal, as "Reagan Democrats" and others came to support the very politician championing policies that would directly harm their own well-being and limit future opportunities. A monstrous, otherworldly predator adopting the physical form of a "dancing clown" might be a bit too on the nose, in fact. The disguised aliens and downtrodden laborers of John Carpenter's *They Live* (1988) may have made for an extremely apt allegory of the Reagan years in the United States, but in many ways, that film oversimplified the problem, as far too many people today would likely not flinch when wearing the glasses that revealed the aliens' true forms or the ideological subtext of magazines and other entertainments. Those are the very things that so many want to vote for, after all, in the monstrously clownish era of Trump and the widespread support for his views.

This is but one interpretation of one recent, noteworthy type of monster. There are many ways of reading the evil clown, as with other forms of monster. As Bould warns, "only fools and knaves would then attempt reduce a monster to a single, fixed meaning. Monsters are polysemic and disorderly; multiple contradictory connotations swirl about them, continually recontextualising. They always escape our control; if they do not, then—as every episode of *Scooby-Doo* shows us—they are not really monsters at all."[35] Very true, but then the invocation of *Scooby-Doo* is itself significant, given that so many of the "monsters" in that series turn out to be real-estate developers, bankers, businessmen, and other capitalist plotters hoping to "scare" away those who might interfere with their selfish, profitable schemes. Under the circumstances, mere ghosts or ghouls might be preferable from the perspective of those hoping to make a life for themselves in such places.

Ideologies of the Undead

In terms of political economy in the age of globalization, further analysis of the role that monsters play in the cultural imagination today would necessarily take the measure of the "infernal machine" that is capitalism itself. Several recent theoretical treatments of *Capital*, including *Marx's Inferno* (William Clare Roberts), *Representing Capital* (Fredric Jameson), *Marx, Capital, and the Madness of Economic Reason* (David Harvey), and *Why Marx Was Right* (Terry Eagleton), have highlighted the degree to which dysfunction is part of the functioning of the capitalist mode of production, and thus Marx's critique, updated and adapted to meet the contingencies of late capitalism, remains crucial to understanding the system that has become so pervasive and powerful that even the thought of its destruction or evanescence seems inconceivable today.

As in the classical Marxian accounts, the base-level terrors of the political economy find their counterparts in the superstructural proliferations to be found in the cultural sphere, among other spaces. In the cultural sphere, then, the emergence, re-emergence, and proliferation of monsters seem to reflect a sense of this doom. For example, Franco Moretti's famous essay "Dialectic of Fear," included in his *Signs Taken For Wonders* (1983), identifies two types of monster, and more specifically two literary characters, as being emblematic of the anxieties associated with capitalism. The types might be labeled the *zombie* and the *vampire*, but the characters are as well known as any in modern cultures: Frankenstein's Creature and Dracula, as invented by Mary Shelley and Bram Stoker, respectively.[36] Revisiting Moretti's argument today, we can see how these key figures have developed into critical embodiments of unnamed terrors in postmodernity, from the nameless terrors of the *lumpenproletariat* to the top-down hierarchy of the blood-sucking capitalist class, which are far less clearly understood now as compared to the nineteenth century. McNally's impressive argument in *Monsters of the Market* indicates the ways that these monsters have come to symbolize aspects of not only industrial capitalism, but also the ever more complex and expansive capitalism in the era of globalization, thus making them into exemplary figures of late capitalist dread.

Moretti's reading established the basic dynamics of class struggle in societies organized by the capitalist mode of production as the lens through which these powerfully representative literary monsters be viewed. The creature in Shelley's *Frankenstein* stands in for the proletariat, and Stoker's Count Dracula embodies a vision of the capitalist bourgeoisie. "Like the proletariat," for example, "the monster is denied a name and an individuality. He is the Frankenstein monster; he belongs wholly to his creator (just as one can speak of a 'Ford worker')." Moretti also notes that the creature is built from disparate parts, assembled, and not a natural being. "Like the proletariat, he is a *collective* and *artificial* creature. He is not found in nature, but built."[37] The creature represents the culmination of the Age of Enlightenment's achievements and terrors, the progeny of modern science and art that takes on a life of its own, in mockery and horror of those who brought it into being. As Moretti puts it,

> Frankenstein's invention is thus a pregnant metaphor of the process of capitalist production, which forms by deforming, civilizes by barbarizing, enriches by impoverishing—a two-sided process in which each affirmation entails a negation. And indeed the monster [...] is always described by *negation*: man is well proportioned, the monster is not; man is beautiful, the monster ugly; man is good, the monster evil. The monster is man turned upside-down, negated.[38]

This fundamental *perversion* of the human form is what makes both the Creature and the modern proletariat monstrous, at once completely unnatural and antisocial, yet somehow also the very substance of the material and social order.

This type of monster is allegorized in such a way that its very existence is menacing, and the terrifying strength and violence attributed to the creature are aligned with a sense of vengefulness and retribution. As Marx and Engels had noted, using a slightly different metaphor, bourgeois society was like "the sorcerer who is no longer able to control the powers of the nether world whom he has called up by his spells."[39] Frankenstein's Creature, along with the variously zombie-like monsters to emerge in his wake, figures forth a more pervasive fear in modern industrial society, which in the context of late capitalism becomes a thoroughly global phenomenon. This may help to explain, in some ways, the increasing number and pervasiveness of different zombie-based horrors, including many visions of a "zombie apocalypse," in recent popular culture. And the *meanings* associated with these "zombies"—some of which, as with the "infected" of *28 Days Later* or *The Last of Us*, are not technically the dead-brought-back-to-life, but which still operate as zombie-like monsters—are as numerous and varied as the creatures themselves. As Bould points out, "[n]ot all zombies require a shot to the head to kill them, and some do not crave a diet of human brains. In fact, the only thing that all zombies have in common is that they *mean*," adding in a timely idiom that "zombies are as allegorical as fuck."[40]

The capitalist as vampire, similarly, is a figure so well known as to be almost a cliché. Marx, in *Capital*, uses the metaphor frequently, as when he observes that "[c]apital is dead labour which, vampire-like, lives only by sucking living labour, and lives the more, the more labour it sucks."[41] And it may not just be the bourgeois capitalist who is implicated by a sort of vampirism, but consumers as well. For example, adding a Freudian element to the Marxist critique, Rob Latham has shown that the erotic or sexualized aspects of the vampire figure also indicate the degree to which commodity consumption itself is bound up in these monstrous images. As Latham observes, "[t]he aggressive orality of the vampire involves an eroticization of images of consumption [...] which may also be seen to evoke historical consumption specifically. The vampire's pleasure comes from biting and drinking—in other words, from acquiring and consuming."[42] The vampire does not just suck blood, but also employs laborers, purchases real estate, and most terribly, spread the vampiric contagion to others.

Moretti's reading of Stoker's *Dracula* goes beyond this generalized figure in noting the degree to which Count Dracula is a vampire specific to the age of monopoly capital, which is to say the late nineteenth century. *Dracula* was published in 1897, at the height of what Lenin had called "the age of imperialism," after all. As Moretti argues, "Dracula is a true monopolist: solitary and despotic, he will brook no competition. Like monopoly capital, his ambition is to subjugate the last vestiges of the liberal era and destroy all forms of economic independence."[43] Dracula, of course, is not only a monster in the sense that he is a vampire, but the monstrosity is compounded by both his foreignness and his aristocracy, elements which combine to threaten the integrity of English national identity and bourgeois individuality, each of which is compromised through the contagion and influence of the vampire's presence. Both living and dead—or, rather, Undead—the vampire occupies the spectrum of society, transforming its members into something new and different.[44] As Moretti says, "[a]ll Dracula's actions really have as their final goal the creation of this 'new order of beings' which finds its most fertile soil, logically enough, in England," one of the birthplaces of modern capitalism and the metropolitan center of the British Empire.[45]

It is thus, perhaps, not difficult to see why Frankenstein's Creature and Dracula remain exemplary literary figures and representative monsters today. Notwithstanding their respective origins in post-Enlightenment fears of science and industry, on the one hand, and the late Victorian anxieties over monopoly capital, nationalism, imperialism, and rapidly shifting social relations associated with them, on the other, these two monsters still serve to demarcate the central zones within the modern (or postmodern) capitalist system's topographies of fear. As McNally observes,

> [c]apitalist market-society overflows with monsters. But no grotesque species so command the imagination as the vampire and the zombie. In fact, these two creatures need to be thought conjointly, as interconnected moments of the monstrous dialectic of modernity. Like Victor Frankenstein and his Creature, the vampire and the zombie are doubles, linked poles of the split society. If vampires are the dreaded beings who might possess us and turn us into their docile servants, zombies represent our haunted self-image, warning us that we might already be lifeless, disempowered agents of alien powers.[46]

Under the circumstances of a global economic system in which the class struggle between proletariat and the capitalist classes is simultaneously extended to a worldwide arena and rendered nearly invisible by ever more mystifying, elaborate, and vast relations of power, these traditional monsters may take on new forms, and yet their messages remain as urgent as ever. As McNally suggests, for instance, "[i]n the image of the zombie lurks a troubled apprehension that capitalist society really is a night of the living dead."[47]

The critical examination of the ideologies of the undead seems all the more relevant in this context. For a variety of reasons, the present moment in world history seems to be particularly hospitable for the dead or the undead, monsters occupying this horrifying liminal space of the in-between, hybrid beings whose manner of simultaneous nonliving and non-dying conjures up terrible visions of our own existential condition in the twenty-first century. Throughout different media in mass culture, as evidenced in popular novels like *Pride and Prejudice and Zombies*, television series such as *The Walking Dead* or *The Last of Us*, or films like *28 Days Later* and its sequel *28 Weeks Later*, *World War Z*, or *Train to Busan*, amongst many others, zombies run rampant, infecting the living and portending an apocalyptic end for humanity. In George R. R. Martin's series of fantasy novels *A Song of Ice and Fire* and its landmark television adaptation *Game of Thrones*, devotees of the Drowned God in the Iron Islands declare, "[w]hat is dead can never die," whilst an army of "the dead" commanded by fearsome Others slowly marches toward an ultimate showdown with the living. Although the tropes of death are likely as old as storytelling, and the encounters between the living, the dead, and the undead have a long history, these twenty-first-century zombie-like figures appear rather timely now as the divisions between leisure and work-time, between activity and passivity, between resistance and capitulation to the system, and between even life and death appear less stark.

Arguably, the ideologies of the undead have become elements of any figural representation of the world as we know it today, such that even a zombie apocalypse and the overthrow of the living by the dead or undead carry with them an almost redemptive quality. Indeed, the predominance of these two types of monsters generated a related subgenre of fantastic horror in which "learning to live with" the monsters—as in the popular television vampire show *True Blood* (2008–14) or the humor-laden zombie films *Shaun of the Dead* (2004) or *Life After Beth* (2014)—becomes simply the way to get along on the present, effectively establishing a properly monstrous "new normal" in the teratocene.

Chimerical Critique

Still other monsters evoke dread and inspire hope in the teratocene. Aatish Taseer has recently suggested that the *chimera* is the preeminent, representative monster of our time. The very word, which once referred to a monster or multiple ones of terrifying proportions, has also become a term for the *impossible*. It is used, even more dismissively, to indicate to a fantastic vision unworthy of our attention at all. But even so, the chimeric fascinates, an "entity that lies beyond human conception." As Taseer writes, "'Chimera,' the word—with a small 'c'—had passed into our lexicon, becoming shorthand for all that was illusory, grotesque, wondrous and out of reach, a three-way bridge between the human, the divine and the netherworldly. Mutants. Monsters. Fantastical beasts. They were all covered by the idea of the chimera."[48] This protean, hybrid creature is not so much a figure to be found within the contemporary world system as a representative of it, one that is all too real in both its concrete monstrosity and in its potential for evoking alternatives realities.

The extraordinary expansions and accumulation of monsters in the era of globalization can be interpreted, at least in part, as an attempt to make sense of, or give form to, the world system itself, which is itself "monstrous" even if it may also seem to some as fantastic, unreal, and impossible. In this sense, the recent rise of monsters—the rise of dystopian horror as a genre or of supernatural terror as a theme—in mass culture can be connected to a sort of cognitive mapping, as Jameson called it. As Jameson has put it in *The Geopolitical Aesthetic*, "all thinking today is *also*, whatever else it is, an attempt to think the world system as such," and he insists "not merely that we ought to strive for it [i.e., a self-consciousness and figural representation of the social totality], but that we do so all the time without being aware of the process."[49] In that book, Jameson showed how conspiracy films, among others, serve as a means for producing such figural representations or cognitive maps of the larger systems in which their events take place, and one can easily imagine that monster movies, horror, and the like might also serve in this manner. But even if this cognitive mapping successfully occurs through a consideration of monsters and the monstrous, that does not mean the world made visible or cognizable is necessarily more comforting or less scary. As Alberto Toscano and Jeff Kinkle have pointed out, "among the first products of a genuine striving for orientation is disorientation, as proximal coordinates come to be troubled by wide, and at times overwhelming vistas."[50] Monsters, like maps, may help us achieve a better sense of the social spaces we inhabit and move within, but they do not immediately make those spaces any less frightful or dreadful. One of the results of cognitive mapping is a completely different, perhaps unforeseen, or previously unimaginable image, and this may be terrifying in its own right. If the old world as we think we know it offers topographies of fear, the reimagined world may well look strange and new, but no less daunting.

That said, Jameson is almost certainly correct to say that we must not only strive for this sense of the big picture, but that we do so anyway whether we intend to or not. In projecting a monstrous system, a system filled with monsters, we are also constructing the framework by which to make sense of this global ensemble, and this activity, even when frightening, comes with its rewards. These may include the new vistas and vantages made possible by the effort, as well as the discovery of new spaces to be explored once those views have been established. Additionally, it should not be forgotten that all this stuff can also be pleasurable. Horror stories, broadly conceived, operate at various affective registers into which *fear* or *angst* insinuates itself, showing how different ways of experiencing horror compel different attitudes toward both it and its underlying conditions. In the course of this analysis, we might see how the experience of fear can metamorphose into the pleasures of critique. As Miéville has argued persuasively, the monstrous world system requires a sense of the otherworldly to help produce alternatives to the tyrannical authority of "what is." In fantasy the impossible is treated as if it were real, thus allowing the possibility of alternatives to the merely actual order of things to be a starting point for critical thinking.

The fantastic is a mode well suited for apprehending a system that masks the social relations of which it is constituted, as with the commodity fetish in Marx's original critique. The chimera is a creature made of many different parts, at once monstrous and scary, but also seemingly a figment of our imaginations. The world system in an era of globalization can also seem almost imaginary, too vast to be "realized" or perhaps to be considered as "real," yet its multilimbed, tentacular reach seems to affect every detail of daily life in even the most remote places, as the supply chain disruptions associated with the global Covid-19 crisis along with other recent phenomena have plainly disclosed. A fantastic, Marxist critique attuned to the dialectic of the impossible and the actual thus befits a system in which monsters are all too real, and the prospects of other worlds seem all too unimaginable.

Conclusion: Crossing the River

Meditating on Gramsci's famous line about "morbid symptoms," historian Donald Sassoon has observed that "[t]he chief characteristic of the interregnum between old and new is uncertainty," adding that "[i]t is like crossing a wide river: the old riverbank is left behind, but the other side is still indistinct; currents might push one back and drowning cannot be ruled out. Unable to anticipate what will happen, one is overcome by fear, anxiety, and panic."[51] Such an anxious crossing is all the more dreadful when one considers all the creatures in the water with you, as well as those to be found along the riverbank in the distance.

Sassoon also notes that, in writing of the old world dying and the new one struggling to be born in 1930, Gramsci may not have been quite as sanguine about that moment's prospects as are the many who quote the lines in reference to the present conjecture today. After all, the "new" that Gramsci was seeing at the time was the rise and spread of fascism, and there was likely much about the "old" that he would like to see preserved and maintained in the future. As Sassoon puts it,

> Marxists traditionally saw crises as opportunities for radical change. Gramsci, so much closer to us, is less optimistic. The conjuncture he was describing was an "interregnum" teeming with "morbid

symptoms," not a potential revolutionary situation. He did not exclude a return to the old, though he hoped—with what he called an "optimism of the will," as opposed to the "pessimism of the intellect"— that the morbid symptoms might offer an opportunity for progress.[52]

Part of the project, then, must be to scrutinize and discern those elements of the new world struggling to be born, while never losing sight of the historical necessity of studiously making sense of the old world in its death throes, observing its diseases and disintegration, and also paying attention to what inevitably remains for us beyond it.

Morbid symptoms refer to indicators of disease, and the very word (etymologically) suggests that the diseases in question would be deadly. No doubt Gramsci had the literal meaning in mind, as well as any figurative associations to be found with the infirmities of the body politic. One might also think of this as "dis-*ease*," the uneasiness or dread with which we encounter so many apparently symptomatic characteristics of the contemporary social order and its ongoing developments. For instance, we could think of the choice by Gramsci's contemporary Sigmund Freud to change the word *Unglück* ("unhappy") to *Unbehagen* ("discontent" or "uneasiness") when he came up with the title for *Civilization and Its Discontents* (*Das Unbehagen in der Kultur*), published in the exact year that Gramsci wrote the "morbid symptoms" line. *Unbehagen* has no exact equivalent in English, but is something like the French *malaise*, itself suggesting a sense of the morbid. This dis-ease is perhaps another instance of the pervasive dread to be found in the teratocene.

Hence, in another ruse of history or dialectical reversal, the mistranslation of Gramsci's original lines as popularized by Žižek's (mis)quotation turns out to be all the more appropriate, for "the time of monsters" is when "a great variety of morbid symptoms appear." It is for us to read those symptoms, to understand these monsters, and to maintain the uneasy and dreadful project of making sense of the world in our time, which is prerequisite to any serious endeavor to forge a different world and future.

Notes

1   For what it is worth, a Google search on February 19, 2023, for the exact phrase came up with over 3,000 hits, although limiting the range of the search to mentions made prior to 2010 produced only a handful, which

strongly suggests that Slavoj Žižek's "quotation" of it that year prompted the subsequent explosion in usage.

2   Slavoj Žižek, "A Permanent Economic Emergency," *New Left Review* 64 (July—August 2010): 95.

3   Antonio Gramsci, *Selections from the Prison Notebooks*, ed. and trans. Quintin Hoare and Geoffrey Nowell Smith (New York: International Books, 1971), 276.

4   Ross Wolfe, "No, Žižek did not attribute a Goebbels quote to Gramsci," *The Charnel House* (June 3, 2015): https://thecharnelhouse. org/2015/07/03/no-Žižek-did-not-attribute-a-goebbels-quote-to-gramsci/ (retrieved February 18, 2023). The title refers to an accusation that Žižek had borrowed from speech in which Goebbels had made reference to an old world dying and a new one coming into being, but as Wolfe notes, the image—old world dying, new world emerging—had a long history already, and he cites examples from both John Reed's *Ten Days That Shook the World* and a 1921 speech by V. I. Lenin, sources with which Gramsci himself would have probably been familiar.

5   On the nuances of Gramsci's observation in the context in which they were made in 1930, see Gilbert Achcar, "Morbid Symptoms: What Did Gramsci Really Mean?," *Notebooks: The Journal for Studies on Power* 1.2 (2022): 379–87.

6   David McNally, *Monsters of the Market: Zombies, Vampires, and Global Capitalism* (Chicago: Haymarket Books, 2012), 1.

7   See Mark Bould, *The Anthropocene Unconscious: Climate, Catastrophe, Culture* (London: Verso, 2021).

8   Donna Haraway, *Staying with the Trouble: Making Kin in the Chthulucene* (Durham: Duke University Press, 2016), 2.

9   See ibid., 169, note 2: "A fastidious Greek speller might insist on the 'h' between the last 'l' and 'u'; but both for English pronunciation and for avoiding the grasp of Lovecraft's Cthulhu, I dropped that 'h.' This is a metaplasm."

10 See Paul J. Crutzen and Eugene F. Stoermer, "The Anthropocene," *Global Change* Newsletter 41 (2000): 17–18; see also Robert T. Tally Jr. and Christine M. Battista, "Ecocritical Geographies, Geocritical Ecologies, and the Spaces of Modernity," in *Ecocriticism and Geocriticism: Overlapping Territories in Environmental and Spatial Literary Studies*, ed. Robert T. Tally Jr. and Christine M. Battista (New York: Palgrave Macmillan, 2016), 1–16.

11 Christopher Nealon, "The Trouble with 'Modernity,'" *Public Books* (May 1, 2015), n. pag. [available online: http://www.publicbooks.org/ nonfiction/the-trouble-with-modernity].

12 Jason W. Moore, "Anthropocene or Capitalocene?" in *Anthropocene or Capitalocene?: Nature, History, and the Crisis of Capitalism*, ed. Jason W. Moore (Oakland: PM Press, 2016), 1–11.

13 See McKenzie Wark, *Molecular Red: Theory in the Anthropocene* (London: Verso, 2015), 223; see also Joshua Clover and Juliana Spahr, *#misanthropocene: 24 Theses* (Oakland: Commune Editions, 2014): https://communeeditions.com/misanthropocene/.

14 Bould, *The Anthropocene Unconscious*, 7–9.

15 Fredric Jameson, *Allegory and Ideology* (London: Verso, 2019), 348.

16 See, for example, Marie-Hélène Huet, *Monstrous Imagination* (Cambridge: Harvard University Press, 1993); Marina Warner, *Managing Monsters: Six Myths of Our Time* (New York: Vintage, 1994); and Jeffrey Jerome Cohen, ed., *Monster Theory: Reading Culture* (Minneapolis: University of Minnesota Press, 1996).

17 Gregory Claeys, *Dystopia: A Natural History* (Oxford: Oxford University Press, 2017), 58.

18 Theodor W. Adorno, *Minima Moralia: Reflections on a Damaged Life*, trans. E. F. N. Jephcott (London: Verso, 2005), 74.

19 Karl Marx, *Capital, Volume 1*, trans. Ben Fowkes (New York: Penguin, 1990), 125, translation modified.

20 China Miéville, "Editorial Introduction: Marxism and Fantasy," *Historical Materialism* 10.4 (2002): 45–6.

21 McNally, *Monsters of the Market*, 13.

22 See William Clare Roberts, *Marx's Inferno: The Political Theory of Capital* (Princeton: Princeton University Press, 2018).

23 Tony Tanner, *Adultery in the Novel: Contract and Transgression* (Baltimore: Johns Hopkins University Press, 1979), 73.

24 Ibid.

25 Miéville, "Editorial Introduction," 42; the quoted phrase "an absurdity which is true," comes from Norman Geras, "Essence and Appearance: Aspects of Fetishism in Marx's *Capital*," *New Left Review* I.65 (January–February 1971): 76.

26 Bould, *The Anthropocene Unconscious*, 27.

27 See, for example, Raymond Williams, *Marxism and Literature* (Oxford: Oxford University Press, 1977), 128–35.

28 Judith [Jack] Halberstam, *Skin Shows: Gothic Horror and the Technology of Monsters* (Durham: Duke University Press, 1995), 21.

29 The actor who played the original Clarabell, Bob Keeshan, went on to become "Captain Kangaroo," and on that children's show he also played "the Town Clown," among other characters.

30 According to the *Online Etymology Dictionary*, *coulrophobia* meaning a "morbid fear of clowns," had appeared "by 2001 (said in Web sites to date from 1990s or even 1980s), a popular term, not from psychology, possibly facetious, though the phenomenon is real enough; said to be built from Greek *kolon* 'limb,' with some supposed sense of 'stilt-walker,' hence 'clown' + *phobia*." Dubious of this etymological explanation, the entry concludes, "[c]oulrophobia looks suspiciously like the sort of thing idle

pseudo-intellectuals invent on the internet and which every smarty-pants takes up thereafter; perhaps it is a mangling of Modern Greek *klooun* 'clown,' which is the English word borrowed into Greek." See https://www. etymonline.com/word/coulrophobia (accessed February 22, 2023).

31   See Amelia Tait, "The Death of Ronald McDonald," *Vice* (October 4, 2021): https://www.vice.com/en/article/v7ew98/what-happened-to-ronald-mcdonald (accessed September 22, 2022).

32   I refer, of course, to Raoul Vaneigem's Situationist *tour-de-force*, "Basic Banalities," in *The Situationist International Anthology*, ed. Ken Knabb (Berkeley, CA: Bureau of Public Secrets, 1981), 117–30, 154–72.

33   See Fredric Jameson, *Postmodernism, or, the Cultural Logic of Late Capitalism* (Durham: Duke University Press, 1991), 279–96.

34   Whitney S. May, "Counterpunch: *IT* as Modern Punch and Judy Show," in *Encountering Pennywise: Critical Perspective's on Stephen King's* IT, ed. Whitney S. May (Oxford: University of Mississippi Press, 2022), 1, 9.

35   Bould, *The Anthropocene Unconscious*, 145, note 4.

36   Franco Moretti, "Dialectic of Fear," in *Signs Taken For Wonders: On the Sociology of Literary Forms*, trans. David Forgacs (London: Verso, 1983), 83–108.

37   Moretti, "Dialectic of Fear," 85.

38   Ibid., 87–8.

39   Karl Marx and Friedrich Engels, *The Communist Manifesto* (London: Penguin, 1998), 57.

40   Bould, *The Anthropocene Unconscious*, 28–9.

41   Marx, *Capital*, 342.

42   Rob Latham, *Consuming Youth: Vampires, Cyborgs, and the Culture of Consumption* (Chicago: University of Chicago Press, 2002), 97.

43   Moretti, "Dialectic of Fear," 92.

44   *The Undead*, in fact, was the original title Stoker had planned to use for *Dracula*. As such, Stoker is generally credited with coining the term in his common usage for the horror genre, even though the label is now likely more often applied to zombies than to vampires. Stoker undoubtedly popularized the term, whereas the charnel-house horrors that went into the making of Frankenstein's Creature were a different sort of reanimation of the formerly dead matter. Notably, ghosts differ even more, as they are given the popular dignity of being dead, even if they have returned from death in a spectral form.

45   Moretti, "Dialectic of Fear," 92.

46   McNally, *Monsters of the Market*, 253.

47   Ibid.

48   Aatish Taseer, "An Age of Monsters: Every time the world is in trouble, one creature takes root in the human imagination: the chimera," *T: The New York Times Style Magazine* (February 19, 2023): 156.

49 Jameson, *The Geopolitical Aesthetic: Space and Cinema in the World System* (London and Bloomington: The British Film Institute and Indiana University Press, 1992), 4, 2.

50 Alberto Toscano, and Jeff Kinkle, *Cartographies of the Absolute* (Winchester: Zero Books, 2015), 25.

51 Donald Sassoon, *Morbid Symptoms: An Anatomy of a World in Crisis* (London: Verso, 2021), 2.

52 Ibid.

Chapter 6

TERATOLOGY AS IDEOLOGY CRITIQUE; OR, A MONSTER UNDER EVERY BED

In popular culture as in the groves of academe, the contemporary scene is crowded with monsters, from alien invaders to the zombie apocalypse, set against the backdrop of darkly fantastic landscapes and dystopian visions. The predominance of the horror genre, broadly conceived, in recent years attests to the profound sense of anxiety and dread permeating late capitalist societies. Horror's popularity as both a genre and a discursive mode is itself a sign of the respect given by readers to authors who refuse to deny the existence of monsters. One could argue that the ostensibly childish fear of monsters serves a more broadly allegorical purpose in contemporary societies. For if there is one thing that most children know, that many adults have forgotten or repressed, it is that monsters are real. This is not a mere suspicion, some dimly descried or indistinct perception, or a vague apprehension of dread. Monsters exist, they are frighteningly close to us, and they mean business. Children's literature has often registered this all-too-real sense of dread. Horror, especially monstrous horror, remains a key theme or genre within and beyond the category of children's literature, which itself occupies a privileged place within the North American publishing industry. Moreover, the outsized dominance of works of fantasy within twentieth—and twenty-first-century prose fiction and popular culture may indicate the degree to which those inhuman beings—dragons, trolls, ogres, vampires, ghosts, zombies, among others—shape our *sense* of the world. As in Mercer Mayer's delightful exploration of this experience in his picture-book by that title, there really is one monster after another.

The presence of monsters and the monstrous could be said to figure forth a sort of allegorical representation of the world system that is useful in coming to terms with the both unreality and many of the realities of the "real world." In this sense, the monstrosity explored through fantastic literature and its criticism could be considered a form of ideology critique, as China Miéville has suggested in his critical examinations of fantasy, science fiction, and social theory. That is, the world as seen through traditional realism is itself unreal, inasmuch as it masks the underlying "truth" in its very surface-level realism. In a world where reality is itself unreal, the non-realism of fantasy may offer the means to get at these hidden truths. Similarly, with horror, these hidden realities may be rendered visible through the emotions of fear, anxiety, or dread, combined with the imaginative process of projecting new models for understanding that allow one to overcome those emotions or to redirect them in productive ways. The horror in the text helps to engender a political or historical sensibility, in which the pervasive feeling of generalized dread may crystallize into a more concrete sense of the underlying reality. It should be noted that this activity, within the text and outside of it, is not rooted in any ethical program, moral didacticism, or social discipline, although these may turn out to be effects. Regardless of what the author, parents, or booksellers might think, the point is not to scare the reader into behaving a certain way, but to create means of giving shape to and understanding the dynamic systems we inhabit. Monsters, by embodying a sort of political unconscious, become a means of demystifying and mapping the social world in an age of globalization.

Signs and Wonders

The English word *monster* can be traced to two, related Latin etymons: *monere* (meaning "to warn") and *monstrare* (meaning "to show"). There are thus elements of premonition and demonstration, and certainly one imagines that the monsters would be something that one may wish to point out or "show" to others precisely in order to "warn" them about some present or future menace. As Jonathan Krell has pointed out, there is a fundamental ambivalence intrinsic to monsters at this etymological and historical level. For "the monster is a kind of warning or portent. However, what we are being warned about is not clear. It seems that the monster can be monstrously malevolent or monstrously marvelous." As he concludes, "the monster may be a sign from God or the work of Satan."[1]

There is another connection between the warning and the showing of monsters, which is that the idea is connected in some way to the spectacle. As Michel Foucault has indicated in his study of the history of madness, madmen and other so-called "monsters" were quietly put on display, in the manner of the freakshow or other such lurid entertainment. "Madness became pure spectacle," writes Foucault, and "[u]p until the early nineteenth century [...] the mad remained monsters—literally things and being worthy of being put on show in public."[2] The connection between monstrosity and visibility has never entirely faded. *Monstrum*, in Latin, already indicated the ominous, the fearful or wondrous, and the thing to be shown was itself a warning. The monstrous was something to see, yes, but also something foreboding, and from this it naturally enlarged itself, becoming an entity both immense and dangerous. The monstrous thus appears as a warning, imbued semiotically with many taboos and proscriptions, while also interceding directly into our midst. As later "Monster Theory" will note, cultural relations to or with monsters speak to societal fears, and as monsters develop, their visibility and functions may change as well. But it also might be quite fitting that, as we find ourselves to be increasingly part of what Guy Debord famously names "the society of the spectacle," we also experience our historical moment as part of a teratocene.[3]

While monstrosity and monsters have always been with us, the monsters of modernity stand out as distinctive figures of cultural significance. The famous etching of Francisco Goya, evocatively labeled "The Sleep of Reason Produces Monsters" (c. 1799), might serve as a point of departure, for the nineteenth century witnessed an explosion of monstrosity, ushering in a veritable teratocene, an age of monsters, as discussed in Chapter 5. In art and literature, not to mention in politics and economics, one finds frequent and regular reference to monsters of all sorts, and the fear of such monsters as often as not represents other terrors of a rapidly changing social sphere and the anxiety over the unforeseeable effects of those changes.[4]

In his fascinating study of fantasy, *A Specter Is Haunting Europe: A Sociohistorical Approach to the Fantastic* (1990), José B. Monléon argues that the post-Enlightenment horror paradigmatically expressed in Goya's famous image comes to reflect and be conditioned by the terrific uncertainties associated with the great social revolutions—especially those associated with the years 1789 and 1848, for instance—and their aftermath in European cultures, not to mention the radical transformations of everyday life associated with growing urbanization, industrialization, and more generally, modernization. As Monléon observes,

> the fears and uncertainties, the monsters of a material and social reality, were neither existential abstractions not expressions of some sort of human (psychological) attributes. Or, if there were, they were also much more. As social production, the fantastic

articulated apprehensions that were deeply attached to the specific
characteristics of capitalist society. The perception of monstrosity
had significant correlations with the way in which dominant culture
defined and redefined its political and economic supremacy, and
depended upon concrete forms of class struggle. On the one hand,
the fantastic "reflected" very real social threats; on the other hand, it
created a space in which those threats could be transformed into
"supernaturalism" and monstrosity, thus helping to reshape the
philosophical premises that sustained the fantastic and effectively
reorient the course of social evolution.[5]

Monstrosity in particular, along with the fantastic more broadly,
became a means of making sense of the new social formations and
relations that emerged and became increasingly dominant in societies
organized in connection with the capitalist mode of production and
its effects. Furthermore, as social life in societies organized according
to the capitalist mode of production itself began to appear more and
more monstrous, as all that was solid melted into air and all that had
been holy was profaned, to cite Marx and Engels's memorable phrasing,
the social system disclosed itself to be a kind of infernal machine,
producing monstrosities and horrors even as it managed to organize
and reorganize social spaces into a living Hell.[6]

If this is the case for the relatively simpler era of industrial capitalism
in the early-to-mid-nineteenth century, how much more *monstrous*, in
terms of both its size and its alterity, has capitalism become after the
rapid and extensive expansions of the capitalist mode of production
during what Lenin called the "age of imperialism" or monopoly
capitalism or, even more so, during the post-Second World War period
of what Ernest Mandel has famously labeled "late capitalism," a moment
typified by the infiltrations for capitalist relations into the most remote
corners of the planet and throughout postmodern societies at almost
every level? In the era of globalization, that is, both the monstrosity and
the accumulation expand exponentially, and arguably the technological
transformations of the past fifty years have rendered even the sense of
the post-Bretton Woods world system of the 1970s that Mandel was
observing as being far too simplistic when compared to our own time.
The baleful necromancy of finance capital and especially financial
derivatives alone may account for whole new levels of complexity and
obscurity in any attempt to "map" the postmodern condition in which
we find ourselves in the twenty-first century.[7]

In order to keep track of these exponentially increasing moving parts of a protean and expanding system, one characterized if not known (since true knowledge of the system is itself becoming harder and harder to ascertain) by its complicated web of interrelated forces operating across continents and oceans, a sort of monstrous mapping project is required. In *The Geopolitical Aesthetic*, Fredric Jameson has elaborated upon the ways that conspiratorial texts, for all the flaw and odious association that "conspiracy theories" conjure up, may function as a sort of cognitive mapping, insofar as the imagined conspiracy is a figurative representation of a system unknowable through everyday perceptions or mainstream depictions: "in the intent to hypothesize, in the desire called cognitive mapping," writes Jameson, "therein lies the beginning of wisdom."[8] The rise and spread of fantastic horror in popular culture might reveal a similarly allegorical function, establishing both the desire for some sense of clarifying overview of a largely if not wholly invisible system, and the desire to overcome that system once and for all.

Monster Theory

I hypothesize that the present fascination with the monstrous in literature, film, and popular culture as a whole is a sign of the unfulfilled desire to map this monstrous system. Monstrosity, horror, and dystopia provide thematic forms or even genres by which the vast system may be made visible or conceived, but of course the image or conception itself relies on a broadly allegorical framework that can enable us grasp in the figures or tropes a more basic notion of the global ensembles of capitalist political, economic, and social relations. What is more, the narratives themselves, equipped with compelling characters and plots, help to mobilize and enact ways of seeing and experiencing the systems in question. The monsters encountered along the way function as part of this semantic universe, thereby making possible those moments of transcoding (even at an unconscious level) of the figurative and the "real" world.

To put it in a potentially oversimplified statement, monsters help us to make sense of our world. In *Skin Shows: Gothic Horror and the Technology of Monsters* (1995), Jack Halberstam asserted that "Monsters are meaning machines," and Halberstam went on to explain that an entity functions as a monster "when it is able to condense as many fear-producing traits in one body as possible into one body."⁹ By engaging with monsters and the monstrous, Halberstam suggests, we participate in a process that defines the contours of our own experiences and understanding of the world, mapping the social spaces while also navigating our way through them.

The monstrous appears as a warning, imbued semiotically with all many of taboos and proscriptions, while also interceding directly into our midst. As later "Monster Theory" will note, cultural relations to or with monsters speak to societal fears, and as monsters develop, their visibility and functions may change as well. Jeffrey Jerome Cohen famously developed seven theses with respect to what he called "Monster Culture." These theses do not so much define what monsters are as they help to situate the monstrous within the larger space of a culture, showing how monsters help us to shape, maneuver within, and make sense of our societies and cultures.

Cohen's seven theses can be briefly summarized and explained in his own words, but it may be useful to list the theses themselves first.

Thesis I. The Monster's Body Is a Cultural Body;
Thesis II. The Monster Always Escapes;
Thesis III. The Monster Is the Harbinger of Category Crisis;
Thesis IV. The Monster Dwells at the Gates of Difference;
Thesis V. The Monster Polices the Borders of the Possible;
Thesis VI. Fear of the Monster Is Really a Kind of Desire; and
Thesis VII. The Monster Stands at the Threshold ... of Becoming.¹⁰

As Cohen elaborates, "The Monster's Body Is a Cultural Body" in that "[t]he monster's body quite literally incorporates fear, desire, anxiety, and fantasy (ataractic or incendiary), giving them life and an uncanny independence" (4). In this way, the monster's very corporeality figures forth the broader social issues of which the monstrous body may then serve as the site of so many symptoms. Often this may be seen as marks on the monster's body, which themselves become signs, or that the bodies themselves are signs, as with figures of bestiality (e.g., werewolves), decay (zombies), and so forth.

Continuing his exploration of these theses, Cohen notes that the recurrence or resurrection of monsters after this or that apparent victory over them testifies to this allegorical significance, as the underlying anxieties represented by the monster cannot be so easily vanquished. And, in Cohen's words, "[t]he monster always escapes because it refuses easy categorization. [...] Full of rebuke to traditional method of organizing knowledge and human experience, the geography of the monster is an imperiling expanse, and therefore always a contested space" (6–7). Unsurprisingly, the monstrous is experienced as a form of radical alterity, an otherness that threatens to destroy identities and familiarities by its very presences. Moreover, as Cohen points out, "[b]y revealing that difference is arbitrary and potentially free-floating, mutable rather than essential, the monster threatens to destroy not just individual members of a society, but the very cultural apparatus through which individuality is constituted and allowed" (12). Along these lines, then, the examples connected to Thesis V show how "[t]he monster prevents mobility (intellectual, geographical, or sexual), delimiting the social spaces through which private bodies may move. [...] The monster of prohibition exists to demarcate the bonds that hold together that system of relations we call culture, to draw horrid attention to that cannot—*must* not—be crossed" (12–13). This observation, in turn, suggests the ways in which fear and desire are so inextricably intertwined in monstrous discourse, where "fantasies of aggression, domination, and inversion are allowed safe expression in a clearly delimited and permanently liminal space" (17).

Cohen concludes this discussion by observing that "Monsters are our children" (20), a nod toward Frankenstein's Creature among many other such beings. This weird intimacy combined with a radical alterity enables monsters to help us understand and speculate upon our own world in new ways. As Cohen puts it, monsters "bring not just a fuller knowledge of our place in history and the history of knowing our place, but they bear self-knowledge, *human* knowledge—and a discourse all the more sacred as it arises from the Outside. The monsters ask us how we perceive the world, and how we have misrepresented what we have attempted to place" (20). As such, we might add, monsters are fundamentally ideological, which is also to say, at the same time, that monsters are fundamental to ideology critique. That is, they can serve to illuminate the contours of the social sphere *as it is* precisely by providing the perspective of *estrangement*, but this otherworldly point of view necessarily estranges the images it depicts, a process that in turn inevitably conjures into being radically alternative ways of seeing. In this sense, monsters can help to evoke new spaces of liberty, "the scandal of qualitative difference," as Herbert Marcuse once put it in reference to utopian thinking,[11] even as they haunt us as we travel though this vale of tears.

Space does not allow for any extensive discussion of trends within popular culture, but it seems that the enduring, and perhaps expanding, popularity of horror as a literary and cinematic genre is itself a sign of the times. The presence of monsters, and of horror more generally, offers a figural representation of the world which reveals the unreality of the so-called "real world." In this sense, the monstrosity explored in horror literature is a form of ideology critique, as Miéville has suggested in his discussion of radical fantasy.[12] That is, the world as seen through realism is itself unreal, inasmuch as it masks the underlying "truth" in its very surface-level realism. In other words, in a world where reality is itself unreal, the non-realism of fantasy may offer the means to get at these hidden or difficult to discern truths. Similarly, with horror, these hidden realities may be rendered visible through fear, combined with the imaginative process of projecting new models for understanding that allow one to overcome the fear. The horror in the text helps to engender a political or historical sensibility, in which the pervasive feeling of generalize fear may crystallize into a more concrete sense of the overarching systems or underlying realities.

One Monster after Another: *An Exemplary Reading*

I would like to use as an example a much loved (by me, at least) little volume for children, Mercer Mayer's 1974 picture-book, *One Monster After Another*.[13] With more than 300 children's books to his name, Mayer is a prolific author and illustrator who has perhaps become most famous for his *Little Critter* and *Little Monster* series, and his distinctively drawn critters or monsters are at once disarmingly cute and altogether weird. *One Monster After Another* appeared before Mayer began these series, so it does not technically belong to either, but the world he creates and depicts in this book is much like that seen in many of his other works. But, as I will argue below, for all the ostensible simplicity and good-natured fun represented by *One Monster After Another*, there is also a figural representation of a scarcely visible world system whose shape is made somewhat discernible through the presence of Mayer's delightfully weird monsters and their activities. In reading about their behavior in this little book, I assert, we may be able to limn a more complex world in which we find ourselves situated and in which we ourselves must operate.

The story is, unsurprisingly, quite simple. On account of the relative obscurity of the text, which some readers may have difficultly laying their hands on, it seems worthwhile to provide a relatively detailed summary. Given the book's modest length, this summary will brief.

Alas, no amount of description or skill in *ekphrasis* can fully do justice to the amusingly strange drawings of the creatures and the world they inhabit, so I encourage readers to seek out copies of *One Monster After Another* or, failing that, to search online for images from the text. As with any picture book, the illustrations are not merely supplementary to the text, but very much part of the substance of the work as a whole, and in this case, the fine detail of even the background or marginal images makes the illustrations well worth studying in greater detail. In any case, no summary can hope to approximate the full power and enjoyment to be found in the original.

One Monster After Another opens with the following lines: "One day Sally Ann wrote a letter to her best friend Lucy Jane. She put it in an envelope and put the envelope into her mailbox." The accompanying illustration shows Sally Ann, on tiptoes, placing her envelope in the mailbox as a bizarre-looking furry creature with pointy ears, prominent tusks, a top hat (!), and a satchel labeled "My Stamps" peers at her from behind a tree. The remainder of the narrative follows the surprising trajectory of this letter as it makes its circuitous way to the intended recipient. As the title suggests, the letter's movements will be influenced by one monster after another, and so they are. Here is a brief summary of the key events in the plot after that opening page, with the names of the particular "monsters" highlighted:

1. Before the mailman arrives to take the letter, a *Stamp-Collecting Trollusk* steals the envelope, and "gabble[s] away with a smirk on his snerk." (The Trollusk was, of course, the furry creature spying on Sally Ann in the first scene of the book.)

2. Before he can rip off the stamp and add it to his collection, a *Letter-Eating Bombanat*, which looks a bit like a cross between a dinosaur, a bat, and a possum, but also wearing a helicopter-beanie and a necktie, swoops down "out of Nowhere"—a sign on a nearby tree indicates "To Nowhere," as if to clarify where this monster came from, while another sign beneath it and pointing the other way reads "and Back Again"—to snatch the envelope from the Trollusk, and then it flies off.

3. But soon, while flying over the *Blue Ocean of Bubbly Goo*, it is snatched by the tentacle of a *Bombanat-Munching Grumley*, an immense anthropomorphic, bespectacled, crustacean-like octopus creature, heaving above the waves. (I highlight the ocean as a "monster" for it seems to serve as such, while also being filled with other creatures.)

4. Before the Grumley can enjoy his freshly caught lunch, it is snagged in a large net and hauled aboard a fishing boat, along with a load of other fish. (The fishermen, presumably, are not monsters. They are merely humans plying their trade.)

5. Moments later, before the boat can reach land, it is struck by a *Furious-Floating Ice-Ferg*, an apparently sentient iceberg Hell-bent on wrecking watercraft.

6. As the vessel begins to sink, the fishing-boat's captain stuffs the letter—remember the letter, which is the true protagonist of this tale?—along with an S.O.S. note, into a bottle and tosses it into the sea.

7. At that point, a *Wild-'n-Windy Typhoonigator*, a sort of monstrous cloud-system with anteater-like "facial" features, sucks up the whole Blue Ocean of Bubbly Goo, along with its contents (including fish, fishermen, paddles, boats, the bottle, the Grumley, and so forth), and blows itself away into the distance.

8. Utterly full, "so full of fishing boats, bottles, and bubbly goo," the Typhoonigator eventually had to disgorge all this stuff, which it does; so, amid everything else in the deluge, down rains the bottle ("KER-PLOP") onto the head of a *Paper-Munching Yalapappus*, a large mammal with fearsome-looking fangs wearing a bib festooned with an image of a knife and fork. "The bottle broke, tinkle-plinkle, and out fell the Captain's note and the letter."

9. The pleasantly surprised Yalapappus quickly consumes the Captain's note, but before he could munch the letter, none other than the Stamp-Collecting Trollusk, "who just happened to be passing by, snatched the letter in his snerk and ran away."

10. The outraged Yalapappus gives chase, and suddenly, the Letter-Eating Bombanat reappears from the sky to snap up the letter once more, only to be captured almost immediately in a large butterfly net by a *Bombanat-Collecting Grithix*, who vaguely resembles a rhinoceros dressed in purple overalls with a bowtie, while the Yalapappus and Trollusk look on in dismay. (The distinctive head of a dodo can be seen observing these events from behind a tree.)

11. "The Grithix, as everybody knows, is a Bombanat collector, not a letter collector." Thus the three other exasperated monsters—the Stamp-Collecting Trollusk, the Paper-Munching Yalapappus, and the captive Letter-Eating Bombanat, lodged firmly under the Grithix's arm—are forced to watch helplessly as the Grithix calmly places the letter in a nearby "official-looking mailbox."

12. Before the box can be stolen—we see the Trollusk and the Yalapappus attempting to carry the mailbox away—an "official mailman" on an "official-looking motorcycle" arrives to stop the would-be thieves.

13. The mailman dutifully opens the mailbox, takes out the letters, and continues on his route, as the monsters gesticulate and wail in varying degrees of outrage. Several textless pages follow with illustrations indicating the letter's continuing journey, as the Trollusk and Yalapappus chase after the mailman, whose motorcycle is visible in the distance.

14. The mailman then delivers the letter to its designated address, as Lucy Jane waves to him from her window, while the monsters— the Yalapappus holds his index finger to his lips, admonishing the Trollusk to be silent—spy on them from the corner of the house.

15. The girl retrieves the letter from her mailbox, opens it, and reads it, oblivious to the monsters lurking at the edge of her home. The missive, the complete contents of which I quote below, is in part an invitation to visit Sally Ann.

16. The final scene shows Lucy Jane, suitcase in one hand and purse (with a familiar-looking envelope protruding from it) in the other, briskly walking down the road as the expectant monsters leer at her from the verge.

So the basic plot of *One Monster After Another* involves the simple act of mailing a letter to one's friend, but in following the letter's movements, a fantastic or otherworldly series of events disclose a vast world apparently unknown to or unseen by the letter-writer and its recipient. As one can see from this adventure, even the most quotidian activity—in this case, mailing a letter to a friend—is bound up in a larger, complex, and dynamic system of biological, social, economic, ecological, and even political relations. Once the letter leaves the writer's hands, it becomes part of this wildly chaotic, incomprehensible aggregation of monstrous activities.

Parenthetically, one might add that the strangeness of all this might be compounded by the relative eccentricity of writing handwritten letters and using "snail mail" in the twenty-first century. It is likely that few young people today still write personal letters such as Sally Ann's, opting instead to send email, text messages, Facebook posts, Snapchat photos, or any number of other means of communication. Had Mayer written a similar story using the media technology available to our own era's Sally Anns and Lucy Janes, presumably the story and its monsters would be very different indeed. But if the monsters involved in the adventures of this letter could be said to represent unseen forces in a broader world system, as I suggest, then how much *more* unclear, complicated, and alienating is a system of relations bound up in a web of global telecommunications and multinational corporate structures? If mysteries abounded concerning the goings-on between the moment we place a physical letter in a mailbox and the instant it is delivered to its addressee, then how much greater the questions and confusions surrounding simple electronic communications, with their reliance on software, servers, databases, "clouds," and so on? (I mention this with due apologies to those experts in both the postal services and email, but the largely unseen character of the systems involved remain pertinent to this discussion, and the "monsters" to be encountered in those largely unseen domains likely remain strange, menacing, and fascinating.) The conditions for the possibility of texting a friend today would undoubtedly appear all the more monstrous than the infrastructure of yesteryear's postal fantasies.

Mayer's *One Monster After Another* concludes with a bit of a joke, or perhaps we could say that, in retrospect, the entire narrative may be seen as the extensive set-up to the joke. The punch line, if it may be so called, is delivered through, and takes the form of, the contents of Sally Ann's letter. On the next to last page of the book, we see a picture of Lucy Jane reading the letter, with the Stamp-Collecting Trollusk and the Paper-Munching Yalapappus peering at her from the corner of her house, and on the verso page we see the handwritten document itself, which reads:

> Dear Lucy Jane,
>> Nothing exciting ever happens around here. Please come and visit.
>> Your best friend,
>>> Sally Ann

Lucy Jane apparently takes Sally Ann up on this offer, for the book ends with an image of her setting forth on her own journey. If the delivery of the letter to Lucy Jane's house is the climax of the narrative, the reading of the letter functions as a denouement. Then, as a sort of *coda*, the illustration on final two pages of *One Monster After Another* depicts Lucy Jane, now in a coat and hat and carrying a suitcase along with a purse from which protrudes the envelope that featured so prominently in this tale, walking down the lane, as our two monsters gaze at her covetously from behind a tree. Punctuating the tale of a remarkably exciting journey, albeit a journey undertaken by a letter rather than by a traditional hero, the letter's actual contents are ironic. Sally Ann's sense that "nothing exciting ever happens" is made possible by her ignorance of the great chain of monstrous being which apparently coincides with the all-too-normal, even boring, world as she experiences it.

Nowhere and Back Again

The punch line-like ending to *One Monster After Another* also hints at a potential "truth," which is that behind the apparently everyday, dull, and tedious processes of social or even biological existence lies an extraordinarily complex, unknown, and perhaps unimaginable system. A feature of our own time is the persistent sense of boredom, even with the cacophonous, kaleidoscopic pandemonium of entertainments and pastimes swirling about many of us at all times. (Or, perhaps, especially so.) As Jameson points out in the opening of his "Totality as Conspiracy,"

> [i]n the widespread paralysis of the collective or social imaginary, to which "nothing occurs" (Karl Kraus) when confronted with the ambitious program of fantasizing an economic system of the scale of the globe itself, the older motif of conspiracy knows a fresh lease on life, as a narrative structure capable of reuniting the minimal basic components: a potentially infinite network, along with a plausible explanation of its invisibility; or in other words: the collective and the epistemological.[14]

In *One Monster After Another*, there is no conspiracy (unless one deem the apparent cooperation between the Trollusk and the Yalapappus to amount to a full-blown "scheme"), but there is a largely hidden, teratological system that coincides with both the ecosystems of the natural world (as we see plenty on non-monstrous animals and plants along the way) and the modern, social systems (in the forms of postal services, commercial activities, and so on). The "adventure" that Sally Ann's letter experiences discloses a system of monsters within or alongside these other systems, which are themselves likely too vast and complex to effectively "map," even as they are also taken for granted at all times.

From the perspective of Sally Ann and Lucy Jane, the transit of the envelope from the writer's home to the recipient's may have well been a simple matter of postal delivery, yet that system is itself vast and, in most cases, not really thought about by those who use it. As with so many such things, it is only when the processes break down, when mail is lost or late or otherwise expelled from the "normal," that we tend to notice, but even in those situations, the extent of the networks involved are probably unknown or underestimated. Both the vastness and the relative invisibility of the intricate network make it a perfect subject for conspiracy theories, as can be seen in Thomas Pynchon's *The Crying of Lot 49* (1966), for example, which makes much of the conspiratorial and labyrinthine world of the mails.[15] The presence of monsters throughout the fabulously interlinked system of adventitious occurrences and happenstance in *One Monster After Another* only helps to underscore, in a cute and humorous way, in this case, the inscrutability of these larger networks and their functioning.

In fact, even without the named monsters in *One Monster After Another*, there are already hints of a strangely tenebrous and sketchy system connecting "Nowhere" and "Back Again," as a pair of road signs indicate in naming certain regions of the tale's fictional geography. For instance, my plot summary left out descriptions of the many other persons, critters (as Mayer will famously call them), and sights that appear in the book. These include a variety on human onlookers, including a postal worker, a birdwatcher, a child dressed as a cowboy, a motorist, picnickers, and various heads poking out of windows. A number of "normal" animals—geese, dogs, rabbits, squirrels, seals, fish, an alligator, and so on—supplement the more monstrous creatures that populate the scenery, and the presence of a dodo, which ought to have been long extinct, suggests a weird crossover between real-world and otherworldly monsters. Diverse structures and businesses appear in the world between Sally Ann's house and Lucy Jane's home, each of which is presumably located in a strictly residential area, but as we follow the letter's bizarre itinerary, we see a windmill, a pizzeria, a hamburger stand, an auto mechanic's garage, a country store, and a gas station, this latter with a sign advertising "Free 150 lb. alligator with each 10 gallons of gas," while another reads "We accept all credit cards." (The national and later global system of banking and finance barely signaled in this referred to credit cards, nestled alongside the ever-so-local "deal" for a free alligator, might be seen as an allusion to that vaster international network of money and power later associated with the term *globalization*, which takes the "monstrous accumulation" of commodities as analyzed by Marx to its planetary limit and frame of reference.) Mayer manages to depict so many things in this otherwise apparently simple little book, everything *including* a kitchen sink, one of which may be seen floating in the Blue Ocean of Bubbly Goo, that one might argue that the author intended to establish an entire world or world-system in which all these instances take place. But regardless of authorial intent, in the relatively limited space between the homes of Sally Ann and Lucy Jane, an entire world system unfolds itself.[16]

This system is made entertaining, if not also intelligible, by the presence, appearance, character, and activities of the various monsters in *One Monster After Another*. Cute as they may be, the monsters themselves register aspects of the human, all-too-human condition, as their needs and desires mirror those of the people. The Stamp-Collecting Trollusk and the Bombanat-Collecting Grithix, presumably, are motivated by mere enthusiasms, devoted as they are to the hobby of collecting, whereas other monsters are likely driven by more pressing biological impulses, such as the need to eat, whether one's preferred food is paper or Bombanats. Along the way, even ecological or environmental forces, as with the Ice-Ferg and the Typhoonigator, become legible reminders of the power of the natural world, which may or may not be at odds with economic endeavors (such as commercial fishing) or political institutions (such as "official-looking" postal services). As an aside, we might today ask whether Typhoonigators have become more common or more damaging as an effect of global warming, just as we might wonder about the environmental health of the Blue Ocean of Bubbly Goo, the sustainability of commercial fishing, and the budgets for social services. That so many of these events, related in rapid sequence, disclose the existence of such a perilous, dog-eat-dog social and natural order, is significant. This ultimately plays up at one and the same time both the dangers of this system and the largely unavoidable, random, or chance nature of those dangers. Throughout all of this, the monsters give color and shape to a system beyond the view, if not beyond the ken, of the Sally Anns and Lucy Janes—and all of the rest of us, of course—who dwell at the Edge of Nowhere and for whom nothing much exciting ever happens. The monsters, one could say, give meaning to a system that not only evades interpretation, but at most times evades notice entirely. Invisible forces are at work everywhere, and the study of such unseen monsters may disclose the mechanisms and processes by which they, and in turn by which our own lives, operate and are mutually affected.

Conclusion: Standing with the Monstrous

I suppose I have been having a bit of fun with a fondly remembered children's book from my own youth, but the overall point about the way in which monsters, along with fantasy and horror more generally, help to give form to a world system that is often untheorized and taken for granted remains. In this, I draw upon some of the critical theory associated now with monsters, from Franco Moretti's well-known essay on the "Dialectic of Fear," which identifies in the figures of Frankenstein's creature and Dracula (or, perhaps, the zombie and the vampire) the terror at the heart of "bourgeois civilization," through Cohen's famous seven theses on "Monster Culture" discussed above, and on to recent approaches to posthumanist or simply posthuman monstrosity, the end-of-the-world narratives that seem to have audiences cheering for the monsters, even if that means eliminating the human race entirely (as I discuss in Chapter 7). The explosion of critical and scholarly work on these and related themes is a testament to their timeliness, and what all of these studies point to is an enhanced concern with the monstrous accumulation that typifies the present social and cultural moment.[17]

If monsters have always been around, then it is also true that they have also meant different things at different times and places. In the present configuration, it seems, monsters are enabling new ways of imagining the world, as the sorts of unseen forces the shape the biosphere and the social strata demand some form of recognition. For instance, the essential features of a capitalist mode of production and its ramifications are rarely immediately apparent. As McNally puts it, "critical theory sets out to see the unseen, to chart the cartography of the invisible," and in his *Monsters of the Market*, that critical theory emerges in the context of a study of society's monsters.[18] Specifically, monsters aid the narrative in embodying a figural representation of the abstract and lived space of the world that reveals the unreality of the so-called "real world." That is, the world as seen through traditional forms of realism is itself unreal, inasmuch as it masks the underlying "truth" in its very surface-level attention to the actually existing state of things as they appear under the sun. In other words, in a world where reality is itself unreal, the non-realism of fantasy may offer the means to get at these hidden truths, what McNally refers to as the *"fantastically real."*[19]

There is also the fundamentally critical role that monsters have played in different cultures as various times. In some cases, of course, this means taking the side of or "standing with" the monstrous, athwart the powers of the "normal" that would seek to expel or incorporate the monster's own inexorable alterity. In his "Halloween and Marxism" talk, Miéville says that "once we start standing with the monstrous, then we're standing with monsters and monstrous-made figures throughout literature and history, because the disavowed throughout history, starting with Grendel being kicked out of Hrothgar's Hall in *Beowulf*, have always had the sneaking sympathy of those suspicious of power."[20] Teratology, in this context, can be a way of piercing the veil, exposing the apparent reality as so much false consciousness, and evoking potential alternatives. It becomes a form of ideology critique, which is perhaps another way of imagining cognitive mapping. Rather than haunting the fringes of our world, these monsters may prove to be central to its functioning. And, along those same lines, the apprehension of these monsters may prove essential for imagining other worlds.

Notes

1 Jonathan Krell, "Monster and Victim: Melusine from the Fourteenth Century to the Age of *Homo Detritus*," in *The Metaphor of the Monster: Interdisciplinary Approaches to Understanding the Monstrous Other in Literature*, ed. Keith Moser and Karina Zelaya (New York: Bloomsbury, 2020), 53.

2 Michel Foucault, *History of Madness*, trans. Jonathan Murphy and Jean Khalfa (London: Routledge, 2009), 145.

3 See Guy Debord, *The Society of the Spectacle*, trans. Ken Knabb (London: Rebel Press, 1983).

4 See, for example, Franco Moretti, "Dialectic of Fear," in *Signs Taken for Wonders: On the Sociology of Literary Forms* (London: Verso, 1983), 83–108.

5 José B. Monléon, *A Specter Is Haunting Europe: A Sociohistorical Approach to the Fantastic* (Princeton: Princeton University Press, 1990), 139.

6 As Fredric Jameson has put it, reflecting on Marx's analyses in *Capital*, "[c]apitalism is thus what is sometimes called an infernal machine, a perpetuum mobile or unnatural miracle, whose strengths turn out to be what is most intolerable about it." See Jameson, *Representing Capital: A Reading of Volume One* (London: Verso, 2012), 146.

7 See, for example, the discussion of financial derivatives in my *Utopia in the Age of Globalization: Space, Narrative, and the World System* (New York: Palgrave Macmillan, 2013), 66–93.

8 Jameson, "Totality as Conspiracy," in *The Geopolitical Aesthetic: Space and Cinema in the World System* (London and Bloomington: The British Film Institute and Indiana University Press, 1992), 3.

9 Judith [Jack] Halberstam, *Skin Shows: Gothic Horror and the Technology of Monsters* (Durham: Duke University Press, 1995), 21.

10 Jeffrey Jerome Cohen, "Monster Culture (Seven Theses)," in *Monster Theory: Reading Culture*, ed. Jeffrey Jerome Cohen (Minneapolis: University of Minnesota Press, 1996), 4, 6, 7, 12, 16, 20, ellipsis in the original. Page numbers in this and the next three paragraphs refer to this article.

11 Herbert Marcuse, "The End of Utopia," in *Five Lectures: Psychoanalysis, Politics, and Utopia*, trans. J. Shapiro and S. Weber (Boston: Beacon Press, 1970), 69.

12 See China Miéville, "Marxism and Fantasy: Editorial Introduction," *Historical Materialism* 10.4 (2002): 39–49.

13 Mercer Mayer, *One Monster After Another*, reprint ed. (Roxbury, CT: Rainbird Press, 1993 [1974]). The pages are unnumbered.

14 Jameson, "Totality as Conspiracy," 9.

15 Thomas Pynchon, *The Crying of Lot 49* (New York: Harper and Row, 1966).

16 Note that all this activity, within the text and outside of it, is not rooted in any ethical program designed to teach the reader a moral lesson. The point of the monsters is not to scare the reader into behaving a certain way, but to create figurative means of understanding the world we live in.

17 For a good overview and selection of recent work, See Jeffrey Andrew Weinstock, ed., *The Monster Theory Reader* (Minneapolis: University of Minnesota Press, 2020). Weinstock's "Introduction: A Genealogy of Monster Theory," is particularly illuminating.

18 McNally, *Monsters of the Market*, 6.

19 Ibid., 7.

20 Miéville, "Marxism and Halloween—Socialism 2013," *YouTube*, uploaded by We Are Many Media, October 30, 3013: https://www.youtube.com/watch?v=paCqiY1jwqc.

Chapter 7

THE END-OF-THE-WORLD AS WORLD SYSTEM

In a scene from a 2015 episode of *The Simpsons*, Homer and Grampa Simpson are sitting in a movie theater, watching a preview in which the voice-over announcer intones portentously, "In a dystopian future … " Without any note of the sarcasm that viewers will supply for themselves, Homer interrupts by saying,

> Finally! A movie about a dystopian future, unlike *The Hunger Games*, *Edge of Tomorrow*, *Oblivion*, *Elysium*, *Snow Piercer*, *The Hunger Games: Catching Fire*, *X-Men: Days of Future Past*, *Enders Game …* *The Road*, *World War Z*, *Children of Men*, *After Earth*, *I Am Legend*, *Mad Max: Fury Road*, *The Maze Runner*, *District Nine*, *The Purge*, *Looper*, *Cloud Atlas*, *Divergent*, *Insurgent*, *The Island*, *Mr. Burns*, *A Post-Electric Play*, and *Chappie*.[1]

As he completes his list—the ellipsis indicates a fade out and fade in, during which indeterminate period of time it is understood that Homer had been continuing to name film titles—a theater employee informs them that the movie they had come to see ended twenty minutes ago. As is also indicated by the now-empty bucket of popcorn on his lap, Homer had been listing dystopian-themed films for some two hours or more. The joke is clear, that films featuring a dystopian future are hardly rare at all these days. In fact, the attentive and knowledgeable viewer would notice that Homer's list includes only films released in the previous ten years. The oldest movie listed, *The Island*, came out in 2005; moreover, eighteen of the twenty-four films named had appeared only during the previous three years. As usual, the satirical wit of *The Simpsons* writers underscores a truth widely recognized: in this case, that a "dystopian future" might be said to be the dominant theme in contemporary popular culture, as evidenced by the Hollywood film industry and its increasingly global audiences.

Imagining the Ending

The dominance of dystopia in popular culture calls to mind famous remark, variously attributed to Fredric Jameson or Slavoj Žižek and by now almost a cliché, about how it is easier to imagine the end of the world than to imagine the end of capitalism. The phrase has become commonplace, and the question of attribution a sort of inside joke. Mark Fisher uses this line as the opening sentence of his *Capitalist Realism* (2009), citing both Jameson and Žižek.[2] In a 2003 essay later included in his revised and expanded collection, *The Ideologies of Theory* (2008), Jameson himself reiterated the claim but introduced it with the wry, indefinite "Someone once said" formulation: "Someone once said that it is easier to imagine the end of the world than to imagine the end of capitalism."[3] Jameson's original formulation, whose slight difference might be said to make all the difference (but I shall return to that later), comes from *The Seeds of Time* (1994): "It seems to be easier for us today to imagine the thoroughgoing deterioration of the earth and of nature than the breakdown of late capitalism; perhaps that is due to some weakness in our imagination."[4]

Meanwhile, Žižek's "original" version of the saying actually quotes Jameson—how this is lost on the many subsequent citers of the formula remains a mystery, but then so many things are attributed to Žižek, after all—in the context of discussing the persistence of ideology in the supposedly post-ideological age we now remember as the early 1990s. As Žižek writes,

> [u]p to a decade or two ago, the system of production-nature (man's productive-exploitative relationship with nature and its resources) was perceived as a constant, whereas everybody was busy imagining different forms of the social organization of production and commerce (Fascism and Communism as alternatives to liberal capitalism); today, as Fredric Jameson has perspicaciously remarked, nobody seriously considers possible alternatives to capitalism any longer, whereas popular imagination is persecuted by visions of the forthcoming "breakdown in nature," of the stoppage of all life on earth—it seems easier to imagine the "end of the world" than a far more modest change in the mode of production, as if liberal capitalism is the "real" that will somehow survive even under conditions of global ecological catastrophe.[5]

It is noteworthy that both Jameson and Žižek place emphasis on the power of the imagination. For all the catchiness of the phrases "end of the world" and "end of capitalism," at issue in this familiar observation is whether and how well we are capable of imagining alternatives to the *status quo* in which we find ourselves at present. As Sean Grattan has observed, "[t]hat the phrase circulates as a somehow unattributable truism says a lot about what kinds of futures might remain unthinkable after the much heralded end of history."[6]

This paradox of the enervated imagination involves a related problem, specifically the crisis of representation implicit in any attempt to give meaningful form to the social totality in the present.[7] The planetary scale alone, as numerous critics have observed, presents almost inconceivably complex and vast networks in which the perceiving subject is wholly entangled.[8] That is to say, the reason we suddenly find it so easy to imagine the "end of the world" and so difficult to imagine the end of our now global, socio-economic system is because the spatio-political figures previously used to stand in for our sense of place or our frame of reference—local, regional, national, or even continental geopolitical zones—no longer function as effectively in our efforts to map the world system in an era of globalization. The system that Jürgen Habermas has referred to as the *postnational constellation* requires a different order of representational techniques and methods, and the fantastic, broadly conceived, makes possible meaningful artificial ensembles, figurative maps, by which to makes sense of an increasingly unimaginable, global social, economic, and cultural sphere.[9] Earlier generations could think in terms of region or nation, a luxury now reserved for the most benighted and reactionary elements of many societies, whose sheer blindness to the ways of the world today can be registered in the perplexities of transnational finance alone, never mind the thoroughly imbricated matters of production, trade, energy policies, diplomatic and military relations, ecological development and degradation, and so on. One reason that the end of the world may be easier to imagine than the end of capitalism is that the former seems more real—this is Fisher's point in using the term "capitalist realism"—partly because many of us feel that we are already experiencing an end-of-the-world in progress. For example, in his diagnosis of the contemporary experience of "living in the end times," Žižek organizes his analysis along the lines of the fabled five stages of grief (Denial, Anger, Bargaining, Depression, and Acceptance), ending on a note of a well-nigh theological politics of grace at the thought of the end.[10]

Along these lines, one could argue that the predominance of dystopian and even apocalyptic themes in contemporary popular culture reflects certain paradoxically comforting aspects of the end of the world. That is, the popularity of these mainstream apocalyptic, post-apocalyptic, and otherwise dystopian films in the twenty-first century indicates a wish-fulfillment that operates at a fairly basic level. In this chapter, I will discuss a few attributes of this desire for end-of-the-world dystopianism, sketching out a few of the ways that such cinematic visions in recent years can serve as figural representations, or ways of making sense, of a world system too vast to comprehend in otherwise meaningful ways.

As with the monsters discussed in earlier chapters, we might connect this apocalyptic desire to Jameson's earlier identification of conspiracy (and, perhaps, even more so the "conspiracy film") as a form of cognitive mapping. In *Postmodernism, or, the Cultural Logic of Late Capitalism*, Jameson noted that "conspiracy theory (and its garish narrative manifestations) must be seen as a degraded attempt—through the figuration of advanced technology—to think the impossible totality of the contemporary world system."[11] Or, as he put it elsewhere, "[c]onspiracy, one is tempted to say, is the poor person's cognitive mapping in the postmodern age; it is a degraded figure of the total logic of late capital, a desperate attempt to represent the latter's system."[12] Yet conspiracy, it might be said, is a fundamentally epistemological genre; it is all about *knowledge*. The conspiracy unmasks the false world of mere appearance to get at the truth, "what's really going on," which more often than not is being deliberately occluded or hidden as part of the very conspiracy that the conspiracy theory or narrative uncovers. Dystopia, which sometimes has that or that sort of conspiracy at its root (as when the dystopian society is formed and governed by a cabal of co-conspirators), is not fundamentally about knowledge. As a narrative form, more often dystopia shares with romance or adventure a hero's quest, if only for survival, with a return or closure that seals the plot, forming a kind of narrative totality that gives definite shape to the world depicted. Hence, dystopian narratives might be said to be less about knowing the world than making sense of it, or, to put it another way, less about *truth* and more about *meaning*.

Such end-of-the-world narratives sometimes exhibit what might be called, paradoxically, "nostalgia for the future," in which readers or viewers are invited to indulge in almost a longing spatial and social organization of imagined, often dystopian, futures. In these dystopian or post-apocalyptic scenes can be found, and *seen*, a clear order of things, complete with a fairly recognizable enemy and thus an easily identifiable hero. This reflects a desire for a simpler past, but it also reflects a longing for the future, or for a time and place where the future held promise. Contemporary dystopian, post-apocalyptic narratives register the dread associated with an unrepresentably vast, incomprehensibly dynamic world system in part by crafting allegories in which the invisible processes of globalization become discernible in a familiar, even homey image of the dystopian state. This may also help to explain why recent dystopian narratives such as *The Hunger Games* (2008) feature overly simplified economies and social divisions (e.g., all coal comes from a single district, all produce from another, etc.), complete with the very conventional if not clichéd totalitarian government with a single despot at its head. Such "monsters" are much easier to imagine and to resist, and this fact may in turn help to explain the great desire for political monsters, one who can be heroically, but relatively easily, deposed or eliminated. Ironically, to imagine oneself living in an "Orwellian society" makes more *sense* than trying to orient oneself in relation to the shifting coordinates of the social totality in the twenty-first century. (Of course, *Nineteen-Eighty-Four* itself shows how the simple monstrosity of Big Brother was a ruse all along, and that everything in that society was much more complicated.) Dystopia, in a way, becomes another form of cognitive mapping, an aesthetic and political program aimed at giving form to the inchoate, protean, neoliberal world order.

In any case, my discussion here will examine three particular aspects of recent apocalyptic or dystopian narrative in film, focusing especially on this idea of the end of the world as being more easily imagined than a transformation of the present socio-economic system. First, there is a basic organization of time into a meaningful whole that comes with "the sense of an ending" (as Frank Kermode would have it), for the positing of a terminus or period retroactively establishes a meaningful narrative that can figure forth a tentative yet meaningful representation of our own historical experience. Second, the fantasy associated with dystopian or apocalyptic narratives frequently offers the reassurance of some type of "order" behind the apparent chaos, which can then be used to make sense of the otherwise complicated global system. In many cases, the broader multinational or global context for the dystopian narrative is reduced to the level of the individual hero, or, as I will discuss below, a more assuring and discrete social unit such as the family or small community. The hero that can save his own family and establish, at a micro-economic or micro-political level, an orderly social organization thus figuratively overcomes the debilitating sense that a chaotic, random, or inscrutable array of forces lie behind our experience and perceptions. Third, relatedly, there is a reassuring simplification, as the vast, complex, and dynamic elements of society are reduced to neatly identified classes and categories. For example, in *Snowpiercer* (2013), the stark divisions of the social classes, with the "scum" toiling in the back and the elite enjoying the luxuries at the front of the train, is far too simple a way of imagining even a fantastic, post-apocalyptic society forced to constitute itself aboard a moving train rolling across a global network of railroad tracks, yet it enables an allegorical representation of class conflict that undoubtedly exists, but remains hidden, in our own world system.[13] What almost certainly ought to be ridiculed as oversimplification may ultimately turn out to be one of the unforeseen political strengths of such dystopian narratives.

This simpler system evokes another potentially desirable outcome, ironically, where the heroic survival by the protagonists offers the utopian vision of a potentially classless society. That is, if the classes can be so distinctively recognizable that the defeat of one by another can be accomplished by taking over a train car, then one can more easily envision a classless society or an approximation of one. Indeed, in the last few years, certain dystopian films and television shows have imagined such a world coming into fruition through the elimination of humans entirely. In a perverse but effective way, the end of humanity itself—or what had perhaps been the ultimate apocalyptic or dystopian theme—becomes an unexpectedly utopian vision. The imagination of a posthuman world points to ways that the all-too-human order of the geopolitical system can be rethought, which opens up the possibility for a politically liberatory critical imagination.

The Consolations of the Apocalypse

The persistence of eschatological thought across diverse cultures and throughout human history suggests a deep-seated desire if not need for definitive terminal point. As Kermode so brilliantly analyzed it in *The Sense of an Ending*, the human obsession with "the End" is a function of our irremediably middling state. "Men, like poets, rush 'into the middest,' *in medias res*, when they are born; they also die *in mediis rebus*, and to make sense of their span they need fictive concords with origins and ends, such as give meaning to lives and to poems. The End they imagine will reflect their irreducibly intermediary preoccupations."[14] In studying the ways that apocalyptic visions relate to fiction, and in particular to the ways that humans make sense of their world (hence, the double-meaning of the book's title), Kermode necessarily understands a certain kind of apocalyptic imagination as universal, and imaginary ends-of-the-world can be found across human cultures and epochs. Nevertheless, Kermode also notes that "there is a powerful eschatological element in modern thought," and he finds that the twentieth century—from its *fin-de-siècle* harbingers of a world transformed and its modernist sensibilities to the millenarianism attendant to the dawn of the twenty-first century—has been especially typified by a sense of crisis. "The moments we call crises are ends and beginnings," Kermode observes. "We are ready, therefore, to accept all manner of evidence that ours is a genuine end, a genuine beginning."[15]

The apocalypticism undergirding the present sense of social and environmental malaise thus has an almost comforting aspect of "making sense," for the organization of our time—the lifetime of an individual subject or the more expansive temporal constructs of an era, epoch, or age, whether social or geological (or both, as with the Anthropocene, for instance)—into a more straightforwardly cognizable plot, with a distinctive beginning, middle, and end, satisfies a basic "desire for narrative," as Jameson has called it, referring to "the impossible attempt to give representation to the multiple and incommensurable temporalities in which each of us exists."[16] Periodization, which requires the identification of discrete beginnings and ends within a grander historical register, or, to put it in spatial terms, which requires the formation of a meaningful segment along a more extensive timeline, itself becomes an important sense-making practice, a "fictive concord" with origins and ends. To put it another way, this time in terms of grammar and usage, the meaningful linguistic unit we think of as a sentence can only be fully meaningful once it has reached the full stop, otherwise known as the *period*, which functions so as to seal the sentence off from whatever follows (thus establishing the end of that sentence's temporal period) and retroactively to establish the significance of what comes before by delineating a boundary. This obviously does not work in the same way for interrogatory sentences and their question marks, among other forms, but the period satisfies a kind of desire even at the level of the page.

As Jameson has also pointed out, "the end of the world may simply be the cover for a very different and more properly Utopian wish-fulfilment," noting the relatively common post-apocalyptic scenario in which "the protagonist and a small band of other survivors of the catastrophe go on to found some smaller and more livable collectivity after the end of modernity and capitalism."[17] In this way, at a figural or allegorical level in the apparently dystopian text, the matter of it being easier to imagine the end of the world than the end of capitalism is neatly resolved in the same fundamental gesture. That is, *thanks* to the end of the world, we can forge a life after capitalism that in many respects fulfills the utopian impulse we had thought we had lost. Speaking of a work by J. G. Ballard, Jameson refers to its "immense eschatological *jouissance*," which is as nice a phrase as any for naming the sheer "fun" associated with the apocalyptic or post-apocalyptic fiction in the twenty-first century, and which in turn may help to explain the tremendous popularity of such works of art in our time.

This is all merely to say that the apocalyptic impulse has as a certain libidinal investment that helps to account for its power and appeal. For true believers, naturally, the end of the world as set forth in whatever religious vision becomes the culmination of not only history but also a life's work. To cite a rather irreverent example, *This is the End* (2013), directed by Seth Rogan and Evan Goldberg, combined the absurd buddy comedy or "bromance" with a Book of Revelations-inspired rapture and apocalypse, in which the main characters find themselves "left behind," presumably owing to their general sinfulness, which is quickly revealed to be primarily just egotism and arrogance.[18] Through acts of self-sacrifice, the principal characters are saved, and the movie ends with an elaborate (and nostalgic) dance party in heaven. This happy ending is actually par for the course in many recent apocalyptic films, as the hero or heroes not only survive the cataclysms, but are somehow also redeemed. For the elect, at least, the end of the world turns out to be good news.[19]

The Allure of the Natural Disaster

Global warming and the new ice age have proven to be evocative themes in what could be considered the subgenre of the environmental apocalypse. As the opening lines of a famous poem by Robert Frost would have it, "Some say the world will end in fire,/ Some say in ice,"[20] and the cinematic apocalypses of recent years have had their share of both, with specular visions of volcanic eruptions and solar flares counterposed to the well-nigh instantaneous freezing of the planet as a result of rapid climate change or nuclear winters. In *Snowpiercer* (2013), the global freeze resulting in a new "Snowball Earth" was caused by human efforts to counteract global warming through technology, so this dystopian narrative effectively squares the circles of intolerable heat and disastrous cold.

The idea of a natural or even supernatural end of the world may be appealing, inasmuch as it displaces the moralizing, blame, and guilt that sometimes accompany many dystopian visions. While it is true that many apocalyptic scenarios today do serve as critiques of and warnings about past and present social or political policies, particularly in the context of climate change, they tend not to have the same sort of bad guys to personally blame for the problem. Mankind itself is somehow to blame, even if there is usually a straw-man villain (e.g., someone speaking in favor of the bad policies) to root against. Man-made climate changes may be making *sharknadoes* more and more likely, but films featuring apocalyptic "natural" disasters are better able to spread the blame, while also depicting heroes to cheer for.

Dystopias brought about by man-made disasters, such as global thermonuclear warfare or even uncontrolled overpopulation, often serve as allegorical remonstrances to the present powers that be or, even more broadly, to the sin of pride, and many of these dutifully include a preachy jeremiad by a character (such as those delivered Jeff Goldblum's character in the *Jurassic Park* series) on the tragic failings and hubris of mankind. The technological threat of 1983's *War Games* offers an earlier, Cold War-era case in point. In that film, the Dabney Coleman character serves as the bad guy, to the extent that one person is a villain, and he represents a military-industrial complex bent on eliminating the possibility of human error; notably, it is the all-too-human emotions of compassion or fear that are the errors he has in mind, as opposed to the idea that humans would be dangerously negligent or too likely to deploy the weapons without due cause. The plan is thus to make the firing of nuclear missiles something controlled exclusively by computers. By ceding human agency, and thus perhaps responsibility, in the opening movements of a nuclear war, the technological system takes over. Individual humans are no longer to blame, although the human reliance on technology proves to be the great failing, a cautionary tale of the old Faust, Frankenstein, or Sorcerer's Apprentice variety. The terror in *War Games* comes with the recognition of how vulnerable we are in relying on these technologies, but technological savvy is also what turns out to save us in the persons of plucky computer hackers. It is the perverse opposite or flipside of the coin from Stanley Kubrick's incisively satirical *Dr. Strangelove, or, How I Learned to Stop Worrying and Love the Bomb* (1964), insofar as the very technology that prevents our "being worried" is the scariest prospect of all.

The transition of a given society from whatever constituted its "normal" state to what will be readily perceived as a dystopian state is often quite gradual and sometimes largely unnoticed. George Orwell's *Nineteen-Eighty-Four* (1949) notoriously omits, or perhaps we should say *forgets*, references to the revolutionary events that would have brought the present system into being. Indeed, the loss of a sense of the past is one of the most dystopian aspects of life under rule of Big Brother in that novel. More dramatically, and at the same time more laconically, Cormac McCarthy's novel *The Road* (2006) begins "after" whatever apocalyptic events must have occurred, placing the characters and the reader in a post-apocalyptic wasteland with no sense of historical transition whatsoever. The characters are trapped in a perpetual here and now in which merely surviving a bit longer appears to be one's sole *raison d'etre*. With the apocalyptic fiction, as distinct from the some of these examples of the dystopian type, the end-of-the-world is a dramatic narrative event, the spectacle itself, and the human plot associated with it involves somehow surviving and outlasting the end. If the apocalyptic event is natural, as opposed to manmade, the fiction can almost take on the comforting form of the *Robinsonade*, with its fundamental theme of man against nature. This old-fashioned figure, paradoxically, can offer a reassuring simplicity to otherwise unfathomable circumstances.

For example, the 2009 film *2012*, directed by Roland Emmerich,[21] who had previously delivered such near-end-of-the-world blockbusters as *Independence Day* (1998), *Godzilla* (1999), and *The Day After Tomorrow* (2004), takes as its point of departure the eschatological prophecy apparently gleaned from the idea that the Mesoamerican calendar developed by Mayan and other civilizations came to an end in what would be the year 2012; hence, that must be *the* end for the whole world. Whereas the earlier, millennial hysteria over "Y2K" involved massive technological malfunctions based on human errors with respect to computer programming—namely, the purported inability of computer programs using two- rather than four-digits to indicate the year to distinguish between 2000 and 1900—the Mayan calendar places the apocalypse in the very *longue durée* of a cyclical history dating back over 5,000 years. The end of the world, in this scenario, is merely the fulfillment of the prophecy or, at a more basic level, the natural running-out of sand it the cosmic hourglass. Presumably, mankind had no say in the matter. *2012* offers a narrative of the world's end as seen through the eyes of a down-at-the-heels science-fiction writer and erstwhile family man turned chauffeur, a combination that allows for a happy balance of light social commentary and heavy explosives.

In the movie, we quickly learn that what may have been seen as a purely natural cataclysm, or the supernatural apocalypse of the Ragnarök variety, is not to be faced with stoic reserve, at least, not by everyone. A prologue set in 2009 shows scientists learning about the impeding overheating of the planet's core, which gives world leaders just enough time to come up with a plan. Jumping to late 2012, chauffeur Jackson Curtis (played with the signature deadpanning of John Cusack) discovers the secret about the impending doom, and—amid cavalcades of special effects-driven disasters, including chasms opening up in the roads, buildings collapsing, and, in particularly vivid image, the entire city of Los Angeles plunging into the Pacific Ocean—he manages to collect members of his estranged family, get them on a plane, and fly them first to Las Vegas, then (thanks to his Russian oligarch/gangster-employer's private jet) to China, where it is thought the spaceships specially built to flee the dying planet are located. These scenes are cross-cut with others showing scientists, government officials, and various relatives in their own responses to the chaos. The main action-adventure plot focuses on Curtis and his family's attempt to reach the ships and escape. In a twist, we discover that the ships are, in fact, *arks*. (And Curtis's son is named *Noah*, of course!) Following a moving scene in which a number people without tickets are allowed to board (but not, presumably, the many billions already dead or left to die), the arks launch into a now global ocean. The film ends with the happy realization that the waters are receding, as mountains (New Ararat?) are visible on the horizon, and Curtis's nuclear family unit is reforged and strengthened.

The happy ending for the various protagonists allows the apocalyptic "end" to serve as a new beginning. In the case of *2012*, the filmmakers are astonishingly *blasé* about the fates of those who did not survive. While the audience is invited to mourn a handful of named characters who die in relatively stoic, if also spectacular ways, the same audience has likely become inured to the massive deathscapes made visible or merely implied by the tidal waves, volcanic eruptions, earthquakes, and other disasters that make up much of the film. More awkwardly, the need to reunite the hero with his estranged family requires that the boyfriend of Curtis's ex-wife first be an asshole (hence, unworthy of her love) and then die (so as to no longer be a romantic rival of the hero), which allows for the archetypal eucatastrophe of the family unit's restoration. The lion may not exactly lie down with the lamb, but at least a divorced couple can get back together at the end of the world. The final line of the movie, downplaying the severity of the nearly global destruction, is given to the hero's young daughter, who had suffered from incontinence, but who now proudly declares that she no longer needs "pull-ups" (a type of diapers that double as underpants). Such a quotidian, indeed intimate detail may seem like a terrible point on which to end the film, but it establishes, at the level of the family that can now allegorically stand in for the "family of man" at large, the restoration of order, health, and happiness. God's in his heaven and all's right with the world, as it were. In any event, the film ends without inviting its viewer to consider the monumental tasks facing these survivors as they try to rebuild civil society *après le deluge*. The family's idyllic reconstitution itself functions as post-apocalyptic happy ending enough.

One might argue that *2012* is really a traditional disaster movie, such as *Airport* (1970) or *The Towering Inferno* (1974), only set on a global scale. In that case, the end-of-the-world scenario enlarges the threat, but the narrative still manages to focus on a handful of would-be survivors. Notably, *2012* and films like it cannot tell the story of what happens after the happy ending, and given the scale of the destruction in *2012*, it hardly seems likely that merely docking the arks on dry land will restore civilization. Thus, as I suggest, the reconciliation of the hero with his wife and children, which is to say, the re-establishment of the bourgeois nuclear family unit, figures forth not only the survival of humanity but the restoration of human civilization *tout court*. Questions about sustenance, healthcare, government, economics, and so on are set aside in favor of the utopian security of the family. As Curtis says to his children during the final scene of the film, "[w]herever we're altogether, that's home."

Nostalgia for the Future

In contrast to the disaster movie, if apocalyptic films could be understood as having their own genre, they tend to be much better understood as *post-apocalyptic* narratives of one variety or another. Hence the conflation with dystopia, although it is true that not all dystopias are the result of global cataclysms. As noted above, many famous dystopia narratives occlude or omit the distinct cause of the dystopian turn in the given society. In some visions, as with the original *Planet of the Apes* (1968), the revelation of the historical turning point is almost a punch line, establishing in retrospect the meaning of what came before in the film. The recent "prequel" trilogy—*Rise of the Planet of the Apes* (2011), *Dawn of the Planet of the Apes* (2014), and *War for the Planet of the Apes* (2017)—meticulously delineates an elaborate historical transition, this time involving not nuclear war but rather bioengineering and medical research, that the original film had relegated to the background. The post-apocalyptic dystopian landscapes might be distinguished from the more overtly political dystopias inasmuch as the former presuppose a breakdown, dissolution, or total overthrow of modern human civilizations, whereas the latter become almost necessary extensions of what could be considered "normal" social organizations. The modern apocalyptic tradition frequently asks its audience to imagine pre-capitalist formations in which the political and economic systems have disintegrated and an almost prehistoric social order obtains, sometimes even returning to Stone- or Bronze-Age technologies. Our classic political dystopias, by contrast, often involve a government and economy that operates all too efficiently, with high-tech transportation and surveillance, and a rigorously rational and orderly division of labor. The simplicity of this, perversely, might be viewed as another desirable aspect of dystopian societies as depicted on film.

In his discussion of utopian vocation, Jameson has noted "the persistent and obsessive search for a simple, single-shot solution to all our ills."[22] The desire to "fix" society as a whole by identifying the key problem to be solved—one thinks of the elimination of money in the classic Utopias, for instance—itself discloses an underlying but powerful desire for simplicity. Indeed, one could argue that, at a fundamental level, the great complexity of social, political, economic, and cultural processes and forms can appear to be the most significant obstacle to our ability to imagine radical alternatives. Thus, it makes sense that utopian schemes would aim for relatively simple solutions, where one or two key alterations could assure the setting aright of so many perceived social maladies. What we might characterize as the oversimplifications of dystopian narratives serves a similar, perversely utopian, purpose. For one of the frequently shared features of post-apocalyptic or otherwise dystopian futures is that the societies involved have become noticeably simpler, whether through a time-travel-like return to a pre-industrial or prehistoric state or through a more futuristic rationalization or bureaucratization of a society, thus rendering it more easily comprehensible. In some cases, a formation that seems to partake of both historical directions is possible, as the high-tech reorganization of a futuristic society engenders seemingly premodern traits or behaviors, such as new tribalisms, religions, or rituals. In any event, the simplification of society in a dystopia can appear to be desirable when compared with the overwhelming and politically disabling sense of our own society's byzantine complexities.

Leaving aside the potentially utopian aspects of post-apocalyptic societies as pre-capitalist formations, not to mention the hybrid forms (such as the *Mad Max* [1979] franchise) in which modern technologies are blended with ancient if not prehistoric social groupings, it seems that recent dystopian narratives take advantage of political simplification in order to help make clearer the fundamental problems with the society. For example, in a United States that has always had trouble managing its ideological commitments to freedom and equality with the realities of its often coercive, obviously inegalitarian economic system, it might help to imagine clearly visible divisions of class, wealth, and power. The easiest way to do that would be a strict, spatial partitioning, with a set number of clearly defined places or regions whose populations would be relatively homogenous and whose movements would be restricted to their respective zones.

In *The Hunger Games* series, for example, the post-US nation of Panem is rather ridiculously divided along geographical lines into districts, each of which is distinctive for its single industry, which is stripped down to the level of mono-commodity production. Thus one district, presumably based in somewhere in Appalachia, is devoted to coal mining, and all of the nation's coal, apparently, is found there. (Presumably, the author is playing on well-known stereotypes of what coal miners must look like and where they must live; in truth, Wyoming produces far more coal than West Virginia, for instance.) Another district of Panem in *The Hunger Games* produces all the fruits and vegetables, while another is responsible for seafood, and so on. The Capitol, seemingly a district that produces nothing, except perhaps entertainment, is also where nearly all the products from the other districts are distributed and consumed.

As unlikely as such a geographical and economic order is, in these narratives it serves to underscore the injustice of the system, while also carefully identifying the various subcultures within the nation based primarily on their economic impact as proletarians. Just as each district is defined by the commodity production associated with it, the individual children competing in the games are also understood to represent a "type" identified with the regional economy of his or her native district. In this way, the dystopian society of Panem allegorically reflects the more global political and economic inequalities, as the United States (or, in an older idiom, the "First World") like Panem's Capitol consumes most of the goods produced cheaply and through mostly exploitative means in various "districts" around the world, in many cases by child labor, which in turn lends greater *pathos* to the spectacle of the Hunger Games themselves. Each zone of production contributes its distinctive champion, a representative of the commodity, in order to entertain those who enjoy the fruits of their labors during the rest of the year. By ludicrously oversimplifying the dystopian order,

The Hunger Games helps to delineate the class lines and order of power within our own societies, at least at the level of the imagination. This simplification also makes the solution seem somewhat more plausible, as the complex systems of economic and political inequality and injustice can be solved by the overthrow of a single despot, a plot design frequently found in fantastic literature.

Much of this comes down to what might be called, paradoxically, nostalgia for the future, to adapt another notion from Jameson. In his *Postmodernism*, Jameson identifies what he calls a "nostalgia for the present" in the ways that postmodern films (especially, but other narratives as well) present the "concept" of a historical epoch, such as "the Fifties," while scarcely registering anything like its actual historical being.[23] It is, rather, an attempt at representing the historical moment of the present in connection to some imagined past. Similarly, in many of these apocalyptic or post-apocalyptic narratives set in the future, there is a projection of an imagined past, often a "simpler" or more "natural" state in which families, tribes, or small groups replace and improve upon the complex social forms of modernity. Often, the post-apocalyptic social order, if the populations are large enough, seems like medieval European societies, complete with kings, knights, vassals, and peasants. It is almost as if, in seeing our own "society" crumble, there is a deep desire for a past social order that "makes sense," regardless of the fact that fewer moderns would actually thrive in such settings. This odd nostalgia, effectively a longing to "return" to a *future* that will remind us of some romantic or dimly imagined past, animates many of these end-of-the-world adventures.

A Posthuman Utopianism

Perhaps some of the undesirable complexity in the current world system is imagined as product of our human (*all-too-human*, as Nietzsche would add) nature. A curious feature of certain recent dystopian visions involves the pervasive sense that a better world is possible without humans in it. This involves a twist on the classic horror to be found in the *Invasion of the Body Snatchers*-type of political allegories, in which the terrifying threat involves aliens or nonhumans taking over and replacing humankind. It also goes beyond the longing to *become* less human, as with Kurt Vonnegut's *Galápagos* (1985), in which the solution to the dystopia of human existence is for humans to evolve into seal-like creatures, which are no longer troubled with the problem of "big brains," but merely concern themselves with catching fish and avoiding sharks.[24] Rather, in such recent science fictional or fantasy works as the popular HBO series *Westworld* (2016–22), *Blade Runner 2049* (2018), and *Jurassic Park: Fallen World* (2018), the inhuman creatures that are robots, replicants, or even dinosaurs are the true heroes, and the audience is positively predisposed to cheer against the human beings in these narratives.

As Sam Adams has discussed in "It's the End of the World as We Know It, and Hollywood Feels Fine," the major studios have stumbled upon a powerful sense that what's truly wrong with our world, what is making it so dystopian in fact, is the presence of the very humans who are buying tickets to see these films. For example, Adams notes that in the original movie version of *Westworld* (1976), the robots known as "hosts" were mindless automatons, and their rebellion functioned as a sort of technological zombie apocalypse; however, in the twenty-first-century television reboot of *Westworld*, "the lines between hosts and guests are purposefully blurred, and not even the characters themselves can be sure which is which, or which is better."[25] Indeed, the audience of this version is encouraged to cheer for the much abused and righteously indignant bioengineered hosts. Similarly, the original *Blade Runner* (1982) depicted replicants as flawed copies of humans, worthy of empathy perhaps, but far from role models, while also raising troubling questions of what makes us human; the sequel *Blade Runner 2049* establishes the replicants as almost definitively the more human (certainly more humane) of the humanoids, with the actual humans proving to be far more soulless, metaphorically speaking. The dinosaurs of *Jurassic Park: Fallen World*, like the apes of the recent *Planet of the Apes* trilogy, also seem to represent an improvement on human control over both the environment and the social order. One might even argue that the popular zombie apocalypse genre, which keeps being refreshed in various creative iterations, such as *The Game of Thrones*'s White Walkers and wights (which, coming as they do from the icy North, have been associated allegorically with the impending threat of climate change), also represents a potentially salubrious or preferable posthuman world system.

The theory of a posthuman world system goes well beyond the scope of this discussion, but it may be worth noting in conclusion that there is clearly a utopian impulse behind the idea of such a dystopian future. The ease with which contemporary filmmakers and audience imagine end-of-the-world scenarios belies a certain desire to construct a meaningful map of the existing world system, a sort of allegorical structure for making sense of the present. While it may be true, as Jameson has suggested, that our inability to envision fully operative, post-capitalist societies may be due to our lack of imagination, it is still the case that our most ideologically delimited narrative forms and political content can nevertheless yield utopian effects, and the dialectic of ideology and utopia (as Jameson famously referred to it) continues to underwrite the imaginative productions today.[26] If the world system today can only become somehow cognizable and narratable in a significant way by figuring forth its inevitable destruction, then that does not so much indicate our inability to imagine alternatives as it does our absolute imperative to do so.

Notes

1   "Let's Go Fly a Coot," *The Simpsons*, directed by Chris Clements and Mike B. Anderson, written by Jeff Westbrook, season 26, episode 20, Fox Broadcasting Company (aired May 3, 2015).

2   Mark Fisher, *Capitalist Realism: Is There No Alternative?* (Winchester: Zero Books, 2009), 2.

3   Fredric Jameson, "Future City," in *The Ideologies of Theory* (London: Verso, 2008), 573.

4   Jameson, *The Seeds of Time* (New York: Columbia University Press, 1994), xii.

5   Slavoj Žižek, "The Spectre of Ideology," in *Mapping Ideology*, ed. Slavoj Žižek (London: Verso, 1994), 1.

6   Sean Austin Grattan, *Hope Isn't Stupid: Utopian Affects in Contemporary American Literature* (Iowa City: University of Iowa Press, 2017), 5.

7   See, for example, my *For a Ruthless Critique of All That Exists: Literature in An Age of Capitalist Realism* (Washington: Zero Books, 2022), 17–39.

8   On "Planetarity" and globalization, see, for example, Gayatri Charavorty Spivak, *Death of a Discipline* (New York: Columbia University Press, 2003); Ursula Heise, *Sense of Place and Sense of Planet: The Environmental Imagination of the Global* (Oxford: Oxford University Press, 2008); Amy J. Elias and Christian Moraru, eds., *The Planetary Turn: Relationality and Geoaesthetics in the Twenty-First Century* (Evanston: Northwestern University Press, 2015); and Christian Moraru, *Reading for the Planet: Toward a Geomethodology* (Ann Arbor: University of Michigan Press, 2015).

9   See Jürgen Habermas, *The Postnational Constellation: Political Essays*, trans. Max Pensky (Cambridge: The MIT Press, 2001); see also my *Topophrenia: Place, Narrative, and the Spatial Imagination* (Bloomington: Indiana University Press, 2019), 155–71.

10 See Žižek, *Living in the End Times* (London: Verso, 2010).

11 Jameson, *Postmodernism, or, the Cultural Logic of Late Capitalism* (Durham: Duke University Press, 1991), 38; see also Jameson, "Totality as Conspiracy," in *The Geopolitical Aesthetic: Cinema and Space in the World System* (Bloomington and London: Indiana University Press and the British Film Institute, 1992), 9–84.

12 Jameson, "Cognitive Mapping," in *Marxism and the Interpretation of Culture*, ed. Cary Nelson and Lawrence Grossberg (Urbana: University of Illinois Press, 1988), 356.

13 *Snowpiercer*, directed by Bong Joon Ho, CJ Entertainment, 2013.

14 Frank Kermode, *The Sense of an Ending: Studies in the Theory of Fiction* (Oxford: Oxford University Press, 1967), 7.

15 Ibid., 95–6.

16 Jameson, "Introduction," in *The Ideologies of Theory: Essays, 1971–1986, Volume 1, The Syntax of History* (Minneapolis: University of Minnesota Press, 1988), xxviii.

17 Jameson, *Archaeologies of the Future: The Desire Called Utopia and Other Science Fictions* (London: Verso, 2005), 199, note 32.

18 *This Is the End*, directed by Seth Rogan and Evan Goldberg, Columbia Pictures, 2013.

19 By contrast the many who die, including even named characters and not just the faceless masses, are imagined as either "bad" people deserving of their fate or as martyrs to be briefly admired, but in any case, all are hastily forgotten.

20 Robert Frost, "Fire and Ice," in *The Poetry of Robert Frost: The Collected Poems*, ed. Edward Connery Lathem (New York: Henry Holt and Company, 1969), 220.

21 *2012*, directed by Roland Emmerich, Columbia Pictures, 2009.

22 Jameson, *Archaeologies of the Future*, 11.

23 See Jameson, *Postmodernism*, 279–96.

24 See, for example, my *Kurt Vonnegut and the American Novel: A Postmodern Iconography* (New York: Bloomsbury, 2011), 131–47.

25 Sam Adams, "It's the End of the World as We Know It, and Hollywood Feels Fine," *Slate* magazine (June 22, 2018): https://slate.com/culture/2018/06/jurassic-world-fallen-kingdom-westworld-and-other-recent-blockbusters-embrace-apocalypse.html.

26 See Jameson, *The Political Unconscious: Narrative as a Socially Symbolic Act* (Ithaca: Cornell University Press, 1981), 281–99.

Chapter 8

IN THE DESERTS OF THE EMPIRE: THE MAP, THE TERRITORY, AND THE HETEROTOPIAN ENCLAVE

In Mohsin Hamid's 2017 novel *Exit West*, a character makes this surprising observation: "The end of the world can be cozy at times." In the context, the protagonists are experiencing the effects of a dystopian yet all-too-real condition, amid civil strife, militant repression, and refugee crises, but in the moment, there is pause, in which a small space is carved out and made habitable, *cozy*. Responding to Saeed's comment, his fellow protagonist Nadia laughs and says, "Yes. Like a cave."[1]

The image of the cave is evocative, signifying not so much a home as a shelter, a hollow at the edge of the elements that can serve as a place of refuge. In dystopian, monstrous, end-of-the-world conditions, finding such a space seems imperative. One might even suggest that only from such a remove, a place that is still part of that world but marginal and closed off in some way, an *enclave* of sorts, could one properly assess the dystopian monstrosity and apocalyptic conditions of the world. One sometimes thinks of utopia in terms of its being an enclave, as when Fredric Jameson proposes that "Utopian space is an imaginary enclave within real social space," which is to say, "Utopian space is itself a result of social and spatial differentiation." Hence, the cozy, cave-like space briefly imagined by Hamid's protagonists can be likened to utopian space, which Jameson refers to as a "pocket of stasis within the ferment and rushing forces of social change."[2] If the world itself is so thoroughly dystopian, then even a recess at one edge of it, if not a self-enclosed and independent enclave, may seem quite utopian in contrast.

Most likely, however, it will be something of a heterotopian enclave, as I discuss below. The space will be one in which many different things coincide, many possibilities exist at once, and nothing definitively good or bad can be guaranteed there. But it is also a space from which to see the world, a privileged vantage that remains both within that world and at enough of a remove to allow for something like a big picture. In other words, it is a space where one can *map* the territory. Facing a dystopian society, in the teratocene, and perhaps at the end of the world, there is a representational dilemma involving how to apprehend and "know" the territory, and thus how to map it. Amidst the residue of the near-total destruction, one may find one's bearings in relation to a seemingly total system.

Unconscionable Maps

Any discussion of the map and the territory, at least insofar as it touches on literary or cultural studies, will frequently turn to the memorable little story by Jorge Luis Borges, tantalizing titled "On Exactitude in Science." It is certainly one of the most recognizable, even most canonical, texts in spatiality studies, broadly conceived, and it always helps to set a properly philosophical tone when thinking about the problem of representation in our world.

At once elegiac and absurd, the fragment—that is, a text presented as if it were a fragment from a larger narrative, but is fact complete unto itself—tells of an imaginary empire in which the passion for mimetic accuracy in mapmaking had reached its zenith with the creation of the ultimate chart, drawn up according to a one-to-one scale, such that the map was coextensive with the territory it was supposed to represent. Citing a fictional source (namely, "Suárez Miranda, *Viajes de varones prudentes*, Libro IV, Cap. XLV, Lérida, 1658"), which already serves to distance the narrative from the presentation of it and add an element of archival authority to the history, Borges writes:

> In that Empire, the Art of Cartography attained such Perfection that the map of a single Province occupied the entirety of a City, and the map of the Empire, the entirety of a Province. In time, those Unconscionable Maps no longer satisfied, and the Cartographers Guilds struck a Map of the Empire whose size was that of the Empire, and which coincided point for point with it. The following Generations, who were not so fond of the Study of Cartography as their Forebears had been, saw that that vast Map was Useless, and not without some Pitilessness was it, that they delivered it up to the Inclemencies of Sun and Winters. In the Deserts of the West, still today, there are Tattered Ruins of that Map, inhabited by Animals and Beggars; in all the Land there is no other Relic of the Disciplines of Geography.[3]

In Borges's vision, a narrative of the absurd "exactitude" in the geographic science of the earlier cartographers—ones so fastidious as to

find even remotely "inaccurate" maps to be *unconscionable*—concludes
with a bleak scene of a desert wasteland, a veritable non-place occupied
by animals, beggars, and the odd scraps of the imperial map.

Borges's story of a map coextensive with its territory has become a
haunting reminder of the absurdity of the quest for perfectly mimetic
representations in cartography and, by extension, in other arts and
sciences. An earlier dramatization of this idea, from Lewis Carroll's
Sylvie and Bruno Concluded, is much more humorous in making a
similar point, as I will discuss below, but here the air of melancholy
or the sense of loss pervades Borges's brief narrative in such a way to
preclude its being seen as a joke (or, at least, not merely as a joke).[4]
Famously, Jean Baudrillard used the Borges fable to illustrate his
conception of late-twentieth-century hyperreality, in which the
simulacrum precedes the genuine article it was supposed to mimic.
For Baudrillard, the map precedes and, in a way, produces the territory.
Baudrillard actually inverts the order depicted in the fable. Whereas
Borges wished to highlight the surreal vision of a representation that
attempted, as it were, not only to replicate but to replace the original,
Baudrillard suggests that, in our time, the simulacrum precedes the
referent entirely. There is no original to be copied. For Baudrillard,
the tattered remains of the territory might be found in the margins of
the map, not vice versa, and thus the deserts are not those of the old
Empire, but of our own "real" world. As he notoriously puts it, in a
manner that found favor with the producers of *The Matrix* films and
other science fiction enthusiasts (Slavoj Žižek among them), we occupy
"the desert of the real itself."[5]

From the perspective of the geographical sciences, these speculations
over the perfect, one-to-one scalar depiction of territorial space in a
map are, quite rightly, amusing absurdities, thought experiments
that remind us that all representation is figurative, metaphorical, or
allegorical.[6] The conceptual dilemma posed by a consideration of
the relationship between the map and the territory is rather simpler
than the hyperreality thesis of Baudrillard, who finds that there are
no originals to be copied, no referent to which the sign refers, and no
"real" territories to be mapped; there are only copies, signs, and maps.
However, most critics are as yet unwilling to give up on referentiality *in
toto*, even if they are willing to question reality as it appears, perhaps by
interrogating the conditions for the possibility of apprehending what
we think of as reality as such. (This is a legacy of Kant, among others.)
At a more practical level, any users of the map recognize the degree to
which the map cannot be "true" to the territory it purports to represent.
But one of the first consequences of the realization that a perfectly

mimetic image of the respective space on a chart is impossible is that we come to realize that we can always imagine *better*—not necessarily more accurate, but more useful—maps. Or, as Jameson put it in his well-known "digression on cartography" in his *Postmodernism* book, when "it becomes clear that there can be no true maps," then, "at the same time it also becomes clear that there can be scientific progress, or better still, a dialectical advance, in the various historical moments of mapmaking."[7] Along these lines, we might say that the failure of the cartographers to create the ultimate, perfect map is actually a boon to map-users, which is to say, everyone. Without a perfect map, we are free to make maps that suit our needs and desires.

Returning to Borges's "On Exactitude in Science," then, we can focus our attention, not so much on the neat idea of a surreal map that is a point-for-point graphic replication of the territory, but on the aftermath of this would-be triumph of geography. In other words, leaving aside the mapmakers with their ambition, ingenuity, and ultimate failures, we can look at the post-geographic age in which the great map was deemed useless and pitilessly "delivered [...] up to the Inclemencies of Sun and Winters." In this epoch, according to Borges's tale, the tattered remnants of the map that can be found here and there in "the Deserts of the West" are all that remains of the "Disciplines of Geography" in that land, which might be taken as a damning indictment of the era and of the people living in it. These are people who have become uninterested in geographical science, who have lost respect for their ancestors' accomplishments, and abandoned the past treasures to the realm of wind and dust. Although Borges does not necessarily report it this way, this is our dystopian age, our monstrous territory, and our postapocalyptic land. We are living in the deserts of the empire.

Deserts of the Real

The vision is elegiac, if not indeed apocalyptic. The deserts of the empire with its scattered, tattered remnants of the old maps conjure up an image of undeniable loss, but it is also that sign of progress, as the epistemic triumphs of a great theory-oriented generation become impractical encumbrances to a later, more pragmatic generation. Proper mapmaking, at least as an adjunct to a formal disciplinary field of geography, ceases. The old Map deteriorates. This era is typified by the open spaces in which those remnants of the map, the scattered and tattered fragments of the great systematic representation of the world which now blow in the wind, form temporary shelters to stray animals and vagabonds. Remnants, remains, residue … that which is left behind. Perhaps ours is the age of the remainder? An epoch of the residual, where the cultural dominants are intolerable and the emergent forms are almost too horrible to imagine. Now seems a perfect time to take note of the traces, those mementoes of former valiant efforts, as the present seems all too dystopian for so many, while the future cannot be imagined apart from a sort of end-of-the-world scenario, an apocalypse without recovery, Armageddon without hope. These fragments of the map, currently littering the deserts and offering the barest shelter to vagrants, might provide clues to an alternative cartography, vistas into another world.

The image of the desert, bestrewn with the ragged detritus of the grand imperial map, evokes bleak austerity. The desert is a kind of non-place, a space of homelessness or estrangement in which the individual or collective subject is forever displaced, without necessarily being able to become reoriented. For instance, the great cultural geographer Yi-Fu Tuan, in *Space and Place: The Perspective of Experience* (1977), has defined *place* as a sort of pause, a resting of the eyes, or an instant of awareness when one isolates, if only momentarily, a portion of otherwise undifferentiated space, and in noticing it as such, imbues it with meaning.[8] At this point, it becomes familiar, like a home, again if only for a moment, whereas the still inchoate spaces surrounding it remains alien, uncanny, menacing, and dangerous. The desert, sometimes literally and often figuratively, conjures up an uncanny sense of a vast, uninhabitable, and unhomely space.

The desert is not a home, though it may be a space through which one must pass, a zone of transgression or of liminality. It might be likened to the "non-places" identified by Marc Augé in his influential study, *Non-Places: Introduction to the Anthropology of Supermodernity* (1995). Augé examines transitory sites, such as airports, train stations, hotels, highways, and supermarkets, which in a sense are not so much *places*—that is, locations instilled with meaning, dense with historical and social reference, the result of creative human endeavor, and so forth—as *non-places*, uniform, homogeneous zones of transit in which modern humans increasingly spend their lives. Occupying these entirely, perhaps all-too-social spaces, we experience another sense of homelessness, a desert of another kind.[9] But more likely, the desert could be characterized as an *atopia*, which Siobhan Carroll has analyzed as spaces "antithetical to habitable place." Carroll adds to the list of manmade atopias such as those mentioned by Augé a number of "natural atopias," such as the North Pole, the middle of the ocean, the desert, or outer space, although she also notes how cyberspace is frequently imagined as a somewhat positive, manmade atopia. Carroll concludes that, whether these atopias are viewed as spaces that either liberate or threaten the individual subject, they have become increasingly useful in "orientating ourselves to the sublime space of the planet and the human networks that span its surface."[10] In the unhomeliness (or uncanniness) of such *atopian* sites we may also come to make sense of the places in which we might feel at home.

In *Being and Time* (1927), Heidegger postulated that our experience of anxiety was intimately tied to the uncanny (*unheimlich*) and thus reflected a profound sense of being "not-at-home."[11] This unease or estrangement is in a way similar to that "homelessness" which Heidegger later identified as the "destiny of the world," a pervasive and troubling condition. In his "Letter on Humanism," Heidegger asserts that a certain homelessness is the condition of contemporary man. The "homeland" that is lacking is understood "in an essential sense, not patriotically or nationalistically but in terms of the history of Being." Ontologically speaking, human beings require a *heimlich* place. "Homelessness," he continues, "is the symptom of the oblivion of Being."[12]

There is a vaguely romantic appeal to this sense of homelessness. It carries something of the flavor of Georg Lukács's "transcendental homelessness" in *The Theory of the Novel* (1920) in which it is used to characterize the condition of man in "a world abandoned by God."[13] In such a world, which lacks the sense of totality given in an earlier epoch (the age of the epic), the novel becomes the form-giving form by which humans can make sense of their world. In my reading of Lukács's work, I have suggested that this might also be imagined as a kind of cognitive mapping, to use Jameson's well-known term.[14] That is, the novel is a form that can be used to give form to the world of limited human perspective and experience by coordinating that experience with a sense of the broader social totality. In this way, it might function in a manner similar to that of a map, which provides a figurative representation of space, often complete with a bird's-eye-view perspective, that can thus enable the individual subject to locate him—or herself in relations both to other places and to a projected, more global space. As Jameson had described a somewhat simplified version of cognitive mapping, drawing on Kevin Lynch's discussion of "wayfinding" and "imageability" in his *The Image of the City*, "[d]isalienation in the traditional city, then, involves the practical reconquest of a sense of place and the construction or reconstruction of an articulated ensemble which can be retained in memory and which the individual subject can map and remap along the moments of mobile, alternative trajectories."[15] And, as Miroslav Holeb has intimated in his poem, "Brief Thoughts on Maps," a map, even the wrong map, may help one find one's way home.[16]

Transferring this idea to the sense of homelessness referred to above, we might suggest that, for those occupying the alien space of the desert, there is an urgent need for a form of mapping that will make possible a sense of place or a "homeliness." It may be ironic to think that, for the "Animals and Beggars" inhabiting them, the "Tattered Ruins of the Map," in fact, are like a home. Can one make oneself "at home" in a map? Aside from the scant shelter from the "Inclemencies of Sun and Winters" that sheer parchment can provide, the fragments of a map may well offer solace, even comfort, to the errant wanderer and his shadow. Dwelling in the deserts of cartography, one necessarily discovers places and projects relations among them, constellating the assorted points into a meaningful ensemble, and thus, perhaps, if not making oneself at home exactly, then making sense of one's own place in the world.

While the desert seems to be a particularly inhospitable place, that does not mean one cannot possibly feel at home there. Not only are there the cultures and populations that have managed to survive, even thrive, in the desert environment, but many have been immediately struck by the beauty of the desert or have developed an affinity for it over time, such that the desert landscape represents, for some, an altogether "homely" territory.

For example, Tuan, in his 1990 Preface to the Morningside Edition of *Topophilia* (which had originally been published in 1974), recounts the narrative of a camping trip he took with several of his fellow graduate students from Berkeley to Death Valley in the early 1950s. Awaking to a sunrise over a landscape utterly foreign to him in his previous personal experience, Tuan reports witnessing "a scene [...] of such unearthly beauty that I felt transported to a supernal realm and yet, paradoxically, also at home, as though I had returned after a long absence."[17] Tuan, who is interested in the phenomenological apprehension or experience of space and place, quite rightly observes that the favored environs for some people might be thoroughly uninhabitable or distasteful to others. The site of one person's topophilia might well engender feelings of topophobia in another. As Tuan continues his meditation on his own affective geography with respect to the ostensible bleak terrain of a place like the Death Valley National Monument, "[t]he desert, including its barren parts and (I would even say) especially those, appeals to me. I see in it purity, timelessness, a generosity of mind and spirit."[18] The geographer admits that his preference for the desert over, say, the rain forest is a prejudice, but such personal or cultural feelings about a space are entirely consistent with the human understanding of and engagement with the environment. Undoubtedly, Tuan says,

> peoples of the desert (nomads as well as sedentary farmers in oases) love their homeland: without exception humans grow attached to their native places, even if these should seem derelict of quality to outsiders. But the desert, despite its barrenness, has had its nonnative admirers. Englishmen, in particular, have loved the desert. In the eighteenth and nineteenth centuries, they roamed adventurously in North Africa and the Middle East, and wrote accounts with enthusiasm and literary flair which have given the desert a glamor that endures into our time [...] Why this attraction for Englishmen? The answers are no doubt complex, but I wish to suggest a psychogeographical factor— the appeal of the opposite. The mist and overpowering greenness of England seems to have created a thirst in some individuals to seek their opposite in desert climate and landscape.[19]

For Tuan, as for Heidegger, the love of place involves a sense of being "at home" there, but Tuan also insists upon the ways that many, including non-natives and absolute strangers, can feel at home in any place, depending on the person and the place.

Prudent Cartographers

Tuan's generally positive disposition and his admiration for T. E. Lawrence's *Seven Pillars of Wisdom* (1926) may have led him to overlook the brazen Orientalism, colonial designs, and frequently racist ideas that accompanied the Englishmen's affinity for North African or Middle Eastern terrain. For example, in *Orientalism*, Edward Said shows how Lawrence's consideration of "the Arab" was in many ways much like the psycho-geography of the desert in Tuan, for this race, like the space it inhabits is primitive, pure, and timeless.[20] Indeed, there is something vaguely ominous in Tuan's otherwise cheery sense of "the appeal of the opposite" when one considers the *mission civilisatrice* that functioned as the ideological foundation of direct imperialist conquest.[21] The otherwise innocent preference for the exotic environment of a foreign land may be revealed to entail, in the fullness of time, the colonization of territories and the extension of empire into new spaces on the map.

Borges's imperial geographers, as we well can surmise, were not merely mapping an Empire out of intellectual curiosity or scientific scruples, but at least in part and perhaps indirectly as a means of extending power over this territory and its inhabitants.

The map is remarkable thing. It is among the most useful and flexible tools available to mankind, offering a strictly figurative representation of a given territory while at the same time serving as the most practical guide. As Gilles Deleuze and Félix Guattari have asserted, "[t]he map is open and connectable in all its dimensions; it is detachable, reversible, susceptible to constant modification. It can be torn, reversed, adapted to any kind of mounting, reworked by an individual, group, or social formation. It can be drawn on a wall, conceived as a work of art, constructed as a political action or as a mediation."[22] One does not normally associate mere works of art, whose realism is at best a measure of the artist's own choices of metaphor or simile, with the everyday, nuts-and-bolts business of going from point *A* to point *B* in the "real world." And yet all recognize the degree to which a map, even the fantastic maps of Borges's fabled cartographers, is an allegorical device. It is a fiction, not unlike a story, that employs any number of figural means to imaginatively depict, not the real territory, but an alternative version of it. Significantly, perhaps, the usefulness of a map is directly related to its being a work of fiction, or in other words a non-mimetic representation of the territory it is supposed to depict.

"What a useful thing a pocket-map is!" remarks the narrator during a memorable scene in Lewis Carroll's *Sylvie and Bruno Concluded*, a scene often thought to be the inspiration for Borges's account in "On Exactitude in Science." In *Sylvie and Bruno Concluded*, Carroll includes as part of a conversion between the titular heroes and one Mein Herr a brief discussion of maps. Mein Herr confesses that he had just lost his way, so that he needed to consult his pocket-map. This then leads to the comment about how useful this item can be, leading Mein Herr to discourse upon the relative value of maps drawn up on different scales:

> "That's another thing we've learned from your Nation," said Mein Herr, "map-making. But we've carried it much further than you. What do you consider the largest map that would be really useful?"
>
> About six inches to the mile.
>
> "Only six inches!" exclaimed Mein Herr. "We very soon got to six yards to the mile. Then we tried a hundred yards to the mile.

And then came the grandest idea of all! We actually made a map of the country, on the scale of a mile to the mile!"

"Have you used it much?" I enquired.

"It has never been spread out, yet," said Mein Herr: "the farmers objected: they said it would cover the whole country, and shut out the sunlight! So we now use the country itself, as its own map, and I assure you it does nearly as well."[23]

As I mentioned above, this version is much more cheerful and humorous. The grand map is drafted, but never unfurled, and the territory is allowed to serve as its own map. In his own variation on the theme of the map coextensive with the territory it purports to represent, Neil Gaiman has extracted a more distinctively literary lesson from these parables, asserting that "[o]ne describes a tale best by telling the tale. [...] The tale is the map which is the territory."[24]

Northrop Frye, in his broader discussion of the ways that literary criticism can be likened to mapmaking with respect to the territory of literature, astutely highlights the word "nearly" in Carroll's story. Much as the farmers and others in Mein Herr's country may feel that they can simply inhabit the map, the urgency of the cartographic imperative cannot easily be suppressed.[25] Furthermore, as Frye puts it, "[s]urely there must be a middle ground between a map that tells us nothing about the territory and a map that attempts to replace it."[26]

The deserts of the empire, those wastelands of representation, speak to the sense of the world system in the present moment. It is not simply that we are unable to represent the global system adequately, but that can only imagine it as something terrible, inhuman, and ultimately fatal. How does one construct a working map under these circumstances? How does one dwell in the remnants of the great maps? Can we find ways to map anew, to produce cartographies of the future worthy of living beings, as opposed to ghosts, the undead, and others who do not truly live.

The work of art itself offers a clue. In his meditation on the origin of the work of art, Heidegger distinguishes between the world and the earth, which may provisionally be understood as the social and historical project of our own existence, on the one hand, and the natural or material conditions of our environment on the other (even if Heidegger would not necessarily put it that way). In some respects, I believe, these might be reimagined as the map and the territory as well. These two spatial dimensions inform not only our being, but also our projects, the means by which we give our lives and works meaning.

In Heidegger's words, "[t]he setting up of a world and the setting forth of earth are the two essential features in the work-being of the work."[27] Jameson has discussed this Heideggerian distinction, underscoring the rift between the terms. As Jameson explains,

[t]he force of Heidegger's account lies in the way in which a constitutive gap between these two dimensions is maintained and even systematically enlarged: the implication that we all live in both dimensions at once, in some irreconcilable simultaneity, at all moments both in History and in Matter, at one and the same time historical beings and "natural" ones, living simultaneously in the meaning-endowment of the historical project and in the meaninglessness of organic life. But this in turn implies not only that no philosophical or aesthetic synthesis between these dimensions is attainable, but also that "idealism" or "metaphysics" can be defined by this impossible project, whose logical alternatives are marked out by the obliteration of history and its assimilation to Nature, or by the transformation of all forms of natural resistance into human, historical terms.[28]

If, for Heidegger, any symbolic means of overcoming this rift or attempts to unify these dimensions of world and earth invariably lead to error, then one might suggest that the alternative lies with inhabiting the rift, "learning to *live* with ghosts" (as Jacques Derrida has put it).[29] Mapping, along with other forms of aesthetic production, is a key means by which we make this space inhabitable for ourselves. In Jameson's words, "[t]he function of the work of art is then to open a space in which we are ourselves called upon to live within this tension and to affirm its reality."[30]

The work of art, in this case, may well be the map itself, which in a perverse turn of events—the ruse of history or the dialectical reversal— turns out to be the territory after all, but only insofar as the artist- cartographer is prudent. Indeed, if the attribution is to be believed (and it is *not*, of course), Borges's "On Exactitude in Science" comes from a work titled *Travels of Prudent Men* by Suárez Miranda, and it makes sense that a prudent traveler in the empire of lost cartography would make note of the remnants of the map scattered across the territory it purported to depict. Prudence dictates caution, after all, particularly with respect to speculation, and the wisdom associated with prudence is always both pragmatic and principled. The prudent artist does not confuse the representation for its referent, and the artist cannot dwell within the work of art. However, the artist gives shape to the world though the work of art, just as the cartographer figures forth the world in attempting to figuratively represent a given territory. In this way, the map and the territory maintain themselves in a somewhat uneasy, yet lasting equipoise in our minds and in our experience. Building a place for ourselves in the deserts of cartography, we dwell in the place that is meaningful only insofar as it may be mapped.

Different Enclaves

As I suggested above, this artistic, creative mapping project is to be undertaken by one who is both part of the world and has some sort of privileged vantage from which to envision it. I am thinking of a sort of heterotopian enclave, neither fully utopian nor dystopian, from which the cartographer can attempt to map the world system. The *heterotopian enclave* is an allusion to Jameson's reference to "Utopian enclave" his monumental study *Archaeologies of the Future*. Jameson there, as elsewhere, notes the way in which traditional utopias are typified by disjunctive breaks, spatial and temporal, as with the trench dug by Thomas More's King Utopus to cut off the "island" of Utopia from the peninsula of which it had been part or the century-long lacuna separating the narrator of Edward Bellamy's *Looking Backward* in the year 2000 from his erstwhile home in 1887. The enclave in this sense offers a space apart from, and perhaps *athwart*, the hegemonic processes that dominate the spaces all around it. As Washington Irving characterized Sleepy Hollow and places like it, "[t]hey are like those little nooks of still water, which border a rapid stream, where we may see the straw and bubble riding quietly at anchor, or slowly revolving in their mimic harbor, undisturbed by the rush of the passing current."[31] In these visions, the utopian enclave offers not only a different space, but a haven from the maelstrom surrounding it.

That is not to say that the enclave is not also perilous. By it its very nature, it is precarious, for example. As Jameson puts it, "[t]he enclave radiates baleful power, but at the same time it is a power that can be eclipsed precisely because it is confined to a limited space."[32] Such a space is readily incorporated within the very systems or structures from which it defined its own character. Elsewhere, while referring in particular to Adorno's utopian view of the aesthetic sphere, Jameson says, "it is a peculiarly transitory and fleeting space, a line of flight that can last but a moment, before being reabsorbed into that nightmarish real world of suffering against which it was an ephemeral protest, and of which it is the briefest dissonant expression."[33]

In the context of dystopia, rather than utopia, and of dystopianism's relations to the multivalenced, complex network of real-and-imagined forces still known as "globalization," the desire for some sort of enclave, no matter how precarious or ephemeral, is all the more urgent. For some, globalization is itself dystopian, and an aspect of its dystopian character is the way—much as Marx had long ago characterized the capitalist system—it tears asunder local differences, spreading a culture (or anti-culture) that is simultaneously cosmopolitan and homogeneous, not to mention totalizing. Coming from an entirely different political and cultural perspective, J. R. R. Tolkien expressed his dismay near the end of the Second World War at the inevitable "Americo-cosmopolitanism," stating in a letter, "I do find this Americo-cosmopolitanism very terrifying. Quâ mind and spirit, and neglecting the piddling fears of timid flesh [...], I am not really sure that its victory is going to be much better for the world as a whole and in the long run."[34] In an ever-burgeoning, dystopian-seeming, homotopic space, perhaps the more desirable, even apparently more utopian "enclave" is fundamentally heterotopian.

Globalization has brought with it a sort of leveling or homogenizing force, yes, but at the same time it had introduced hitherto unthinkable diversity and difference into nearly all sectors of social existence. A recent collection edited by Simon Ferdinand, Irina Souch, and Daan Wesselman, *Heterotopia and Globalization in the Twenty-First Century* (2020), confronts that paradox. In their Introduction, the editors offer the example of a Bohemian or "hipster" coffee house in Amsterdam, but one which could just as easily appear in New York, Shanghai, Lagos, Tel Aviv, or Buenos Aires. Its space and character are marked by *difference*; that is, the whole point of the enterprise is to *be* different from its surroundings, and the global spread of such utterly similar if not identical places *of difference* is a feature of the present century. The editors refer to this as "discrepant emplacements," and they draw upon Michel Foucault's influential concept of *heterotopia* in order to "grasp the clashing, incongruous spatiality of contemporary globalization."[35]

Foucault himself never really developed this concept more fully in his own work, and it is therefore somewhat odd that the idea has become so valuable to critics. Foucault mentions "heterotopia" briefly in *The Order of Things* (1966) and gave a lecture devoted to the subject, "*Des espaces autres*" ("Of Other Spaces"), in 1967, but that lecture was not until 1984 (translated into English in 1986), so for a full seventeen years even Foucault himself apparently saw little need to have "heterotopias" discussed further. Notably, Foucault's rather spatial studies of the 1970s—*Discipline and Punish*, in examining "the birth of the prison," could be imagined as a study of a particularly significant heterotopian form, after all—but the term is not mentioned in Foucault's published writings of that era, not even once. Nevertheless, heterotopia has become a key concept for cultural geography, urban studies, and the humanities over the past thirty-five years in part because it seems to capture many different possibilities in a single term. As the editors of *Heterotopia and Globalization* assert, "heterotopias are discrete segments of larger discursive totalities" (such as the geographical space of a nation state, for instance), and in relation to those totalities, "heterotopias manifest their own distinct logics, moods, and norms," which in turn may "refract, disturb, but also accentuate aspects of the wider social or discursive totality."[36] In a way, then, heterotopias are already imagined *as* enclaves, set apart from the presumably homotopic spaces surrounding them.

Marx's discussion of this sort of thing is part and parcel of the "all that is solid melts into air, all that is holy is profaned" features of the age. As he and Engels say in *The Communist Manifesto*, "[t]he need of a constantly expanding market for its products chases the bourgeoisie over the entire surface of the globe. It must nestle everywhere, settle everywhere, establish connections everywhere."[37] This observation leads into the famous paragraph in which the authors examine the "world market," which had given all places a "cosmopolitan character," and thus set the stage for the advent of a "world literature."

However, this expansion outwards into foreign zones is a counterpart to the urbanization Marx and Engels go on to discuss a moment later, when they make their infamous "idiocy of rural life" comment. This is a process of centralization, even as its effects are quite diffuse. Marx and Engels observe that

> [t]he bourgeoisie keeps more and more doing away with the scattered state of the population, of the means of production, and of property. It has agglomerated population, centralised the means of production, and has concentrated property in a few hands. The necessary consequence of this was political centralisation. Independent, or but loosely connected provinces, with separate interests, laws,

governments, and systems of taxation, became lumped together into one nation, with one government, one code of laws, one national class-interest, one frontier, and one customs tariff.[38]

The centralization Marx and Engels here envision, which implies the formation of a *capitalist enclave* in the form of a politico-economic metropolis, has its dialectical counterpart in the dispersion of power across both the countryside and the globe.

One could imagine this as a kind of simultaneous motion of centripetal and centrifugal forces, where the very powers of centralization that have facilitated the burgeoning urbanization and the rise of the great metropolises are matched and supplemented by the powers that have extended capital beyond national borders and to the extreme ends of the earth, all the way to the deserts of the empire, as it were. In Marxism, indeed, the two tendencies must be understood as part of a larger dialectical process in which the system unites the only *apparently* contradictory forms of here and there, near and far, home and away, or center and periphery. The imaginary space of the enclave then lies in between these extremes, while at the same time occupying both. To be there is to be "in the middest," a heterotopian space that partakes of many others all at once.

The term *heterotopia* has been used in a variety of ways in recent decades, and it has become a keyword within spatially oriented critical theory and practice. Foucault is credited with the concept, but it must be acknowledged that his own advocacy of the concept is somewhat ambiguous. For one thing, Foucault first used the term as if it were the name for an important concept for philosophy, only to drop it entirely for the rest of his career. He had first used the term in *The Order of Things*, but his most famous exposition of the concept comes from the 1967 lecture, "Of Other Spaces." Arguably, Foucault himself thus found the concept unhelpful for his post-1967 researches, and yet it has proved quite influential in postmodern social theory, particularly in the works of Edward W. Soja, who uses it as the basis for his notion of "thirdspace."[39] It may be that heterotopia is connected to what Jameson called "that new spatiality implicit in the postmodern," and Soja makes a strong case for connection these ideas.[40]

In the Preface to *The Order of Things*, Foucault introduces the term "heterotopia" by explicitly contrasting it with utopia. As Foucault puts it, "*Utopias* afford consolation: although they have no real locality there is nevertheless a fantastic, untroubled region in which they are able to unfold; they open up cities with vast avenues, superbly planted gardens, countries where life is easy, even though the road to them is chimerical."[41] In contrast, Foucault asserts,

> *Heterotopias* are disturbing, probably because they secretly undermine language, because they make it impossible to name this *and* that, because they shatter or tangle common names, because they destroy "syntax" in advance, and not only the syntax with which we construct sentences but also that less apparent syntax which causes words and things (next to and also opposite one another) to 'hold together.'[42]

Foucault argues that this is why "utopias permit fables and discourse," whereas heterotopias "dissolve our myths and sterilize the lyricism of our sentences."[43]

Dystopias, as well, are known for producing fables, and the twentieth century often found it difficult to distinguish between utopia and dystopia, despite the many formal differences in their narratives. Much of the discourse surrounding radically alternative social formations has ranged between the poles of utopian and dystopian visions, while a heterotopian alternative to both may be difficult to imagine. Could it be an enclave apart from both? Or would it be merely a version of the central space of capital, as with the local-yet-cosmopolitan coffee houses?

The metropolitan center, which forms the true core of the elaborately structured world system, can be figured as utopian, heterotopian, and dystopian all at once. In Marx's sense of the expansions of capital and the sheer scale involved with the world market, the earlier country/city or rural/urban distinction is extrapolated onto a planetary level, as becomes apparent when transcoded into Immanuel Wallerstein's tripartite scheme of core, semi-periphery, and periphery.[44] The core, in this sense, represents the urban capital, especially the great metropolis, whereas the periphery neatly aligns with a conception of rustic simplicity, so much so that this geographical metaphor also takes on a historical dimension, such that travelers from the core to the periphery view themselves as moving from the most up-to-date, modern, and *present* plane of existence into a space that is associated, if not confused, with the past. (The semi-periphery, then, represents an intermediary stage of development, one most likely moving from a less remote past to a more proximate present, but which could well be in danger of relapse.) Ethnography and anthropology combine with travel narratives and tales of adventure to find "primitive" cultures in exotic locales, effectively turning these peoples and cultures into living fossils, fit for paleontological or archaeological investigation as much as merely cultural or social inquiry. Movement through space effectively becomes movement through time, and the various stages of history can be apprehended synchronically by establishing a well-developed map and archive. These different spaces, too, get refigured as somehow *heterotopian* enclaves.

And yet, as history has shown, these spaces can succumb to new forms of local, regional, or nationalist ideologies and thus to this or that type of dystopia, very quickly. The reactionaries, in effect defining themselves as distinct from a putatively hegemonic "norm" wind up reacting to difference itself, thereby affirming some kind of "authentic" identity, thus also re-establishing various national myths and symbols on the very terrain of a postnational, would-be heterotopian space. In the very heart of the heterotopian enclave, it seems, some fairly hideous monsters can be found lurking.

Despite frequent allusions to *heterotopia* as a progressive or even revolutionary site, Foucault himself made clear that there is nothing particularly good or bad about such places. Yes, in them, the possibilities of new social structures might emerge, but we know that these may not always be desirable. The heterotopian enclave, like the utopian one, evokes a tentative, provisional, and limited space of alterity, but ultimately these spaces must remain part of, and engaged with, the spaces of the world system itself. How those who find themselves situated in such enclaves deal with the larger system of which they are part will, as the saying goes, "make all the difference."

Haunting Spaces

Inhabiting these spaces will require a sober assessment of that which is residual as well as what may be emerging, and in our dystopian times, perhaps, few will view that which is emergent as hopeful signs for the future. Rebecca Solnit has recently observed that that widespread dystopian sensibility has cast a pall over the very idea of a better space and time to come. "Even the affluent live in a world where confidence in the future, and in the society and institutions around us, is fading— and where a sense of security, social connectedness, mental and physical health, and other measures of well-being are often dismal." But speaking in particularly of the looming environmental situation, which is of global concern, Solnit goes on to explain, "[t]o respond to the climate crisis—a disaster on a more immense scale than anything our species has faced—we can and must summon what people facing disasters have: a sense of meaning, of deep connection and generosity, of being truly alive in the face of uncertainty. Of joy."[45]

This is an inspiring message, but it is not always easy to find joy in the struggle itself, particularly when faced with dystopian, monstrous, and apocalyptic conditions. In such cases, as we have seen, merely attempting to map the system, to understand it and interpret it, seems close to impossible, and the idea of wholesale change, restructuring or revolutionizing it, seems close to unimaginable. The heterotopian enclave, a *cozy* space amid the end-of-the-world landscape, may be the best we can hope for in the interregnum between the old dying world and whatever is coming. In such places, the power of the residual can be seen all the more clearly.

Reflecting upon what he understands to be "the age of the novel," which ended some time ago (perhaps in the 1950s, in fact), Jonathan Arac has affirmed that this is not so much a cause for despondency or for nostalgia as it is an opportunity to produce altogether new and exciting work in the theory and history of the novel. As he puts it, "[w]e love to write histories that cheer on the emergent and challenge the dominant, but have we yet explored how to write histories of the residual? Perhaps this explains why deconstruction exercised such appeal. Deconstruction loved to think the residual. Teleology yields to haunting in Derrida's return to Marx."[46] Arac here refers to Derrida's *Specters of Marx*, in which Derrida plays on the notion of a "hauntology," but also to the attention paid in deconstruction to such things as the *trace*, which is in effect the presence of an absence, a residue. Along these lines, as I quoted above, Derrida suggests that if we are to "live otherwise, and better," it will require that we "learn to live *with* ghosts."[47]

The idea of haunting, as with ghosts, certainly conjures up the notion of an absent presence as well, where the dead and gone are somehow here again, and to be haunted is to have this spectral residue assert itself in our own time and space. But we also know the term *haunt* to refer to a place, a site in which one spends indefinite time, or a location one frequents or stays. There is clearly something vaguely eerie about such a concept, but at the same time, something quite cozy as well. After all, in everyday language, one feels quite at home in one's haunts, even if by definition a haunt is not one's actual home.

The animals and beggars who shelter in the tattered remains of the grand imperial map of Borges's fable do not seem like particularly hopeful figures, but in finding shelter, amidst the harsh conditions of the deserts of the empire, amongst monsters of unimaginably varied forms, and faced with the apparently imminent end of the world, such survivors demonstrate what it means to live with ghosts, to write histories of the residual. In this, they—which is to say *we*, living in our own dark times—represent those who, in seeking some heterotopian enclaves, find ourselves all the more worldly, all the more *of* this world, and thus in a position to help shape its future, no matter how limited our current powers to do so seem. Mapping the territory again, which we will likely find ourselves doing anyhow, seems as good a place to start as any.

Notes

1   Mohsin Hamid, *Exit West* (New York: Penguin, 2017), 83.
2   Fredric Jameson, *Archaeologies of the Future: The Desire Called Utopia and Other Science Fictions* (London: Verso, 2005), 15.
3   Jorge Luis Borges, "On Exactitude in Science," in *Collected Fictions*, trans. Andrew Hurley (New York: Penguin, 1999), 325. Borges cites a fictional source: Suárez Miranda, *Viajes de varones prudentes*, Libro IV, Cap. XLV, Lérida, 1658.
4   Lewis Carroll, *Sylvie and Bruno Concluded* (London: Macmillan, 1893), 169.
5   Jean Baudrillard, *Simulacra and Simulation*, trans. Sheila Faria Glaser (Ann Arbor: University of Michigan Press, 1994), 1–2, italics in original. In *The Matrix* (1999), directed by the Wachowskis, a character introduces another to the fact that what is taken for human reality and lived experience is in fact only a great computer simulation, punctuating this surprising news with the line, "Welcome to the desert of the real." This phrase was used as the title of 2002 book by Slavoj Žižek, in which the author employed a Lacanian and Marxist analysis of the terrorist attacks of September 11, 2001, and the media responses to them. See Žižek, *Welcome to the Desert of the Real: Five Essays on September 11* (London: Verso, 2002).
6   See, for example, J. B. Harley, *The New Nature of Maps: Essays in the History of Cartography*, ed. Paul Laxton (Baltimore: Johns Hopkins University Press, 2001).
7   Jameson, *Postmodernism, or, the Cultural Logic of Late Capitalism* (Durham: Duke University Press, 1991), 52.
8   Yi-Fu Tuan, *Space and Place: The Perspective of Experience* (Minneapolis: University of Minnesota Press, 1977), 161–2.
9   See Marc Augé, *Non-Place: Introduction to an Anthropology of Supermodernity*, trans. John Howe (London: Verso, 1995).

10 Siobhan Carroll, "Atopia / Non-Place," *The Routledge Handbook of Literature and Space*, ed. Robert T. Tally Jr. (London: Routledge, 2017), 159, 164–5.

11 See Martin Heidegger, *Being and Time*, trans. John Macquarrie and Edward Robinson (New York: Harper and Row, 1962), 233.

12 Martin Heidegger, "Letter on Humanism," trans. Frank A. Capuzzi, in Heidegger, *Basic Writings*, ed. David Farrell Krell (New York: Harper and Row, 1977), 217–19.

13 Georg Lukács, *The Theory of the Novel*, trans. Anna Bostock (Cambridge: MIT Press, 1971), 88.

14 See my "Lukács's Literary Cartography: Spatiality, Cognitive Mapping, and *The Theory of the Novel*," *Mediations* 29.2 (Spring 2016), 113–24.

15 Jameson, *Postmodernism*, 51.

16 See Miroslav Holub, "Brief Thoughts on Maps," trans. Jarmila and Ian Milner, *Times Literary Supplement* (February 4, 1977): 118. This poem relates the story, itself a retelling of a tale formerly told by the Nobel Prize winner Albert Szent-Györgi, of a Hungarian reconnaissance unit, hopelessly lost in a snowstorm in the Alps during the First World War. At the brink of despair and resigning themselves to death, they find a map that one soldier had kept in his pocket. Using it to locate their bearings, the soldiers manage to make it back safely to camp. There the commanding officer, who had been wracked with anguish and guilt over the loss of his troops, asked to see this miraculous map that had saved their lives. A soldier handed it over, and it was revealed to be a map, not of the Alps, but of the Pyrenees. The moral of the story appears to differ among its tellers. Szent-Györgi's point in originally recounting the anecdote was to show that, in science, even errors or false starts can lead to success. Holub's broader intention in retelling the tale, however, may have been to show how, in the words of his poem, "life is on its way somewhere or another," regardless of one's sense of orientation.

17 Tuan, *Topophilia* (New York: Columbia University Press, 1990), xi.

18 Ibid.

19 Ibid., xii.

20 See, for example, Edward Said, *Orientalism* (New York: Vintage, 1978), 229–31.

21 Ibid., 54–7.

22 Gilles Deleuze and Félix Guattari, *A Thousand Plateaus*, trans. Brian Massumi (Minneapolis: University of Minnesota Press, 1987), 12.

23 Carroll, *Sylvie and Bruno Concluded*, 168–9.

24 Neil Gaiman, *Fragile Things: Short Fictions and Wonders* (New York: HarperCollins, 2006), xix–xx.

25 See my *Topophrenia: Place, Narrative, and the Spatial Imagination* (Bloomington: Indiana University Press, 2018), especially 1–14.

26 Northrop Frye, "Maps and Territories," in *The Secular Scripture and Other Writings on Critical Theory, 1976–1991*, ed. Joseph Adamson and Jean Wilson (Toronto: University of Toronto Press, 2006), 439.

27 Heidegger, "The Origin of the Work of Art," trans. Albert Hofstadter, in Heidegger, *Basic Writings*, 172.

28 Jameson, *Raymond Chandler: The Detections of Totality* (London: Verso, 2016), 77.

29 See Jacques Derrida, *Specters of Marx: The State of the Debt, The Work of Mourning, and the New International*, trans. Peggy Kamuf (London: Routledge, 1994), xviii: "If it—learning to live—remains to be done, it can happen only between life and death. Neither in life nor in death *alone*. What happens between the two, and between all the 'two's' one likes, such as life and death, can only *maintain itself* with some ghost, can *only talk with or about* some ghost. So it would be necessary to learn spirits […] to learn to live *with* ghosts, in the upkeep, the conversation, the company, or the companionship, the commerce without commerce of ghosts. To live otherwise, and better."

30 Jameson, *Raymond Chandler*, 78.

31 Washington Irving, *The Sketch-Book of Geoffrey Crayon, Esq.*, ed. Haskell S. Springer (New York: Penguin Books, 1988), 272.

32 Jameson, *Archaeologies of the Future*, 17.

33 Ibid., 173.

34 J. R. R. Tolkien, *The Letters of J. R. R. Tolkien*, ed. Humphrey Carpenter (Boston: Houghton Mifflin, 2000), 65.

35 Simon Ferdinand, Irina Souch, and Daan Wesselman, eds. *Heterotopia and Globalization in the Twenty-First Century* (London: Routledge, 2020), 2.

36 Ibid.

37 Karl Marx and Friedrich Engels, *The Communist Manifesto* (London: Penguin, 1998), 54.

38 Ibid., 56.

39 See, for example, Edward Soja, *Thirdspace: Journeys to Los Angeles and Other Real-and-Imagined Places* (Oxford: Blackwell, 1996).

40 Jameson, *Postmodernism*, 418; see also Soja, *Postmodern Geographies: The Reassertion of Space in Critical Social Theory* (London: Verso, 1989).

41 Michel Foucault, *The Order of Things: An Archaeology of the Human Sciences*, trans. anon. (New York: Vintage, 1973), xviii.

42 Ibid.

43 Ibid.

44 See Immanuel Wallerstein, *The Modern World System*, 3 volumes (Cambridge: Academic Press, 1974).

45 Solnit, "What if Climate Change Meant Not Doom—But Abundance," *Washington Post* (March 15, 2023): https://www.washingtonpost.com/opinions/2023/03/15/rebecca-solnit-climate-change-wealth-abundance/.

46 Jonathan Arac, "Literary History in a Global Age," *New Literary History* 39.3 (Summer 2008): 757.

47 Derrida, *Specters of Marx*, xvii–xviii.

CONCLUSION:
GOLD-BEARING RUBBLE

In what was to be the last letter he wrote to Gershom Scholem, Walter Benjamin expressed a fundamentally utopian sentiment amid the dystopian horrors they were experiencing in 1940. Encouraging his friend to persist in his writing projects even in such bleak times, Benjamin said, "[e]very line we succeed in publishing today—no matter how uncertain the future to which we entrust it—is a victory wrenched from the powers of darkness."[1]

It is a powerful line, all the more so when one thinks of Benjamin's own fate later that year. More so, one might think of the fact that, right around the time he sent the letter, Benjamin was working on what would become one of his most famous and influential essays, "*Über den Begriff der Geschichte*" ("On the Concept of History," also known in English as "Theses on the Philosophy of History"), written in early 1940 but published only years later. Here, among other insights and figures, Benjamin introduces his famous image of "the Angel of History" while reflecting upon Paul Klee's painting *Angelus Novus*, but also using a stanza of Scholem's earlier poem (itself a reflection on Klee's painting), "*Gruss vom Angelus*" or "Greetings from Angelus," as an epigraph for that section: "My wing is ready for flight, / I would rather to turn back, / If I stayed in mortal time, / I would have little luck."[2] Benjamin, likely thinking of both Klee's and Scholem's "Angelus" at once, pictures the angel of history:

> His face is turned toward the past. Where we perceive a chain of events, he sees one single catastrophe which unceasingly piles rubble on top of rubble and hurls it before his feet. The angel would like to stay, awaken the dead, and make whole what has been smashed. But a storm is blowing from Paradise; it has caught itself up in his wings and is so strong that the angel can no longer close them. This storm propels him into the future to which his back is turned, while a pile of debris before him grows skyward. This storm is what we call progress.[3]

Benjamin was at times a utopian himself, but his fable about the angel of history is suffused with a melancholy for which he is also known, and perhaps given the circumstances of the time, a more dystopian attitude makes sense. To see history itself as one continuous and everlastingly destructive catastrophe, to see that as the inevitable result of what humans wish to call progress, is to recognize whither all this supposed progress has led, noting that the highest achievements of the modern world are fraught with horrors and that "[t]here is no document of civilization which is not at the same time a document of barbarism."[4] As Benjamin's friends Max Horkheimer and Theodor W. Adorno put it, "[i]n the most general sense of progressive thought, the Enlightenment has always aimed at liberating men [...] Yet the fully enlightened earth radiates disaster triumphant."[5]

Disaster triumphant seems like a pretty good label for a dystopian era. Although Benjamin's melancholic sense of the present occasionally would seem to invite some sort of nostalgia, here in his concept of history as a perpetual wreckage admits little hope in that direction, even if the prospects for the future hardly appear to be brighter. In some ways, the rejection of romantic nostalgia is arguably itself utopian, in a speculative or prospective direction, such that it admits of no going back by letting us know that what we would be going back to is itself merely more disaster and destruction. And yet a fearful attitude toward the past, much like a pessimistic vision of the future, can be politically crippling as well. The discrepant temporalities of utopian and dystopian thinking frequently clash, intersect, or become blurry in the fogginess of both nostalgia and prognostication that we experience in any given present.

Specters of the past, as well as of the future, predominate the cultural discourse. The sense that our societies and our lives may be "returning" to a dark time in the past has itself become a pervasive fear, even among those who consider themselves politically conservative, which traditionally meant cleaving to the values of the past. (Hence the success in some quarters of the slogan "make America great again," for instance, a phrase that combines some utopian past with a utopian future in its thoroughly dystopian sense of the present. Although that slogan has become a sign of the most invidious forms of right-wing bigotry, many among the liberal or left-wing in the United States have occasionally found themselves nostalgic for the time of New Deal-era commitments to the commonweal, support for public education, widespread unionization, and so on.) Yet even the most reactionary conservatives have expressed fears of returning to past situations or conditions that they find objectionable, and of course partisans of all stripes can mine the annals of history for things to cherish and abhor with equal aplomb.

In a recent article focusing on the putative fear within the United States of the current economic system's "returning" to that of the 1970s, Aaron Timms uses the term *nostophobia* to indicate this "fear of the past" (or, more literally, a fear of the return to a past), even as this fearful emotion in practice conjures up mostly fantastic visions in lieu of the actual historical conditions. "Nostophobia papers over the damaging legacy of those years while distorting the truth of the 1970s, which were also the decade of worker power, a rising ecological consciousness, and grassroots political experimentation," writes Timms. "Most importantly, it obscures the degree to which the unresolved questions of that decade still bedevil the West. A return to the 1970s is in some sense impossible, because the 1970s never really ended."[6]

Timms observes that "[t]he rise of nostophobia may also reflect a shriveling of hopes among Americans today for the future." The neoliberal order, undergirded as it is by the ideologies of meritocracy, individualism, and quantification, contributes mightily to the widespread feeling that change at a fundamental level is impossible, and that therefore any efforts at change are futile and ultimately undesirable. As Timms continues, regarding the shift in attitudes since just the 1970s in the United States,

[f]orty years later, that optimism has been drained from the body politic: Most Americans today expect income inequality to widen and living standards to decline or stagnate over the next 30 years. The rapid acceleration of climate change has extended the province of collective dread to the planet as a whole. Now inflation—which increases the pressure of time, intensifies anxiety about the future, and "redistributes fortune's favors so as to frustrate design and disappoint expectation," as Keynes once put it—has reemerged, after its decades-long hibernation, to compound the gloom. Nostophobia is the morbid symptom of a society that's stuck—culturally stagnant and economically self-cannibalizing. Wedged by anxieties in all directions, fearful of what's passed and terrified by what's next, Americans no longer have anywhere to look for inspiration. Not even the past will save us now. Unless, of course, it will.[7]

This final line could be said to represent Timms's own utopianism, insofar as the lessons of the past still hold out promise for future developments. It is as if the past, here seen as the economic and social circumstances of the 1970s, were the rubble in which traces of gold can be detected, excavated, and put to use today in furtherance of a more satisfying tomorrow.

"Gold-bearing rubble" is Ernst Bloch's powerful metaphor for finding the traces of the utopian amid the devastations that our history has set before us. Such a figure offers us a way of getting around both the nostalgia for a supposedly more glorious past and some nostophobia with respect to our troubled histories, for it would have us recognize the degree to which "History is what hurts," as Jameson so famously put it,[8] not trying to mask the charnel-house of history or its continuous catastrophes that have piled their rubble sky-high at the feet of our present situation. But it offers us a way of seeing, both in history itself and in our cautious, meticulous, and fitful study of that history, those elements of the past that may be of use to our present, and to helping forge new possibilities for the future. This works just as well with cultural forms like novels and films as for history, for the fiction of dread—in representing the dystopian conditions, monstrous accumulations, and apocalyptic landscapes—provides us with piles and piles of rubble worth exploring, and it also points us to the many glimmerings among the debris that may yet yield gold. Sifting through the rubble, we can reaffirm the power of critical and speculative practice, "the lastingly subversive and utopian contents" of such fiction, theory, and criticism today.[9]

In what has become a widely circulated quotation, Rebecca Solnit affirms the value of hope as a spur to action, more like the Sartrean existential sense of a project than of mere optimism about future outcomes or happenstance. As Solnit writes:

> Hope is not a lottery ticket you can sit on the sofa and clutch, feeling lucky. It is an axe you break down doors with in an emergency. Hope should shove you out the door, because it will take everything you have to steer the future away from endless war, from the annihilation of the earth's treasures and the grinding down of the poor and marginal. Hope just means another world might be possible, not promised, not guaranteed. Hope calls for action; action is impossible without hope. At the beginning of his massive 1930s treatise on hope, the German philosopher Ernst Bloch wrote, "The work of this emotion requires people who throw themselves actively into what is becoming, to which they themselves belong." To hope is to give yourself to the future, and that commitment to the future is what makes the present inhabitable.[10]

This revisionary sense of "hope," prying it away from pie-eyed optimists and from cynical detractors alike, is especially appropriate in a dystopian condition, for the very hopelessness that characterizes much of the gloominess of the present can be found in our skepticism over what "hope" means. Like dread, in fact, it is less a way of dreaming about the future than a means of dealing with the present, its threats as well as its promises.

Jameson has said that "we need to develop an anxiety about losing the future which is analogous to Orwell's anxiety about the loss of the past and of memory."[11] The fiction of dread, with its intense focus on a dystopian present—often figured forth as a more or less near-future scenario—is particularly well suited to heightening our awareness, if not also our anxiety itself, of the anxiety about the loss of a future. Perversely, perhaps, such fare may even reignite the sort of utopianism that animated popular culture at the end of the nineteenth century, when so much that seemed promising about "modern" society confronted directly the horrors of poverty, disease, injustice, racism and sexism, and so on. Edward Bellamy's famous allegory of the coach in the first chapter of *Looking Backward*—it depicts how masses of humanity were forced to pull the great carriage, whose driver was hunger, along an endless, sandy, hilly road, whilst the wealthy rode comfortably and even left their cushy seats for their children after them, but even they feared the possibility that, at any moment, a bump or jostle would cause them to fall and have to take up the ropes themselves—is as dystopian a picture as we might see, even though it was meant to simply call attention to the plain conditions of the present. But this led Bellamy to imagine what could be, if only in projected into another century, if those in that present did what was needed to change things. That is Solnit's sense of hope, which comes from the recognition of our dystopian *status quo* and from the anxieties we ought to feel about our potential loss of the future.

Benjamin's desire to wrench victory from "the powers of darkness" in his own *finsteren Zeiten* demonstrates the power of dystopian theory and practice to foster potentially utopian aims.[12] The fiction of dread as it plays out through novels or films or theory, operates in this way too, for it allows us to map our world at this time, to diagnose the malaise of the present, to identify the monsters that menace but also give shape to our social order, and to register our anxieties with respect to the ends of our world alongside our hopes for its reconstitution. The dread animating this creative work sparks the imagination, much like China Miéville's canny octopuses who undoubtedly consider their futures all the more promising while they have coconut shells in hand (er, tentacle),[13] and this is itself the necessary step in the right direction when it comes to our efforts to fashion this world and its future into a better place, after all. This idea is, in some respects, the dialectical complement to Bloch's notion of gold-bearing rubble, insofar as it attempts to find what there may be of value in a future we no longer dare to believe possible, and yet in seeking it, we make of that apparently rubble-strewn future, a dystopian landscape filled with monsters and teetering on the edge of the world's end itself, a space that is not only inhabitable, but actually worth living in.

Notes

1   Gershom Scholem, ed., *The Correspondence of Walter Benjamin and Gershom Scholem, 1932–1940*, trans. Gary Smith and Andre Lefevere (Cambridge: Harvard University Press, 1992), 262.
2   Quoted in Walter Benjamin, "Theses on the Philosophy of History," in *Illuminations*, trans. Harry Zohn (New York: Schocken Books, 1969), 257, translation modified.
3   Benjamin, "Theses on the History of Philosophy," 257–8, translation modified.
4   Ibid., 256.
5   Max Horkheimer and Theodor W. Adorno, *Dialectic of Enlightenment*, trans. John Cumming (New York: Continuum, 1987), 3.
6   Aaron Timms, "We're Haunted by the Economy of the 1970s," *The New Republic* (October 31, 2022): https://newrepublic.com/ article/168050/1970s-stagflation-haunts-politics-today.
7   Ibid.
8   Fredric Jameson, *The Political Unconscious: Narrative as a Socially Symbolic Act* (Ithaca: Cornell University Press, 1981), 102.
9   Ernst Bloch, *Heritage of Our Times*, trans. Neville and Stephen Plaice (Berkeley: University of California Press, 1991), 116. I am grateful to Caroline Edwards for adverting my attention to this passage, and to her own excellent work on Bloch, utopianism, and twenty-first-century literature; see, for example, Edwards, "Uncovering the 'gold-bearing rubble': Ernst Bloch's Literary Criticism," in *Utopianism, Modernism, and Literature in the Twentieth Century*, ed. Alice Reeve-Tucker and Nathan Waddell (Basingstoke: Palgrave Macmillan, 2013), 182–203.
10 Rebecca Solnit, *Hope in the Dark: Untold Histories, Wild Possibilities*, 3rd ed. (Chicago: Haymarket Books, 2016), 4; the quotation from Bloch comes from *The Principle of Hope, Volume One*, trans. Neville Plaice, Stephen Plaice, and Paul Knight (Cambridge: The MIT Press, 1986), 3.

11 Jameson, *Archaeologies of the Future: The Desire Called Utopia and Other Science Fictions* (London: Verso, 2005), 233.

12 As Phillip E. Wegner discusses, the *finsteren Zeiten* ("dark times") refers to a line from Bertolt Brecht's poem, *"An die Nachgeborenen"* (i.e., "To Those Born After"), the opening line of which reads *Wirklich, ich lebe in finsteren Zeiten!* ("Truly, I live in dark times!"). See Wegner, *Invoking Hope: Theory and Utopia in Dark Times* (Minneapolis: University of Minnesota Press, 2020), 1.

13 See Chapter 1, *infra*; see also China Miéville, "Marxism and Halloween—Socialism 2013," *YouTube*, uploaded by We Are Many Media, October 30, 3013: https://www.youtube.com/watch?v=paCqiY1jwqc.

INDEX